# Mageborn: The Blacksmith's Son

By

Michael G. Manning

Photography and Cover by Donna Manning
Illustrations by Michael Manning


ISBN 978-1463684341
LCCN

Printed in the United States of America.

# Acknowledgements

I would like to thank my family and friends for their continued support. I would not have been able to write this without their encouragement. I'd particularly like to thank my mother for her lifelong support and my wife for her encouragement, not to mention her photography and artistic skills in designing the cover.

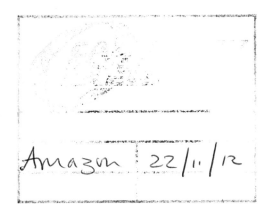

# Prologue

Elena di'Cameron was worried about her husband. He seemed fine when he returned from dinner that evening, but now he was ill. Normally she would have dined in the hall with him and her family. They were visiting her parents, the Count and Countess di'Cameron, but her baby had been fussy. Rather than drag him downstairs she had fed him in her room and taken a light meal there for herself.

Tyndal, her husband and counselor to the King of Lothion, had returned right after dinner complaining of tiredness and had gone to bed early. A few hours later she woke to the sound of him retching violently. "Tyndal? What's wrong?" She sat up and lit a lamp. He sat on the floor, holding the chamber pot as he heaved. She was shocked at his appearance. His face was pale and his black hair was damp with sweat. As she looked on he convulsed again, but his stomach was already empty.

She went to him and wiped his face with a towel, "You don't look good. Let me get the physician."

He waved his hands, "I just want some water, I don't need a healer."

"I'll get some for you." There was no use arguing with him; she would call for the physician while she got the water. He could complain later, the stubborn fool. She crossed the antechamber and stepped out into the hallway. Her parent's rooms were across from hers and the door was slightly ajar. *That's odd,* she thought, but she continued down the hall, intent on her goal.

As she rounded the corner she saw two men in black garb entering one of the empty rooms. Stepping back quickly she knew things were very badly wrong. Then she remembered her parent's door. Rushing, she was back to it within seconds and thrusting it open she burst into the room. The doorway led into a small sitting room; the layout was similar to her own rooms. It was empty. A scream came from the bedroom and the opposite door flew open, as her mother struggled to get through. She was held from behind by another of the black garbed men and the front of her nightdress was soaked with blood. In the space of a heartbeat Elena saw her mother's head jerked back and smoothly the man drew a short blade across her neck in a circular motion.

# Prologue

Blood fountained from her ruined neck and the Countess di'Cameron sagged to the floor. In Elena's heart a voice was screaming but no sound came from her lips; her teeth were clenched and her jaw set. The assassin looked at her grinning, the woman before him was no challenge, barehanded and still in her nightgown. Two short strides and he was to her, his open hand reaching for her hair. He barely lived long enough to regret his mistake.

Elena was one of the Anath'Meridum, the secretive guardians that protected the line of Illeniel, and a lethal warrior with or without weapons. She stepped into him and her palm struck him in the chin, snapping his head back. The force of it caused him to topple backward, off balance. She stayed close, giving him no space as he stumbled. Holding his shirt she ripped his other dagger from its sheath and pushed him to the floor while sliding the blade into his chest, just under the sternum. A second thrust under his chin made sure he would not rise again.

Her mother was dead; she knew that before she got to her. Her father the Count was dead on the floor of his bedroom, and the blood pooling on the floor shone blackly in the candlelight. Elena came near to collapsing then as the sight overwhelmed her, but a flash of light from behind kept her from giving in to her emotions. Returning the way she had come she saw the hallway fill with incandescent fire and the screams of dying men found her ears.

The flames vanished as quickly as they had appeared and she ducked her head out, scanning the hall. Two men lay smouldering on the floor outside her own room, and Tyndal stood clutching the door frame. He was having difficulty staying upright. Gradually he sagged downward holding his stomach. More men ran past, one leaping over Tyndal to enter her bedroom while the other two paused to finish the dying wizard. They never saw her stepping out from the other bedroom.

One raised his sword to strike Tyndal while the other looked on. Behind them an angel of death rose up in a white nightgown, blond hair framing flashing blue eyes as Elena struck. The dagger went into the kidney of the man watching her husband while her free hand jerked backward on the collar of the one raising his sword. Her bare foot was planted behind his right boot and he fell backwards. He never got the chance to get up; the dagger was back and in his throat before he had finished striking the ground.

# Prologue

Tyndal was staring at her as she raised her head, loose hair hanging like a golden cloak over her shoulders. Her eyes met his and he tried to speak, "Our son..." his voice was dry and weak. She took up the dead man's sword and raced past Tyndal without a sound. The nursery door was open and within she could see a dark form, the third man, holding a sword over the crib.

This one heard her coming and faced her head on, forgetting his target momentarily. Steel flashed in the dim room for tense seconds, seconds that felt like hours. He was good... few swordsmen could have held her at bay so long… but he knew he was losing. A moment more and she would have him. Desperate he stepped to the side and feinted, not at her, swinging instead for the crib with its tiny occupant. Elena made the choice every mother would make, not that it was a choice, for there was no thought in it. The instinct of every woman in history that had ever held babe to breast made this choice for her, not that she would have changed it. She lunged, seeking to block the sword that sought her son's life and barely she made it, but it left her off balance and exposed. The assassin's riposte took her in the stomach, steel ripping her gown and the flesh beneath. Her own sword whipped back as she retreated, slicing into his face.

The assassin screamed, blood running from his right eye. The pain and blood disoriented him for just a moment, and he tried to defend himself as Elena came back. She was clutching her stomach with her left hand to keep everything in, while her right drove him mercilessly backward with the sword. Her face was lit with rage and fury as she struck at him. "You will ***not*** have my son!" She struck again and this time his response was too slow; she batted his clumsy defense aside and pierced his heart, driving the sword between his ribs and out between his shoulder blades, pinning the dead man to the wall.

Elena had no time for dying; she went to the crib, still trying to keep herself together. Because of her stomach she only had one hand, so she dropped the sword and tried to comfort her son with her free hand. She heard a noise behind her and if it had been another assassin she might have been undone, but it was Tyndal. He looked like death warmed over as he made his way into the small room. "Your belly..." he said as he gasped for air.

# Prologue

"Never mind that, you look worse than me, and that's saying something." She smiled at him, the same smile that had won his heart years before, then she leaned back against the wall and slid down. Loss of blood had begun to make her dizzy.

Tyndal sat down beside her and tried to ease her flat onto the floor, but the skin of her stomach separated as she straightened out, drawing a choked cry from her. "Dear gods Lena! I can't fix this... it's too much..." Tyndal Ardeth'Illeniel was the most powerful wizard alive then, but his knowledge of the healing arts was limited, and his own body was dying. The meal at Castle Cameron had been poisoned, and every man woman and child within the keep that had eaten it was dying as well.

He put aside his pain, focusing as he drew his finger across her belly like a knife. The skin drew together and closed at his touch and within a moment only a silver line remained to show where she had been cut. Elena's pain subsided and she looked into Tyndal's face. It was covered in sweat and drawn by pain and exhaustion. Still his brilliant blue eyes looked on her with the same sharp intellect that had always fascinated her. This man, her husband, was dying and she could do nothing.

Able to sit up now she drew him to her, tears brimming in her eyes. They held each other for a long minute, till he began heaving again and pushed her away. He was bringing up blood now. After an eternity he stopped and managed to speak, "You've got to take our son and go."

Some women might have argued or wept, but Elena di'Cameron did not. She was Anath'Meridum, and she knew what had to be done. Nodding she rose and tested her wound. The skin and muscle seemed whole but a deeper burning told her that more was yet wrong within her. Tyndal leaned over the crib and picked up their son. He swayed a bit as he stood there, making her concerned he might fall with the tiny child, but he kept his feet. "Grow strong my son; live and make me proud." He kissed his son on the cheek and handed him to Elena. "I love you both."

"Forever," she replied and kissed him quickly.

Taking her free hand Tyndal led her into the bedroom. She left him for a moment and gathered a few things. Dressing quickly she put on simple breeches and a plain tunic, then she slipped her surcoat over it. She buckled on her sword and joined her husband; he had gone out onto the balcony.

Standing there she looked at the man she had pledged her life to protect. The man she had to leave behind. Doubt assailed her, “Are you sure?”

“There is no other way. I am dying already; you must break your vow. You have to escape if our son is to live,” he replied. Tears stood out in his eyes.

Elena looked away, then she went back inside. She pushed the furniture in the anteroom against the door then went to reclaim the assassin’s sword. She put the stranger’s weapon in her sheath and then returned to Tyndal, holding her own sword in her hand. She held out the blade to him and their eyes met. “I, Elena di’Cameron forsake my bond and I ask for your release.” She spoke the words no Anath’Meridum had ever spoken.

Tyndal reached out placing his hand over the blade, “I, Tyndal Ardeth’Illeniel release you.” As he spoke the blade glowed for a moment before going dark, then it shattered like glass. “My strength is almost gone Elena, you have to hurry.”

Dropping the hilt she embraced him and then took their child from his arms. "How is this going to work?" She wasn't sure how he planned to get her down; the balcony stood nearly a hundred feet above the courtyard below.

"You will be light, like thistledown. You'll have to jump, but my magic will keep you safe till you reach the ground. I'm sorry, its all I have strength for..." he said. He spoke a few words in the ancient tongue and put his hand on her brow.

"I love you," she said and put her hand to the rail, holding their son close with the other.

"I know. You carry my heart in you, and my life in your arms. I do not die tonight, so long as you live." He kissed her and then she jumped, drifting down like a feather in a light wind. As she floated downward she heard a noise come from the room above and Tyndal turned back to the bedroom. Men were forcing the door inward, pushing the furniture aside. Tyndal walked toward them with fire dripping from his hands. A second later he was lost to her sight as she drifted lower.

# Prologue

The night grew bright for a moment as flames shot from the balcony. The fire grew, brighter and brighter till it seemed as bright as the sun, consuming their bedroom and a large portion of that floor of the keep. Then it dimmed, fading back to an orange glow as the keep began to burn from within. Tyndal Ardeth'Illeniel, the last wizard of Lothion, was no more.

Elena reached the ground and gazed upward a moment longer. Then she looked away and began running for the stables. She wept silently as she ran, holding her infant son. It would have been shameful for someone to have seen one of her order crying, but then, she was Anath'Meridum no longer.

She reached the stable in less than a minute and ducked inside. Amazingly the place was empty. Wasting no time she saddled one of her father's coursers, fast horses bred for the hunt. It wasn't easy to mount carrying her babe, but she managed it somehow and then they were out, racing away with the wind whipping her hair back.

They rode across the castle yard and through the gatehouse. There were men and horses gathered outside but she caught them by surprise and was past before they could try to stop her. Looking back over her shoulder she could see them mounting to follow, shouting at her to stop. She paid them no heed and rode on, flying headlong into the night.

She rode through the night, pushing her mount, hoping to outdistance her pursuers. Sometime near dawn her horse faltered and nearly fell, forcing her to stop. She dismounted hastily before her mount collapsed. She had ridden it to death. The horse was blowing hard and its mouth was covered in froth but she had no time to mourn it. It sank to its knees, and trying hard not to think, Elena opened the artery in its neck, giving it a quick release.

*I have seen nothing but death this night, and I have nothing but more of it ahead of me,* she thought. Another day she might have shed tears to have slain such a beautiful animal, but there were none left in her. She lifted her son and began to walk. As the hours drew on the pain in her belly grew worse till it felt as though her stomach was on fire. Something was broken inside but she could only hope it wasn't enough to kill her before she reached Lancaster.

The Duke of Lancaster was her father's liege-lord and the closest place she could hope to find refuge.

Eventually she found herself on the road again, and she walked eastward into the rising sun. She was uncertain where she had met the road, so she couldn't be sure how many more miles it was to reach Lancaster. She kept walking. She could see smoke rising beyond the next hill so there must be a dwelling nearby.

An hour later she was having trouble thinking clearly. Her mouth was dry and her body was hot. Fever had set in and she feared that she would collapse before reaching help. Glancing over her shoulder she saw a man following, a hundred yards back. By his clothes she could tell he was one of the assassins from the night before.

Adrenaline gave her a moment of clarity and she sped up. He was afoot so she figured he must have ridden his horse to death trying to catch her during the night. She felt a moment's pity for the animal. Her body was weak, too weak, and even the adrenaline failed to give her enough strength. The man drew steadily closer and she knew the result was inevitable.

He was only twenty yards back now, and she could hear him breathing hard as he approached. Neither of them had the strength to run, making their competition into a grotesque parody of a sportsman's race. He was striding heavily while she stumbled along. "Goddammit just stop!" he shouted at her. "Quit now bitch and I'll make your last minutes pleasant before you die."

Elena di'Cameron was no fool. She could not continue and she had no strength to fight. Setting her son down she turned back. Five steps... then ten... she collapsed as he approached. She lay face down with the sword she had taken cradled beneath her. She would not think of it as her own sword; that sword had been broken. She heaved great lungfuls of air and dust from the road as she tried to get some strength back. Her only hope was that he was stupid enough to have some sport of her before he killed her.

She waited till he stood above her, hoping he would pause. She seemed helpless, which was almost the full truth. Standing there he decided he was too tired for fun and drew his sword. Elena rolled and thrust upward, trying to impale him either in the groin or stomach. It very nearly succeeded, but her arms failed her and the strike was too slow. He kicked her sword aside and then came down hard, planting his knees on her shoulders. She felt her collarbone snap and screamed with what air she had left.

## Prologue

Pinning her to the ground he drew out a small knife, "I'll finish your kid with this after you're dead witch!" His eyes held no trace of sanity. She tried to spit in his face but her mouth was dry and there was nothing left. Then an arrow sprouted in his chest. He seemed surprised, looking at it in astonishment. Dropping the knife he tried to pull it out when a second arrow appeared in his throat. He fell off of her, dead before his head found the road. Elena tried to get up, but nothing worked. She could hear her son crying as her sight grew dim. Darkness closed around her and she sank into oblivion.

Some nameless time later she awoke. She attempted to move and her collarbone shifted, grinding. The pain forced her into stillness and she lay there taking stock of her surroundings. "Don't try to move. Your body has been through too much," a voice said.

A woman sat beside the bed. They were in a small room, some farmer's cottage perhaps by the look of it. She rinsed a cloth and placed it back on Elena's forehead. "Your body is taken with a terrible fever. I thought for a while you might never awaken."

Elena stared at her; the woman had a kind face, with strong features, "My baby..."

"Shhhh, don't worry he's ok. He's right here. A good strong boy you have; he's been crying lustily since Royce brought you in." She leaned over and lifted Elena's son from a makeshift bed they had set up in the room. Elena wasn't able to hold him so the woman settled him beside her, where she could feel him with her hand.

"I need to tell you some things," she started.

"Nah nah, don't work yourself up. Your body is working hard to fight the fever. You need to rest. There will be plenty of time later," the woman reassured her.

"No, there won't." Elena said, "I'm hurt deep inside. Down here..." She tried to gesture to her stomach but it hurt too much to move. She was tired, bone tired, but she kept talking, and slowly she explained who she was to the woman caring for her.

After a time she learned that the woman was named Meredith Eldridge, Miri for short, and her husband Royce had found Elena on the road. He was a blacksmith and had been on his way to take a cask of nails and other sundries to the castle at Lancaster.

Fortunately he always took his bow with him on such trips. The two women spoke for over an hour before Elena could no longer continue and lapsed into a troubled sleep.

The next day her fever was worse but Miri still held out hope for her. Elena convinced them to let her have pen and paper but the struggle to sit up and write was almost too much for her. She fought her pain and weariness and eventually she found a position sitting at the table which didn't hurt as much. Her left arm was useless but she could still grip the pen in her right, as long as she didn't move it too far while writing.

She wrote two letters. One for her son, and a much shorter note to the Duke of Lancaster. At last Miri helped her back to bed, exhausted. "Don't tell him Miri... not till he's older."

"What's that love?" Miri tried to sooth her.

"Don't tell him about me, till he's older. Let him be happy. When he must know, give him my letter." She was emphatic.

"Shush now, you can tell him yourself when you're better. You'll stay here with us and when you get your strength you can help me with the place," Miri smiled and stroked Elena's hair. "You just rest yourself, and someday soon we'll have a picnic. Spring is here and it's so lovely out. The flowers are blooming and the air is full of sweet smells." Elena fell softly asleep while Miri talked. She felt like a girl again, with her own mother singing her to sleep. After a while Miri got up and went to start dinner.

Elena never woke. She passed quietly away that night. Her son woke the Eldridges the next morning with his crying. It seemed he knew somehow that she was gone.

# Chapter 1

*The ideas examined within these pages were originally meant to explore the nature of magic alone, until deeper examination revealed the connection between the 'aythar' that is spoken of by wizards, and the miracles and supernatural occurrences found in all faiths and religions. No one was more surprised than myself, at this connection between the 'natural' and the 'supernatural' and it formed the basis of my loss of faith and the beginning of my fall into heresy. Therefore be warned, if you are a man of faith or religion, a cleric, monk, priest or holy man of any type, stop here. Read no further, for the ideas and science presented within will doubtless erode the very necessary foundations required for any sincere connection with the gods.*

*~Marcus the Heretic,*
*On the Nature of Faith and Magic*

I never felt like an unusual child, which I suppose is true of everyone, at least up to a point. Growing up I was inquisitive and adventurous as most boys are, but as I grew my mother made some observations, "He's a very quiet child." I don't remember the first time she said that, but it immediately struck me as true. In fact I was very introspective, despite my amiable nature and easy smile. As I got older she went so far as to describe me as someone born with an "old soul", whatever that meant. Mostly I just thought a lot, which set me apart from the other children a bit, but not enough that I felt a difference or a gap. Looking back it seems clear that my native caution and introspective nature are probably what kept me alive.

My father's name is Royce, Royce Eldridge, and he is a blacksmith by trade. I've often wondered if he regretted his vocation, since it seemed he loved horses more than metal and would use any excuse to slip away to the city to see the races. He had also spent a bit more money than would be wise purchasing high bred horses of his own. My mother, Meredith is her name, chided him about that, but she didn't really mind. In truth she loved horses just as much and it was during one of his trips to see the races, as a younger man, that he had met her. Unfortunately after they married they were unable to have children, but as fate would have it my father found me years later, on another of his trips into the city. As he tells the story I was just a lone babe, abandoned on the roadside not far outside of town. My young mother had put me there, where I could easily be seen and heard, in hopes that some farmer's wife might happen upon me. I'll probably never know exactly why she chose to do so, but things have worked out well for me anyway, so I have never borne her any ill will.

Royce and Meredith were happy to have a child of their own and being an only child I got a bit more attention than most children. If my parents had been wealthy I would have probably been completely spoiled, but as it was I was simply happy. Most of our neighbors didn't realize I was adopted, but my parents never kept it a secret from me. I was proud to be an Eldridge and I worked hard to please my father. He made a point of letting me watch him work in the smithy, familiarizing me with the tools and methods of his trade. I found the ruddy glow of hot iron fascinating, watching it slowly take shape under his patient hands. Being a smith's son it was naturally assumed that someday I would follow him in the craft, and I had no objection. If things had turned out differently I might be working at a forge even now, happily shaping metal to make my living.

As I grew from a curious boy into an awkward adolescent it became apparent that I might have some difficulty at the work. I had many natural talents. I was unusually intelligent, something that most adults noticed within minutes of talking to me. I had a good eye for metal and a natural gift when it came to crafting or building. My hands were sure and skilled, an artist's hands my mother called them. That lay at the heart of the problem; although I was long of limb, I was not particularly stout. I worked hard helping my father at the bellows but no matter how much my mother fed me I never seemed to fill out. It seemed I was doomed to remain a gangly youth forever. Still, I was skillful enough that given time I would probably have managed to become a competent smith, if not for what happened that spring, when the rivers were swollen with rain.

The day had dawned bright and full of promise, as spring days are wont to do. The rains had been especially heavy that year, my sixteenth year, but they had ended a few days ago and the whole world seemed alive and shining. The sun was warm while the air still held a crisp chill left over from winter. All in all it seemed a terrible waste to be cooped up in the smithy with my father. I suspect that is why my mother sent me out to look for herbs. She had always been kind and I think even then she knew my youthful spirit was too large to be bounded by the orderly confines of the smithy. So it was with a spring in my step and a wicker basket in my hands that I went out to explore the fields and woods near our home. I knew the area well of course, but I enjoyed every chance I got to roam about, and I knew my mother wouldn't expect me back very soon.

I spent the morning roaming about the fields, picking a variety of greens and dandelions that I knew my mother liked to use in her cooking, but as noon neared I decided to venture down to the river in search of angelica, a medicinal herb. I had no notion of what I would find there that day. I passed through a heavily wooded area that was close to the Glenmae River. The land rose up before reaching the river, so I was still unable to see the banks when I heard the sound of a horse in distress. The horse was blowing and nickering loudly, with a pitch that indicated it was full in the throes of panic. If you have spent much time around horses you probably have an idea what I mean. I immediately broke into a run, youthful daydreams forgotten. I still don't regret what I did that day, but looking back I wonder how things might have turned out if I had taken a different path and avoided the river.

Coming over the rise I saw a young man about my own age standing at the bank of the river, swearing loudly at the surging waters. I suppose it might be more correct to say he stood at the 'new' bank of the river, for it appeared that a large portion of what had been the bank had been swept away, undercut by the rushing water. I still could not see the horse, but the boy I knew, for he was my best friend, Marcus. Even at this distance I could see his face was white with fear. Within half a minute I had reached him, and though I shook his shoulder he looked at me blankly, as if he didn't know me. It took him a moment to recognize me and collect his wits enough to speak coherently, "Mort!" I should probably mention at this point that my name is Mordecai, but most of my friends at this age had taken to calling me 'Mort'. "I'll never get her out of there Mort! She's going to die and it's my fault!"

The 'she' he was referring to was his father's prized mare, Dawnstar, although we just called her Star. She was a beautiful roan, with a star-like blaze on her forehead. She was also one of the most expensive acquisitions in his father's large stable of horses. His father, the Duke of Lancaster had bought her expressly for her bloodline, to improve his own stock, for she came from a famous line of racehorses. I was sure that Marcus wasn't supposed to be riding her, but little things like rules rarely stopped my friend when he had a notion to do something.

It was easy to guess at the rough details of what had happened. He had ridden her close, to watch the river as it raced along. He had gotten off and led her close to the bank, as the mare had enough sense to balk at being ridden so close to the roaring water. That was when disaster struck. The weakened river bank had collapsed under the weight of the horse, and while Marcus had managed to scramble back out of the way, the mare had not been so lucky. She was trapped in the river, struggling to keep her head above the water. The torrent had swept her up against a fallen tree where she was trapped, unable to climb up the steep muddy bank. Star's panicked cries wrenched at my heart as she desperately strove to keep her head above water.

Without thinking I began scrambling down the slippery embankment, trying to get close. It should be readily apparent that my thinking at this point was not clear as there was no possible way I could free the trapped horse. The crumbling bank was steep and narrow at the water's edge, which would make it impossible to get the horse out of the water, even if I were strong enough to accomplish such a thing. At the moment she was near to being swept under the lower edge of the fallen oak, which would lead to a swift drowning as she would most likely be caught in the large limbs dipping into the water. Still I approached her without a clear plan, drawn by her plight.

"Mort! You're gonna get yourself killed!" Marcus was usually the more reckless of the two of us, but today he was showing a lot more intelligence than I seemed to possess. "Get back up here before I have to explain your death as well!" For a moment I considered his words, and I realized he was right. I started to turn, to make my way back, common sense finally overcoming my foolishness, but then I met Star's eyes. That was when my life changed. That was the moment that swept everything before it aside and set me, and my friends on a course that we could never turn back from. The historians would have much less to write about if I had not looked into that frightened mare's eyes.

At this point I'm not sure how to describe what I experienced. Probably some of you who read this have been through moments of crisis and felt the surge of emotions that sweep over you in an instant, the timeless moment of clarity in which you can think a thousand things in the blink of an eye. This was one of those moments, and as I looked into that noble creature's eyes I felt as if a window into my own soul had opened. My world shrank, until it contained nothing, nothing at all but Star and myself. Her eyes were wild with fear and her breathing was loud as her lungs heaved, despite the rushing water. My own body seemed light and insubstantial, and soon I lost all sensation of it, falling into her gaze. Now there was only Star, and Mordecai was gone, as if he had never existed. My body and indeed my very 'self' were no more, everything had been replaced. I should rephrase that, my body still existed, but it was different now, much heavier and it was cold. I could feel my heart pounding so hard I thought it might burst from my chest. I was mostly submerged in the cold river, and I could feel it chilling me, sapping my strength as it pushed me against the tree, drawing me downward with an inexorable pull.

I could see a young man on the river bank, slowly sinking down, like a puppet with its strings cut. He was slipping into the water as well, and I wondered who he was. I fought to stay above the water and in my desperation I had one clear thought. If I just had something firm to stand upon, I might be able to get myself up and out of that freezing water. My hands hit something hard, next my feet found it as well and I began to rise. Stepping up I found something else solid to stand on and I began to walk out of the river. As I emerged my hands felt strange and looking down I realized they were now hooves. That seemed rather silly, since I was quite sure I wouldn't be able to climb up the embankment without hands, so instead I walked up the river until I came to a place where the bank rose at a gentler slope and I chose that spot to walk out.

Looking back I saw a second man, and I recognized him. It was Marcus, and he was dragging the other boy out of the river and back up the embankment, although he wasn't having much success. The mud was steep and crumbling; it would be impossible for him to carry the other person back up it. Instead he was trying to get under the stranger and push him up and over the edge where it had crumbled away. It was obvious that he would never be able to get him up high enough so I decided to help him. Walking up the rise I got close to the edge and looked over at him struggling with the young man's limp body. He pushed him up again and since my hands seemed to be useless, I stretched my head down and grabbed the teen by the collar, using my teeth. Had my neck always been this long? Pulling back I got him awkwardly onto the grass and dragged him until I was sure the ground was firm.

By now Marc had gotten himself up as well and he was shouting something at me. Looking at him I realized the colors were strange. It was definitely my friend but he looked different to me. Glancing down I stared at the unconscious stranger. There was something familiar about his face. He had long gangly arms and legs and his head was covered with thick black hair. At last it hit me, and a cold shock ran through me as I recognized myself lying there upon the ground. With that realization I felt a surging sensation and felt myself rushing toward my empty body, and then there was only darkness.

Sunlight filtered in through my closed eyelids, which made me wonder how I could have slept so late. Normally my mother would have awakened me with the dawn to start my daily chores. The bed was comfortable however, so I decided to sleep a little longer and see how long I could manage before she came to rouse me. Then I felt warm breath on my face and heard a snort, as if one of my father's horses had somehow gotten into my room, but that couldn't be… could it? I cracked one eye and was startled to see Star looming over me, with Marc sitting on the other side of me.

"Thank the gods you've woken," he said. "I had begun to think you were going to pass over to the other side." His face held a slight smile, though I could see tension written in his expression.

"Why am I lying on the ground?" Even as I said this I realized it was true; I was lying on the damp grass, not far from the river. I started to sit up and everything began to twist and turn around me as waves of dizziness washed over me. I have a stubborn streak though, so I sat up anyway and stayed that way till the world quit whirling about.

"I was hoping you could tell me that," he replied. "For some reason you felt you could drag an entire horse out of the river by yourself, and even worse, you promptly passed out as soon as you got to the edge of the water. You nearly drowned."

"How did Star get out?" I had a strong suspicion that I knew exactly how she'd escaped the river, but I still couldn't believe it.

"The best I can tell she's been possessed by a water spirit." Marc stared pointedly at me as he said that, and I knew him well enough to tell he had a different opinion. "Right after you passed out she walked up and out of the water, walking over the top of it about thirty yards before she made her way onto dry ground." He paused then, as if to see what I might say, but I held my tongue. "Then she walked back up over the top and proceeded to drag you up and over the edge of the embankment with her teeth. All in all I'd say her behavior was rather unhorse-like."

I looked down, unsure what to say, "Well…"

# Chapter 1

"You might as well tell me. I've already seen several unbelievable things today; I'm not likely to call you a liar at this point." Marc and I had been friends since we were small children, so trust wasn't an issue; it was simply that I couldn't understand what had occurred either. I gave up attempting to understand, and just described my experience as best I could. It took a while, but Marc was a good listener. After a while I ran out of words and just sat there, looking at Star grazing nearby.

Marc looked pensive. He had a brilliant mind, when he chose to employ it, and I could see the gears turning as I watched. Finally he spoke, "Let's lay it out in plain view. You sent your spirit into the horse and took control of her body. Then you used some sort of magic to allow Star to walk on top of the water…"

"Now hold up," I interrupted, "I didn't use any magic, nor would I know how to!"

"What else would you call it Mort?" He stared at me; his gaze was direct and unwavering.

"Ok, well obviously something amazing happened, but that doesn't mean that I was the cause, source or principle agent behind the..." I had lapsed into our most familiar form of speech, the type we used when discussing matters of science or philosophy. He wasn't buying into my circumlocutions though.

"Bullshit," he interrupted.

"What?"

"You heard me, bullshit. Don't try to talk your way around it. You're not talking to your parents, or any of the other dullards we know, so don't try and feed me a bunch of crap. You need to own up to it and face what happened head on. *You* did it. *You* did something miraculous, and that makes you either a saint or a wizard. Given your general lack of piety I'm leaning toward the latter."

"You're crazy," I replied intelligently, "I don't know the first thing about magic."

Marc smiled, "I don't either, but I do know one thing."

"Such as?"

"Wizards are born not taught, so lack of knowledge is no defense." Deep down I suspected he might be right. We were both full of questions, but the experience with the river had left us cold, wet and tired. We agreed to keep the details of what had happened secret, at least until we could figure things out.

# Chapter 1

“Come to the keep tomorrow and we’ll go through Father’s library,” he said. Marcus’ father was the Duke of Lancaster, a fact I frequently tried to forget.

“I can’t. I’m supposed to help Dad with a load of pig-iron tomorrow.”

“Tomorrow evening then. In fact, tell your parents you’ll be staying with me for a few days," he replied.

"I can't do that. What will they think?"

"They'll think it's wonderful their son is hobnobbing with the nobility." Marcus never held his higher social station against me, but he had no qualms about making full use of its advantages either. “Listen, I’ll send a runner over this evening with a fancy invitation. Your father will be so impressed he won’t even consider refusing.” Marcus grinned at me with his usual irrepressible smile.

“I think your plan leaves a bit to be desired,” I replied. “Don’t you need some sort of excuse or reason for the invitation?” My parents knew about our odd friendship as it had never been a secret. Marcus and I had met when we were boys, playing in the courtyard of the Duke’s keep during one of my father’s delivery trips. We hit it off immediately, although I’ve never been sure why. I suspect it was because he was the first child my own age with enough imagination and wit to keep up with my elaborate games of pretend. Soon after that my parents began getting 'requests' from the Duchess for my presence to help entertain her son. The Duke and his wife were remarkably forward thinking when it came to 'mingling' of the classes, but still as we entered our teenage years I had seen less and less of Marcus as he was required to spend more time with people of proper breeding.

"Hah! You're coming over for a social gathering and boar hunt my father arranged for this week." Marcus had an incredibly smug expression on his face, as if he had impressed himself with his own cleverness. The idea wasn't that clever so I knew he was hiding something.

"You just made that up didn't you," I accused.

"Not a chance!" He had a definite glimmer in his eye. "Father planned this party two months ago. Young men and ladies of gentle breeding from all over the realm will be descending on our noble duchy this week."

That gave him away. "Young...oh wait! You sneaky bastard! This is one of those 'mixers' your parents have been sending you to in order to properly socialize you with the gentry!" In point of fact Marcus resented the social gatherings his parents forced him to attend and spent most of his timing describing them to me as dull occasions attended by dimwitted fops obsessed with their own self-importance. I was sure he secretly enjoyed them at least somewhat; he merely presented them in a negative light to make me feel better since I couldn't attend. Which raised a question. "Wait, wait, I'm confused. How do you intend to bring a commoner along for this thing?" The 'commoner' of course was me; I had no illusions about my social standing.

Marc snickered, "Ah my friend, this time is different! *My* father is hosting this event and since it is my home I can bring anyone I wish." That effectively ended my last good argument. He got up and began leading Star away. He could have ridden her, but he was an excellent horseman and it never even occurred to him to do so after her ordeal in the river. "I'll have the invitation over in a couple of hours. I'll send a coach for you tomorrow evening."

I shook my head, embarrassed, and tried to think of a good parting remark. My wit failed me however, so I had to settle for a simple, "See you tomorrow." I began walking home, trying to figure out how I was going to explain this to my parents.

# Chapter 2

*Any meaningful study of magic must begin with those most proficient in its use, mages or wizards, as those more educated in its use are called. Those individuals who for uncounted generations have been passing knowledge, from master to apprentice, regarding how to effectively use and shape the forces of magic, or as they refer to it, the 'aythar'. According to their teachings, aythar is the vital force present in all living things, and in some part also in inanimate objects, although to a lesser degree. It is the core force behind things we describe with many different names such as: energy, spirit, life-force, élan, passion, magic, and faith.*

*~Marcus the Heretic,*
*On the Nature of Faith and Magic*

The next evening arrived more quickly than I'd imagined and there was the coach, pulling up near our house. My father had actually been rather pleased by my news. He had a fair opinion of the Duke already, and I'm sure he saw this as an opportunity to acquire more favorable terms and business for the smithy. It certainly can't hurt having your son be friends with the next Duke. Mother was a bit more anxious. She seemed certain I would commit some serious breach of etiquette and get myself and possibly the family into trouble. I tried my best to reassure her, but looking back I see now she was much wiser than I had ever given her credit for.

Stepping into the coach I was surprised to see Marc already within. He gave me a wide grin, "Hullo! Ready to start your adventures?"

I answered in a sour tone, "This isn't some romance where we're off to slay dragons and rescue damsels you know."

"Says you, but I have a rather more optimistic view on these matters. Besides which, there will indeed be some fair damsels at Castle Lancaster over the next few days, some of whom may well need a rescue," he replied.

"From what?"

"Not what, who!"

I sighed, my friend had developed a definite talent with women over the past year, or so I had heard. "You'd best be careful; tupping the town girls is a far cry from besmirching the honor of a nobleman's daughter."

## Chapter 2

He didn't answer that, just grinned at me. We rode in silence for a while, till the bailey came into sight and the outer walls drew closer. I was staring out the coach window when something caught my eye. "Marc! Look at that." I pointed out the window, toward the nearing archway.

Marc poked his head out the window to look in the direction I had pointed, "What?"

"The wall, what are those odd symbols? See them glowing like phosphor?" I was pointing again, trying to show him the glowing runes limning the archway ahead of us.

"I don't see a thing," he said as he sat back down, "describe them to me." I did the best I could and by the time I was done we were through the gate and heading for the stables. "Oh! Of course!" he said.

"Of course what!? Don't leave me wondering dammit." The glowing runes had put me on edge.

"You saw the castle wards. Father told me about them, but apparently only people with the 'sight' can see them. I'm guessing that includes wizards," he answered, rolling his eyes up and to the side, as if to indicate he didn't know any wizards.

"I'm not a.... Wait, they weren't there last week when I came to town. Did your father hire some sorcerer to enspell the walls these past few days?"

Marc stared back at me, "No. The wards are old. They were placed decades ago by some wizard my grandfather employed for a short time."

"Then why couldn't I see them before now?"

"Well you didn't used to possess livestock and walk on water either. Ah! I know! Did you just finish puberty? I noticed the other day you don't look quite as girly any more...check your balls, are you getting fuzzy down there?" He ducked, laughing, as I threw my travel sack at him.

The coach stopped and a footman held the door for us to step down, so we tabled our discussion for later. Stepping into the courtyard I saw a familiar face. "Dorian!" I called out to a stalwart looking man crossing over to us. Dorian Thornbear was actually the same age as Marc and I. He was not quite as tall as me, standing about five foot ten inches, but he had quite a bit more muscle than either of us. He was the son of the Duke's seneschal and because of his martial prowess he had already been accepted into the lord's service as a man at arms. The stiff leathers he wore along with the spear in his hands were visible evidence of this.

"Ho! Master Marcus! Who let this ragamuffin in here?" Dorian said this with a light tone; we had all been friends since I had begun visiting the keep as a child.

Marc spoke, "I've invited Mort to spend the week."

"You going to bunk with me again Mort?" Usually in the past I'd stay with Dorian's family if I was sleeping at the keep. Technically his family was minor gentry, but they were a lot less intimidating than the Duke's family. Plus our fathers were close friends.

I started to reply with a yes but Marc interrupted me with a hand on my shoulder, "Not this time Dorian, I've convinced him to let me put him up in one of the guest rooms."

Dorian frowned, "Will there be enough room with all the visiting peers this week?"

"Certainly," Marc replied.

"But..." I started to object.

"Shhh! Don't argue, besides you need to be in the main keep if we're to visit the library at night without creating a lot of questions among the castle guard," Marc glanced at Dorian who's eyebrows had gone up at this. "We're on a secret mission!" he whispered in a conspiratorial tone.

"Really?" Dorian Thornbear was one of the bravest and most loyal friends I had ever known, but he had a certain lack of guile built into him. He was honest to a fault, perhaps that's what made him a bit gullible. Not that the young lord of Lancaster was trying to fool him, it was just that Dorian tended to take such things over-seriously. We wound up standing in a sort of huddle near the back of the coach as Marc and I filled Dorian in on the events of the past few days. The three of us had always been as thick as thieves, but I had some concern that Dorian might give away my secret. Deception had never been his strong suit.

"Now what would you lads be conspiring at!?" The loud voice of Marc's father, Lord James, the Duke of Lancaster came booming from behind us. He was a man of moderate build, with sandy brown hair and blue eyes. He laughed as Dorian whirled to look back at him.

## Chapter 2

"Nothing your grace!" Dorian ducked his head as he replied.

"You look well your grace. Thank you for the invitation." I gave a formal bow; I have always had a knack for keeping a cool head.

"You are welcome, young Eldridge. Please give your father my best wishes when you see him again. I trust you will enjoy your stay with us." The Duke was unusual among most of the peerage in that he treated all his vassals and even yeomen with courtesy and respect, though he had no requirement to do so. It was a fact that had made him extremely well liked among the people of Lancaster.

"Father! Why do you insist on scaring my friends?" Marc was a bit annoyed with the Duke.

"Hah!" The duke exclaimed, "It's every man's right to embarrass his son. Would you deny me the simple pleasures of life in my dotage?"

James Lancaster was still in his late thirties, and still quite hale, which his son was quick to point out, "When you've actually gone senile Father you'll know it because we'll have you put out to pasture." They spoke for a bit more before the duke finally relented and left us to our own devices. Dorian had to report for duty, something he remembered rather quickly after the duke had surprised us, so he excused himself and we were on our own again.

"Let me show you the room I've got picked out. You'll love it." Marc led the way through the keep and up the stairs. I followed, curious despite myself, although I had visited many times over the years I had never been given a room inside the keep itself. When we finally came to a stop outside the door I realized we were extremely close to the Lancaster family quarter.

"Are you sure this is right? Isn't this near your family's rooms?" I asked.

"Indeed, my door is right over there," Marc pointed across the hall. He opened the door and shoved me in before I could start objecting. The room itself was ostentatious, at least by my standards. It held a large four poster bed, dressing table, chair, a desk and some sort of odd couch-like piece. I had no idea what it was, but I discovered later it was called a 'divan'.

"There's no way you can put me in this room," I said, looking over at my friend. "You've got nobility from all over the realm coming tomorrow and every one of them rates higher than me. If someone finds out you've put the smith's son in this sort of room it'll create all sorts of hell."

## Chapter 2

"Bah, you're right of course, but we have to place them in rooms according to their rank and status. Do you know who our most distinguished guest is going to be?"

"Not a clue, I'm common remember?"

"No you're not, but the world hasn't realized it yet. His lordship Devon Tremont, son and heir of the Duke of Tremont will be our most privileged guest. Protocol would dictate that he should have the best room we have to offer."

"So let me stay with the Thornbears like I usually do."

"Not possible," he remarked, "Gregory Pern, son of Admiral Pern will be staying with them."

"I'll be fine in a broom closet then." I was being sarcastic, but I actually meant what I said.

Marcus looked at me seriously, "Listen, Devon Tremont is the biggest prat I've ever met. I absolutely refuse to have that asshole sleeping across the hall from me. You on the other hand are my best friend, and infinitely more worthy, in my humble opinion."

"You wouldn't know humble if it walked up and kicked you in the shins. But thanks for the compliment.

You still can't put me in here, it'll cause an incident." I knew I was right, and surely he realized it as well.

"You're right. It would. *If* anyone knew you were a complete nobody. As it stands you are unknown gentry, who happened to be staying here prior to their arrival. Your rank and status are unknown and you were already in residence when they arrived. It would be rude to relocate you unless you were some common lout with no standing." He was smirking at me now.

"I *am* a common lout with no standing."

"I know that, and you know that, but no one else does," he answered.

"Most everyone living in this castle knows me!"

"I talked to Mother last night. She's agreed that for this week you are Master Eldridge, a scholar and distant cousin. No one needs to know more than that, and she'll make sure everyone plays along."

"What about the servants?" I said.

"People of breeding do not talk to the servants," he said this with an aristocratic tone and tilted his head back slightly. "Besides I already let them know as well, just to be sure." He winked at me.

## Chapter 2

After that I gave up. I had known Marc long enough to realize there was no dissuading him from his wild schemes once he had made up his mind. I only hoped it didn't turn out badly. We talked for a while longer and made plans to start searching the library that night after dinner. Once we had talked it all out he left and I had the room to myself, so I promptly lay down and took a nap. I had to admit, it was the most comfortable bed I'd ever slept upon.

Sometime later I woke; someone was standing at the bedside. I was slightly confused and it took me a moment to remember where I was. Looking around I realized there was a young woman looking at me with a slightly embarrassed expression. "Sir if you wouldn't mind getting up, dinner will be served in half an hour."

Still groggy I sat up and collected my wits as best I could. I glanced at the maid again. She was beautiful in a healthy and unpretentious way that few possess. Soft brown curls creeping down her slender neck framed a delicate face with faintly rosy cheeks. Then I felt stupid, I knew her! "Penny! What are you doing here?" Penelope was her name but in town we all knew her as Penny. She was the cooper's daughter and one of the most sought after girls in Lancaster. Not that any of the boys had caught her eye yet; she was as discerning as she was beautiful.

"Pardon me sir; I just took service with the Duke's household this past winter." She lowered her eyes meekly. The Penny I knew was anything but meek, amiable yes, sweet-spirited certainly, kind usually but not always.

"That's two 'sirs' now Penny, one more and I'll tell the Lady Genevieve who was stealing her roses a few years back." When we were eleven or so she and I had been playing in the garden behind the keep. Her grace, the Duchess of Lancaster, or Lady Ginny as we knew her then, kept a beautiful flower garden. Dorian had been with us and when Penny proposed we steal some roses for her I had thought he might die of fright. Dorian had been a big worrier even then. In the end I picked three roses, one for each of us, although Dorian was too nervous to keep his.

"I never! You took those roses!" she exclaimed.

"Well, you put me up to it," I answered dryly.

"Mort they might fire me if you tell that story." She looked nervous but I could see her natural spirit starting to reassert itself.

"Relax, I was just kidding. Now explain to me how you wound up as a retainer for the Lancasters." Actually if I had paused to give it thought it wasn't hard to figure out. The servants in the keep were generally well compensated and the work was usually better than what you could find in town. All things considered a job here was a stroke of luck for anyone that managed to get one. The pay was generous and whoever she married someday would be blessed with a second income.

"My Da's business hasn't been going well lately, he hurt his back last year and we were having trouble making enough to keep food on the table, much less pay the tax man. So when I heard the castle had a position come open, I put in for it. Anyway! Stop distracting me; you'll get me in trouble for sure. And don't you dare mention that story about the roses again!" She said this with a tone of annoyance, but her eyes held a smile in them. "I'm supposed to tell you that your clothes are laid out for you on the dressing table and you'd best get moving if you expect to be dressed in time for dinner."

Now I was off balance again, "Clothes?" I said stupidly.

"You can't be wearing *those* if you expect to rub elbows with the Duke's family, much less the guests who'll arrive tomorrow." She wrinkled her nose as she indicated my simple attire. I had worn my best tunic which only had a few patched spots. Mother had even washed it for me this morning so there weren't any stains.

"There's nothing wrong with my clothes," I replied grumpily.

"Not if you're planning to muck out the stables," she retorted, "but for *Master* Eldridge, scholar and gentleman they simple won't do." She indicated the clothes laid out for me with a sweep of her hand. There on the dressing table was a fine dark grey doublet and hose, accented with black lacing and ebony buttons. Soft cloth shoes completed the outfit.

*Oh hell no,* I thought to myself.

Penny was something of a mind reader it seems, or my face gave away my thoughts. She tried another tactic, "Please Master Eldridge! You simply must be properly dressed or else I'll get in ever so much trouble." She looked at me with large brown eyes that seemed about to brim over with tears. Had she always had such large eyes?

"What the hell is wrong with you?" I growled.

"Please Master Eldridge; I would be so grateful if you would just deign to wear these garments." The

## Chapter 2

Penny I knew never acted like this. In fact I remembered her being more of a tomboy. Glancing down I could see she had developed in more ways than one. I blushed a bit then.

"Fine dammit, just get out and let me get dressed." I was angrier at my own reaction than I was at her.

Her face lit up happily in that annoying way women have when they get what they want. "I'll just wait in the hall."

"Damn right you will." I muttered to myself. I stripped off my clothes and began struggling with the unfamiliar clothes. The hose and shoes I managed without a problem. The white under tunic was simple enough, but when I got to the doublet things got complicated. It had entirely too many buttons and laces and soon I was hopelessly lost.

"Penny," I called, "are you still there? I think I need some help."

"I've heard that before," she teased as she peeked into the room. "I knew you'd be calling for help before too long. Here now, stand up straight! Face the mirror… no, not there, I need light from the window to see properly." She took charge and began sorting out the mess I'd made of the doublet. Standing behind me she reached around me to draw up the laces holding the front together, looking over my shoulder to see her hands in the mirror.

I could feel her hair tickling my neck as she worked to tighten up the laces, something which caused me to develop all sorts of unwelcome thoughts. She didn't seem to notice thankfully. "When did you get so tall Mordecai?" she said, her breath warm beside my ear. I was pretty sure the softness behind me was a product of the development I'd noticed in her before. My cheeks flushed. "What were you thinking?" she continued without waiting for me to answer, "You have to tuck the shirt in before you tie up the hose." She slipped her hands in around my waist and deftly began tucking the shirt in. I yelped in an entirely manly manner and jumped away.

"I can do that!" I said, and then continued by putting my foot in my mouth. "I hope you don't dress all the guests like that."

"Of course not you dolt! That's what valets are for!" She looked angry and perhaps a little embarrassed although I wasn't sure.

"Well then why are you here?" My clever wit was in fine form this evening.

## Chapter 2

"Marcus thought you might like to see a friendly face rather than deal with a stranger! Honestly Mort, what do you think I am? Some sort of doxy?" Some men claim angry women are attractive but I've never been one of them. Penny was scowling at me as I tried to figure out how she had gotten from what I had said to the idea that she was some sort of prostitute.

"Wait Penny, I'm sorry. I didn't mean it like that. I was startled and I feel out of place here. I spoke out of turn." At last my legendary charms were returning to save me. She glared at me for a second longer and then her features softened a bit.

"I guess I can understand that, this place can be intimidating." She relaxed and then when I wasn't expecting it she punched me on the shoulder. "There, we're even now." For a moment things felt like they did when we were kids, back when things were simpler. "What startled you though?" she asked.

Sometimes you can be too comfortable expressing yourself around your friends, "Well last time I saw you, you were just this big gap toothed tomboy and now you're… well… you…" Yep I had done it again. Did I mention I'm a genius?

"Tomboy?" She was obviously sorting through and trying to figure out if I had insulted her again. "I guess I was, but what does that have to do with anything? I'm still the same for the most part. We're both taller after all. Are you trying to say I look funny?"

"No, no… you look great! I mean really really great, beautiful in fact, so much so that I feel a bit awkward." I turned red as my inner voice replayed what I had just said back to me. By now she understood what I was getting at, and I swear for an instant I saw her smile before she blushed and turned her back on me. I'm sure I imagined it.

"Apology accepted," she replied, "and thank you for the compliment." She walked to the door before looking back, "You'd best hurry or you'll be late for dinner, *Master* Eldridge." I snatched up a pillow and threw it at her, but she shut the door before it got there. I'll never understand women, but I guess having one for a friend isn't so bad.

I gave myself a last look over in the mirror. The change was astonishing. A tall dark haired man stared back at me, blue eyes standing out in stark contrast. I was still a bit lanky, but the doublet did a lot to address that and I had to admit the grey looked good on me. There was a knock at the door and I found a small boy outside the room.

# Chapter 2

"An it please you sir, it's time for dinner, Master Marcus said you'd be wanting to know." He was a scruffy young boy somewhere between eight and ten years old. One of his front teeth was missing, giving him an off-kilter grin.

"What's your name boy?" I said, sounding so much like an adult I almost believed it myself.

His answer came with a faint lisp, "Timothy sir."

"Lead the way Timothy," I replied, and gave him a deep bow. Sensing my mood Timothy put on airs himself and we strode down the corridors and hallways like great lords. At least until we encountered the Duchess along the way. We dropped our act then and I gave Timothy a wink as he left. I walked with her grace the rest of the way, in a much more somber mood.

Luckily I knew my way around the keep fairly well so I had no trouble finding the great hall. I would have seated myself at the servants table, where I obviously belonged, but Marc caught me as I entered and steered me to the high table. It felt like everyone in the room was staring at me as I sat down. The duke occupied the head of the table, with his lady wife sitting at the first seat on his right. Across from her Lord and

Lady Thornbear were placed and I wound up seated next to her with Marcus to my left. The duke's other children, Ariadne and Roland sat across from me and Father Tonnsdale, the castle chaplain sat at the foot of the table. This being the first time I had ever sat at the high table, I felt distinctly conspicuous.

The dinner conversation was quiet and revolved entirely around the arrival of their guests the next day. Thankfully no one expected me to give an opinion as I was quite out of my depth. I did keep my ears open and learned a bit however. It seemed the events of the coming week were primarily being staged in order to familiarize Marcus, and to a lesser degree his siblings with other notables around their age. Given that the estates of the landed nobility were separated by great distances each nobleman would host events such as this to allow the young to socialize with their peers. Hopefully this would help them form important friendships that would serve them in the politics of later life, not to mention the possibility of finding a marriage partner. None of this was stated directly of course, but I'm a quick learner and I managed to pick up on the undercurrents.

Things were going well, the soup course was done and I was mostly finished with the second course, a lovely fish and parsnips dish, when Father Tonnsdale leaned forward. He was pontificating on the lack of merit to be found in some of the heathen religions many noble houses still held to, when his silver star slipped out of his robes and came into view. Unlike the last time I had seen it, now it was glowing with a soft gold radiance. Surprised I choked and then coughed, getting some of the parsnips into my nose. They were seasoned with a bit of horseradish, so the resulting burn made my eyes water and I fought to keep from spitting out my food.

Marc thumped me on the back while I regained my composure. Father Tonnsdale addressed me, "Are you all right Master Eldridge?"

"Yes Father, I'm sorry, your necklace caught me off guard. I never noticed it glowing like that before." As soon as the words left my mouth I knew I had said too much.

"How unusual! I have heard that certain individuals can see the light granted by our Lady, but it is a rare gift. Do you by chance have the sight Master Eldridge?" He was staring at me intently.

Ariadne, Marc's younger sister spoke then, "Don't be silly Father, we've known Mort for years and he's never shown any sign of having the sight." The duchess glared at her daughter for using my nickname at the table.

Marc interrupted, "Actually, I've been meaning to ask you about it Father Tonnsdale, this past week Mordecai has begun seeing things, like the castle wards." Nice, he'd managed to tell everyone at the high table. At least he hadn't mentioned the incident with the horse, but then I rather doubted he'd want his father knowing he had nearly lost his prize brood mare.

"How old are you Mordecai?" the priest asked me.

"Sixteen sir, I turn seventeen later this month." I answered.

"Peculiar, in most cases the sight manifests itself around age twelve or thirteen at the latest, during the tempestuous period around puberty. It's fairly rare in itself but of the few dozen cases I've heard of none were later than that."

"I'm sure it's just a temporary phase Father." I was beginning to wish I could make myself invisible.

"I doubt that. You might consider a career in the Church. A gift such as yours is highly prized and its use in the service of our Lady is helpful to avoid accusations of witchcraft and sorcery later on."

The duchess rescued me then, "Let the lad enjoy his dinner Father. You're frightening him with talk of witchcraft. It is hardly a fit topic for the dinner table." Lord Thornbear grunted in agreement with her and the dinner conversation gradually turned away from me and onto more comfortable venues.

Things went smoothly after that, dessert was a lemon syllabub, a sweet cream concoction I had never heard of before but of which I heartily approved. When they began to serve the after dinner drinks Marc signaled me quietly that it was time to leave so we made our excuses and rose from the table.

"Mordecai," the Duke stopped me, "please call on me in the morning. I'd like to discuss some things with you before the guests arrive tomorrow."

"Of course your grace," I bowed and kept my features neutral. I managed to get the rest of the way from the great hall without having a heart attack.

"Don't fret about it Mort, he just wants to make sure everything is clear concerning your identity this week," my friend reassured me.

"Speak for yourself," I replied, "he's not my father, to me he's the grand and powerful Duke of Lancaster." We made our way to the library.

# Chapter 3

*Of particular importance to those who work with aythar, is a full understanding of its interactions with human beings. Accordingly several characteristics have been described and named to understand this interaction. The first and most important characteristic is 'capacitance', which refers to the amount of aythar present or stored within a given person. The amount is not fixed and varies from moment to moment but never exceeds a certain limit. That limit varies greatly from person to person, but in most humans is quite small. Let me add here that all 'living' beings contain some amount of aythar, or else they would be dead, and even corpses contain some amount, although much smaller by many orders of magnitude.*

*~Marcus the Heretic,*
*On the Nature of Faith and Magic*

I had been there before, at first when Marc undertook to improve my education. My parents had taught me to read at a young age but the finer arts of geometry and grammar were beyond them. I think he dragged me along at first to provide a distraction from the work his tutor had set for him, but over time it became clear I had a real knack for language and mathematics. Later the Duchess encouraged Marc to invite me since his progress greatly improved when I was involved. As a result I was probably the best educated peasant ever to emerge from Lancaster.

Still the Duke's library was one of the best in the kingdom, and neither of us really knew the extent and breadth of the volumes it contained. Being young we just started searching titles and hoping to find something relevant. Marc started thumbing through histories hoping to find some mention of past wizards while I wound up getting bogged down in an herbal compendium. I always had a weakness for plants. Eventually I broke away from that and began searching again when Marc called me back.

"Hey Mort I found something!" It turned out to be a history of the university at Albamarl, which was the capital of Lothion. "According to this, the university used to have a college of magic," he said.

"Is it still there?" I asked.

"No apparently there was a plague and rumors got around that the wizards had something to do with it, the college was destroyed by an angry mob. Looks like most of the faculty were burned at the stake."

## Chapter 3

"Why do I want to be a wizard again?"

"Because it's terribly impressive! There are very few left now, and otherwise how will I ever find a magical counselor when I become duke?" He gave me one of his famously charming grins.

"Your father doesn't have a 'magical' counselor" I replied.

"Only because there are none to be found anymore. My grandfather had one though. Oh look here! You aren't a wizard after all!" That got my attention. "According to this you're a mage."

"What's the difference?"

"Anyone with a moderate amount of latent ability is a mage, a wizard is a mage who's been educated and learned to harness his powers properly."

I laughed, "So I'm ignorant! We knew that already." We skimmed through the rest of the book but as to the fate of the wizards that survived the burning of the college there was nothing to be found.

"Let's keep looking, I know Vestrius kept some books here somewhere," Marc said.

"Vestrius?" I asked.

"Grandfather's pet wizard," Marc answered.

I made a slow tour of the shelves when I noticed something odd, back near the corner, beside one of the wooden bookcases was a faintly glowing symbol. "Hey come check this out," I called. Then I reached forward to touch it. A moment later I found myself sitting at a reading table back in the front room of the library. Marc was looking at me oddly.

"What the hell is wrong with you?" he said.

"Why?"

Exasperated he went on, "A moment ago you called me over to that side room where the grammars are kept and then you just walked out and sat down over here with nary a word of explanation, that's what!"

"I did?" Confusion had become my regular companion these past few days.

"The legends of absentminded wizards are becoming truer every day," he replied. "Come on, let's see what you forgot, professor dimwit." We got up and went back into the small side chamber that he said I had called to him from.

Looking around for a few minutes I spotted the glowing rune again, "Hello what's this?" I reached out to touch it again. A moment later I found myself sitting at the reading table again. Marc was sitting across from me with a bemused expression.

"I'll start by saying you are never going to cut it as a mage or whatever if you keep touching strange wards," he said.

"Weren't we just in here a bit ago?" I queried.

"There's the great mind I've come to respect. Welcome back Mordecai, master of the obvious!" Sarcasm was not one of his more becoming qualities. Now that I think on it, it's probably not one of mine either. He quickly explained what had happened, so we went back to take another look.

This time I didn't touch the rune, "Can you see it?" I asked him.

"No."

"Try touching it and see what happens," I suggested.

"Not a chance, what if I forgot something important!"

"Like what?"

"Like maybe the first time I lay with a woman!" Marc answered.

"What the heck? When did that happen? You're not a virgin anymore?" I was stunned.

"And you are?" he replied, arching his eyebrows.

"Shut up, let's get back to business." I stared at the rune while he chuckled behind me. Finally I tried something different. Holding my hand out, I brought it near the rune but didn't touch it. As it came near to the glow I could feel a pressure growing in my mind. *Forget.* A faint whispering came to me, but I held firm. Taking a deep breath I tried to exert a pressure similar to the one I felt, only directed outward, back at the rune. For several long moments I could feel a tension building, not only in my mind but in the air around me, then the world exploded.

I found myself lying on my back with Marc looming over me holding a pry bar. "You are either the stupidest or the luckiest bastard I've ever known," he said. I sat up and looked at the spot where the symbol had been. It was notably absent, but a scorched area marred the wall now.

"Where'd you get the pry bar?"

## Chapter 3

"I went to get it before I knew you were trying to blow yourself up. Give me a hand, there's an iron ring behind the spot where that magical doodad was." He let me put my hand on it first, and then when it was apparent that nothing else was going to explode he helped me to pull. We tugged for a few seconds and then the paneling opened along a seam, a small cupboard was revealed. Inside were three leather bound books. The first two were about ten inches on a side and about an inch thick. The third was massive, fully eighteen inches tall and three or four inches thick, it was covered in glowing symbols, the only part of it I could read was the title, *A Grammar of Lycian.* The other two were untitled.

Marc started to reach in but I put my hand on his arm, "Don't" He glanced at me then withdrew his hand. Carefully I reached in and pulled out the two smaller books; since they weren't glowing I guessed they might be safe. I left the larger book inside.

"Is it warded?" Marc asked.

"It has something all over it, and it glows like a bonfire." After some discussion we closed the panel and left the other book inside. Hopefully I would learn enough to peruse it safely later. It was getting late so we decided to quit for the evening. I took the two books with me to my room.

"Promise me you won't look at them without me." Marc had a serious expression. "If something happens while you're reading it someone should be around to drag you away or put out the fire."

I met his gaze and tried to be serious, "Don't worry, I'll wait." A dozen smart ass comments ran through my head but for a change I kept them to myself.

Once I was safely ensconced in my room I began examining the books. I had initially intended to keep my promise, but curiosity had gotten the better of me. Since nothing had happened after opening the covers I figured I might as well see what I could discover. The first book turned out to be a journal, written by Vestrius himself. The second seemed to be some sort of book of spells, most of it was written in plain English, but interspersed were glowing words and symbols I had no experience with. It also contained a lot of diagrams. As soon as I saw the glowing parts I decided it should wait, so I returned to the journal.

My decision turned out to be the correct one. Unlike most journals in which someone writes their daily thoughts and such, this one turned out to be more like a lab notebook. Vestrius had been apprenticed as a teenager to another wizard named Grummond. The first task he had been given was the keeping of a journal, to record what he learned each day. I could not imagine anything more useful to me at this point. I began to read.

Vestrius' first days as an apprentice were quite illuminating for me, and made it clear to me what the importance of the third book was. *A Grammar of Lycian* was exactly that, a book detailing the grammar and vocabulary of Lycian, a long extinct language. The journal also made clear why the book glowed. Wizards are taught to use language, written and verbal, to manifest their power. Since using one's native tongue would be dangerous in the extreme the custom was to use a dead language. Lycian had become the de facto language of magic hundreds of years ago and knowledge of it was maintained for that purpose only. Because of its long use, even the writing had acquired a sort of residual power, which could prove dangerous sometimes even in the hands of those without the gift, but to a much lesser degree.

I resolved to collect the third book the next day; I would need to study it if I was to follow along with Vestrius' journal.

Penelope
Cooper

# Chapter 4

*The second characteristic is called 'emittance' and refers to the rate or ability of a person to channel or 'use' a given quantity of aythar. Unlike capacitance, emittance is not a universal trait in all human beings. Some persons, popularly called 'stoics', have no emittance whatsoever, and as a result are completely unable to use, sense or manipulate magic in any way. Luckily such persons are rare, most likely occurring no more than at a rate of one or two persons per hundred. One beneficial side effect of this is that stoics are impossible to manipulate in more subtle ways, such as via enchantments or other magics affecting the mind or spirit. This makes them invaluable in certain roles, particularly in judicial settings. They are of course, still susceptible to other forms of magic, but no more so than any other physical being or object would be.*

*The vast majority of humanity has a very low emittance, such that without extensive training or exposure they are largely unable to manipulate aythar to any significant degree. Similarly they have difficulty even perceiving things which are purely magical in nature. Such persons are able to use magical devices, and with extensive training even use some aythar directly, but to a very limited degree.*

*~Marcus the Heretic,*
*On the Nature of Faith and Magic*

I awoke to sunshine streaming in through the open window. Squinting at the bright light I attempted to cover my head with one of the decorative pillows that I had shoved to the side the night before. Someone snatched it away from me.

"For the love of all that's holy!" I burrowed under the covers, seeking to hide from the light. I had never been a particularly late sleeper but I had stayed up till nearly dawn the night before. Someone else had different ideas and I found myself struggling to keep the covers up, while my assailant tried to peel them back.

"Oh no you don't! Mordecai Eldridge you wake up this instant! I'm done covering for you this morning, you've already missed your meeting with the Duke and if you think…"

"What?" I let go of the blankets and sat up. My attacker, Penny, abruptly fell backward and tripped over the chair, taking the covers with her.

"Ow!" she exclaimed as she came down hard on her derriere. At this point a few things require explanation. Most common folk sleep naked, as I was now, pajamas and night clothes being a luxury. As Penny stood back up I became uncomfortably aware of this, not to mention the fact that my little soldier was giving his best morning salute. I was suddenly grateful for the abundance of decorative pillows and made quick use of one to hide my condition. Penny was kind enough to look away.

"Listen Penny, I know we've been friends a long time, but don't you think it would be better to knock next time?" I'd be damned it I was going to be embarrassed. I was clearly the victim in this situation.

"I did knock! I knocked at seven; I came back and knocked at eight and again at nine! You were called to meet with the Duke at nine thirty but I told him you were ill. I don't think he believed me at first, but Marcus told him he'd kept you up late drinking." She looked extremely put out but I noticed she hadn't offered me back the covers. Instead she kept darting glances at my legs, well I presumed it was my legs. I repositioned the pillow to make sure I was covered. "Finally I just came in at ten," she continued, "to clean and air out the room. You were sleeping like one of the dead."

She was determined to ruin my righteous indignation. "What time is it now?" I asked a bit sheepishly.

"Midday." Her raised eyebrow and pursed lips informed me that she thought noon was entirely too late to be waking.

"Noon?" My earlier resolve to not be embarrassed deserted me. "I'm sorry Penny. Look I appreciate everything you've done for me, would you mind leaving so I can get dressed?" I glanced over at the dressing table. The night before, scratch that, the morning before I had gotten into an epic struggle escaping the devilish clutches of the doublet. It appeared she had sorted out the tangled mess I had victoriously left at the foot of the bed.

"You're going to need my help, but I'll wait over here till you've got your hose and shirt on." She turned her back to me and faced the dressing table, so I got busy putting on the clothes I could safely manage. Too late I remembered that the dressing table had a large mirror on it, looking over my shoulder I could see her surreptitiously watching me in it. I'm not sure why, but I kept my mouth shut and finished dressing, probably I'd had enough of embarrassing conversations. I made sure to tuck my shirt in this time.

# Chapter 4

Minutes later she was helping me to lace up the doublet. Despite our prior experience I still found her closeness unsettling. I remembered Marc's admission regarding his lack of virginity and I couldn't help but wonder. *Could it have been Penny?* I kept my idiot mouth closed this time. The thought bothered me anyway.

"What kept you up all night?" The words startled me, coming as they did from right next to my ear. *I'm going to have to get Benchley to help me dress tomorrow.* I thought to myself. Benchley was the valet that assisted Marc with his own wardrobe. Shutting my eyes for a moment I organized my thoughts.

"Pardon?" Sometimes my cleverness amazes even me.

"Don't," she answered.

"Don't what?" Having settled on the 'dumb' defense I figured I'd keep going.

She finished up the laces and stepped away, eyeing my clothes critically. "Keep shutting me out Mort and you'll regret it one day."

I decided that I might still have a chance with feigning ignorance, "Honestly Penny I don't know what you're referring to, you heard Marcus, we stayed up late drinking and I had more than might be wise…" I never got to finish, her hand caught me with a stinging slap that left my cheek tingling and turned my head half way around.

"Goddammit Mordecai! I'll put up with a lot, but don't stand there and lie to my face! You tell Marc and Dorian everything but you can't be bothered to trust me! Why? Is it the tits?" She was gesticulating wildly and she punctuated this remark by lifting the anatomy in question. "You think I'm some empty headed girl you can't be bothered to trust?"

I was backpedalling quickly, caught completely off-guard by the unbridled fury in her voice. "No of course not Penny! I trust you, I mean we grew up together, you being a woman has nothing to do with this. We've always been close friends if…"

"Close!?" she interrupted. "That's why you went out of your way to visit whenever you came to town the past two years? That's why you knew my Ma died last year of the consumption? That's why you knew Da wasn't able to work anymore and that I had taken a job here? You came to see Dorian. You made countless trips to talk to Marcus! I just wasn't good enough to bother talking to?" The scope of our conversation had grown to encompass a lot more than my secret research. In truth I had avoided Penny the last couple of years, mostly because things had gotten increasingly awkward with the onset of puberty. She had changed in ways that set us apart, and as she blossomed she had only gotten more popular with the men in town. I had never liked competition and truthfully she was way out of my league.

"Did you think maybe I didn't need a friend too?" She was winding down now and I could see tears in her eyes.

"Penny I'm sorry, you're right," our conversations were developing a definite pattern, "I figured you had plenty of friends. Every boy in town has been trying to court you, surely…"

"I didn't need suitors, I needed a friend." She looked directly at me as she said this, and for a moment I wanted to hold her. *Stupid! She tells you she needs a friend and the first thing you think of is making a pass at her.* Being born male truly is a curse sometimes.

"Fair enough, I agree with you. If I were you I'd be somewhere else, I obviously don't merit your friendship, so why are you here Penelope?" She was right, but I was tired of arguing. I couldn't possibly apologize for not being there for her during her hardships. Besides she'd probably be better off if she stopped worrying about me.

"Asshole! I'm here because you're the only true friend I have! And don't think you're going to run me out of here like that; we're friends until I say we're not! Even if I have to beat you into telling me what's going on with you!"

I gave up. "What do you want to know?"

She looked at me suspiciously, "No tricks, I already know more than you think so you'd better be honest."

"Deal."

"Why were you in the library last night?" That surprised me, she obviously didn't miss much.

"How did you know that?" I asked.

"You weren't drinking, and I found two strange books in the reading desk. If I didn't know better I'd think you were in league with dark gods, the stuff in one of those books looked suspicious." Remind me never to underestimate women. "Now stop dissembling and tell me what you've been whispering about with Marc and Dorian."

## Chapter 4

"I doubt you'd believe it. Maybe it would be better if I showed you," I replied. "Go close the curtains; this will be easier to see if it's darker." To her credit she didn't ask any questions although she did look at me oddly as she pulled the drapes shut. "Come sit on the bed with me, this will take me a moment."

"I saw *that* earlier if that's what you want to show me," she said sarcastically.

"Just hush for a second and let me concentrate." I had read through the first few days of Vestrius' apprenticeship last night and although I hadn't studied the Lycian vocabulary yet, his journal included the first few words he had learned, and their application. I closed my eyes and tried to relax my mind. I held up my hand and cupped my palm. *"Lyet"* I vocalized and focused on the empty air in my hand. A warm glow formed there, dim but visible, rather disappointing. *"Lyet!"* I said again, putting more force into it. The light flared becoming a brilliant incandescent ball too bright to look at. I closed my eyes but the glare was strong enough to show through my eyelids. Penny's response was more interesting.

"Shit!" She leapt backwards across the bed and fell over onto the floor on the other side. That made twice she'd landed on her backside in less than an hour.

I left the ball of light hovering there in the air and moved to help her up. Truth be told I hadn't figured out how to move it yet, I'd had enough trouble working out how to turn it off last night when I tried it the first time.

Everything looked strange in the harsh white light, it cast shadows that made her face seem strange. The worst part was the fear I saw in her eyes. I could only imagine what I must look like in the glare. "Now you see why I had such trouble telling you?" I tried to smile, to put a familiar face on, to reassure her, but that only made it worse. She was backing away, edging toward the door.

"Wait Penny, this isn't as bad as you think. Here, let me put out this light, then I'll try and explain better." I gestured at the light, *"Haseth"* The light went out abruptly plunging the room into relative darkness since our eyes were still accustomed to the glare.

I heard her give out a yelp and then there was a loud thump. *That would be the divan I'll wager.* There was a loud knock and the door flew open.

Marc stomped into the room, "Alright you slugabed, its high time you got up! If you sleep any longer… huh?" Penny ducked past him and ran from the room. My eyes were finally adjusting to the dimmer light and I could see Marc staring at me from the doorway. I'll be the first to admit things didn't look good. The bed was a complete mess, with blankets still on the floor. The divan had flipped over onto its side. *I knew it was the divan,* I thought to myself.

"Was that Penny?" he asked turning in a circle.

*Oh damn! I knew it had to be her he was talking about last night, and this looks bad.* My thoughts were racing, "It isn't what it appears."

"And what would that be? That you're chasing the staff around your bedroom with the curtains drawn in the middle of the day?" He seemed a bit miffed but not nearly as much as I would have been if I thought someone was poaching my game. "Listen Mort, we've both known Penny a long time but she's been through a lot recently. You shouldn't give her a hard time. I meant to tell you this earlier but she lost her Ma not long back and since then…"

Obviously I was destined to travel from one misunderstanding to the next in this life. "No, no, no! I was explaining my situation to her and it upset her." It took almost ten minutes to describe what had happened. It would have been quicker but he has a bad habit of interrupting.

"So you came straight back here and immediately ignored our promise to wait?" He was shaking his head.

"That pretty well sums it up," I said this with my most charming smile.

"You understand I had to tell my father that we were up drinking late last night and you passed out from an excess of wine?" he replied, pointedly ignoring my overwhelming charisma.

That took the wind out of my sails, "He probably thinks I'm a drunkard now eh?"

"I doubt that Mort, but he certainly thinks you can't handle your wine," he gave me an evil grin. "Come on, I told Father I'd fetch you up before our noble guests start arriving." Since I was already dressed we headed for the door, but I did pause to set the divan back on its legs.

As we left he turned to me, "And if I ever find you chasing Penny around your chambers again I'll toss you out on your ass. The other maids I might forgive, but Penny is special."

"Dammit I told you that's not what happened!"

Chapter 4

Marc winked at me, “I know, it’s just fun to see you get flustered. You know, now that I think on it… if it had been some other maid, I don’t think the misunderstanding would have bothered you nearly as much.”

“What’s that supposed to mean,” I snapped back.

“Nothing my friend, nothing at all.” He put his arm around my shoulders as we walked down the hall. Well he tried; I’m still taller, so he had to settle for thumping me between the shoulders.

# Chapter 5

*Rarely, some are born with a moderate to high emittance but with a low capacitance. This trait occurs with no more frequency than one in a hundred. Those born with it usually do not become aware of it until puberty, when their bodies begin to mature, although occasionally it becomes active even earlier. The primary trait found in those with a high emittance is known to the common folk as 'the sight'. This refers to their ability to sense and see things of a purely magical nature. They sometimes manifest precognitive abilities or other forms of prescience and clairvoyance. Most become mystics, soothsayers, and fortune tellers. Some enter the clergy or priesthoods of various religions as their ability allows them to channel the powers of their gods. Thus are born the legends of 'saints'. Such would likely have been my own destiny if fate and my own intellectual curiosity had not interfered.*

*~Marcus the Heretic,*
*On the Nature of Faith and Magic*

My audience with the Duke had gone much as I'd expected. He made light of my late sleeping, passing it off as the 'excess of youth', but I was still sure I had disappointed him. In any case he made sure that I was aware that he and the Duchess both were colluding in misrepresenting my social status. As Marc had said earlier, I was to represent myself as a traveling scholar and avoid questions as to my exact place in society; they for their part would divert questions by remarking that I was a distant cousin of some sort.

Looking back I cannot help but wonder at their nonchalance at deceiving so many people about my social standing. It seems incredible from the standpoint of a lowly blacksmith's son, but when I consider it from their lofty station it makes a bit more sense. It quite literally was no big deal to them; the Lancasters were second in rank only to the royal family itself. Who would gainsay them? Who would bother to question the rank of an unknown scholar? And if the truth should out, what of it? They could pass it off as a minor joke and the worst consequence might be some ruffled feathers. For my part, it scared the living shit out of me, and I felt as if I had my neck on the executioners block.

I took a free moment that afternoon to continue reading and do some experimentation. One of the more interesting things Vestrius had learned early in his apprenticeship was a spell to put others into a magical slumber. Apparently it was a simple feat and one taught early because of its general usefulness. It could be used defensively against men and beasts or to escape from delicate situations. It also had the advantage of plausible deniability, assuming that all the witnesses were included in the effect. Grummond made a point of telling Vestrius that it would have no effect on 'stoics' but I had yet to find out what that meant.

I set out to find a suitable target for experimentation. I initially considered Marcus or Dorian but I put that idea aside. I was still uncertain of my abilities and I didn't want to risk putting them into some sort of permanent coma. I settled for sitting at the window and attempting to put birds to sleep. My first target was a blackbird that was kind enough to land on the windowsill.

I focused my will and looked at the bird, *"Shibal."* It collapsed as though someone had struck it with a well-aimed stone. I watched it for several minutes to see if it would waken. It didn't. The spell was supposed to last a while, depending upon how much power the caster put into it, but I had no idea if the size of the creature was a factor. I tried waking the bird with loud noises but it remained stubbornly asleep. I was pretty sure that was not normally the case with sleeping birds. Finally I picked it up and made sure it was still breathing. It seemed to be fine, with the exception of being a very sound sleeper. I tried shaking it a bit and then I poked it.

"Ow! Shit!" the bird woke and promptly bit my finger. It flew around the room for several minutes while I chased it, trying to herd it toward the open window. Eventually it found the exit and I sat down to consider what I had learned. I definitely wouldn't be bringing more birds into the room, my finger was still throbbing painfully.

I decided to try again, this time on something further away. I spotted a hawk circling overhead. *"Shibal."* The bird faltered for a moment but quickly recovered. I wasn't sure if it was because of the distance or whether it was more difficult to put it to sleep because it was flying. I drew myself inward mentally and focused my intention on the bird, *"Shibal!"* The hawk dropped from the sky like a stone. I felt more than heard the hard 'whump' as it hit the stone courtyard. *Bollocks! I killed it.* I quickly drew back from the window, lest someone see me and make the connection. The story of the burning of the college in Albamarl had left an impression on me.

A knock sounded on my door and I started. Surely no one could have seen the hawk and gotten up here already? I opened it and found Dorian standing there.

"You need to come down in a few minutes Mort. The first of the guests are here and Marc wants you there to greet them with him." He glanced around the room. The bed was still in disarray and the pillows were scattered. "Looks like you've been making friends with the cleaning staff already."

I wondered for a moment if he had been talking to Marc. "Dorian you trust me right?" I tugged him into the room and shut the door.

"Well sure. You remember that time you and Marc dragged me out to old man Wilkin's farm to help you steal pumpkins?" He had an endearing habit of repeating our childhood stories every time he got the chance, or annoying habit, depending on the circumstances.

"Yeah yeah, here come sit down for a second." I hustled him over to the divan.

"You and Marc told me you were gonna use the pumpkins to scare the crap out of…" he started to continue the story. Normally I wouldn't have minded but I had heard it a dozen times already and I had other things on my mind.

*"Shibal,"* I intoned seriously. Nothing happened.

"…Sir Kelton while he was standing watch that night," Dorian continued without missing a beat. It might have been because I was staring at him intently, he probably thought I was listening. A second knock interrupted my thoughts.

Benchley, Marc's valet stood in the doorway, "His Lordship thought you might need some help getting ready," he said. I guess Penny had changed her mind about dressing me, or perhaps Marc had.

A sudden thought occurred to me, "Actually Benchley I'm already properly dressed but you could give me a hand with the bed. I haven't a clue how to get the sheets and pillows back the way they were." I waved in the general direction of the disaster zone I was calling a bed.

Benchley stood a bit straighter and I realized I had probably insulted him since such tasks were usually the domain of the chamber maids. He was a 'gentleman's gentleman' after all. He kept his tongue though, and walked over to pick up the coverlets. I watched him carefully, biding my time. Meanwhile Dorian had stopped his story and was looking at me with an odd expression; he knew I was up to something now.

As soon as Benchley leaned over the bed to smooth the sheets I spoke, *"Shibal."* He collapsed across the mattress as if he had been poleaxed.

"Sweet Mother!" Dorian stood up and stared at Benchley, then looked at me, his mouth agape. Then he silently mouthed, "What did you do?" as if we were in danger of being overheard. Honestly, his overly serious expressions are half the reason I love Dorian.

I spent the next few minutes explaining what I had done. One nice thing about Dorian, as opposed to Marc, is that he doesn't interrupt. He listened intently, his eyes growing wider as I talked. My demonstration had definitely sent him into a state of high anxiety, but the other thing I love about Dorian is his intense loyalty.

"I better go stand guard in the hallway to make sure no one comes in," he said in a hushed tone. I tried to convince him that wouldn't be necessary, since there was nothing more incriminating in the room than a sleeping manservant, but you can't shake these ideas from him once he gets his mind set on them.

Once he had left the room I stepped over to Benchley. My first thought was to awaken him with a shake, since that was what had worked with the bird, but then I figured I should use the opportunity to get more information from my experiment. I tried shouting first, that didn't work but it did draw a worried Dorian back in from the hallway. "What are you doing?" he silently mouthed at me.

"Nothing, go back to the hall," I silently mouthed back. Lord, now he had me doing it too! He went back out so I decided to try gently shaking the sleeping valet. After a moment I had to get more vigorous, for it seemed I had put Benchley into a deep slumber. That didn't work either. Finally I went and got a slender straight pin from the dressing table. I've never been sure why they keep those there, but it came in handy.

"Gah!" Benchley uttered a most ungentlemanly sound and sat straight up from the bed. I quickly hid the pin I had just plunged into his posterior. "What happened to me?" He seemed very confused.

"It appears that you fainted Benchley. Do you think perhaps you might be working to hard lately? You might do well to get some more rest." I did my best to look concerned for his well being as I gently ushered him to the door.

"What about the bed sir?" he asked.

"Never mind that," I replied, "the chamber maids can get it in the morning."

"Very good sir," he ambled down the corridor while I watched him go.

Dorian nudged me, "If we don't get moving you're going to miss greeting the Duke's guests."

"Oh, right!" I shut the door and we headed down.

As we walked he looked over at me, "We're going to need to talk about this later."

"Be sure to invite Penny to the meeting," I muttered sarcastically to myself.

"What? I didn't hear you," he said.

"Nothing, I was talking to myself." Inwardly I did resolve to try and make sure I included her more in the future. Her speech earlier had made me feel like a complete jerk. All of this assumed of course that she didn't think I was an agent of the dark gods. The last I had seen her she had been putting as much distance between us as possible.

I wound up standing at the steps leading into the main keep with the Duke and his family. The Lord and Lady Thornbear were there as well, which left me feeling distinctly out of place. While the coaches drew up the Duchess was kind enough to explain my role.

She was a striking woman in appearance despite her middling years and she placed her hand over mine as she spoke, "As the guests get out of the carriages James and I will greet them one by one. Each person standing here will escort one of the guests into the front hall and then show them to the sun room upstairs." In case you've forgotten, James was her husband, the Duke, although she was the only person I had ever heard refer to him by his given name. The sun room was a brightly lit parlor upstairs near the Duke's rooms. "Mordecai, you will escort Rose Hightower."

"Yes your grace."

"Do you remember how to address her?" the Duchess had some qualities that reminded me of my own mother.

"I address her as Lady Hightower," I said confidently.

# Chapter 5

"No, Mordecai. Lady Hightower is her mother, you address her simply as Lady Rose," she remonstrated me.

"Yes your grace, Lady Rose." I knew that, but I was nervous.

By then the first coach had drawn up and the occupants were getting out. Naturally the first was Devon Tremont, the son of Duke Tremont. The Duke of Tremont was the only peer of the realm who had equal standing with the Duke of Lancaster; accordingly his son and heir had equivalent standing to Marcus. I took that to mean I should be exceedingly polite. The Duke and his wife greeted him warmly and Marc stepped forward to escort him upstairs.

Knowing Marc as well as I did I could tell he didn't like Devon immediately. "Devon," Marc tipped his head slightly in greeting, "It is good to see you again." Something told me that was exactly the opposite of how he felt, but he hid it so well I doubt anyone could have discerned it.

"Marcus, well met. I see you are in good health…still." Devon replied. The slight pause before the word 'still' made it abundantly clear he wished it were otherwise. I watched him intently as they mounted the steps. He was of middling height with a lean athletic build and light brown hair. The moment I laid eyes upon the young lord I nearly gasped. He carried about him a strange radiance, almost a purplish aura and something about it made me feel mildly ill. I had never encountered anything like it before. For a moment his eyes met mine and they narrowed, I wondered what he might be seeing, as there was certainly nothing remarkable about me.

The moment passed and he continued up the stairs. My reverie was interrupted by the next guest, Stephen Airedale, the son of Count Airedale. He was an impressive young man with light blond hair and steel grey eyes. He was also the first person to emerge that was my equal in height, possibly he was taller. Marc's sister Ariadne offered him her arm and the two of them proceeded up the stairs chatting amiably. Her mother had trained her well and I could see she would someday be a formidable socialite.

The next to get out was Master Gregory Pern, the son of the famous Admiral Pern. As the son of a military commander his standing within the aristocratic circles was minor, his father had been a commoner originally after all. Regardless, his father's powerful shadow had a long reach and there were rumors that Gregory might be granted a minor title in the future. Before we go on I have to confess, if I sound knowledgeable about the aristocracy it is not through any great knowledge of my own. Marcus had tutored me on our guests that afternoon with some help from his sister.

Master Pern was being led away by Lady Thornbear who seemed quite comfortable on the arm of a handsome young man. She winked at me as they went by. Meanwhile her husband, Lord Thornbear had stepped up to escort Lady Elizabeth Balistair, daughter of Earl Balistair. She was lovely in her own right, although I would have said her nose was a bit too long and her green eyes were unsettling. She was also excessively tall for a woman, probably near five foot eleven inches. Not that that was a bad thing, but being as tall or taller than most men would make finding a husband difficult, and finding a husband would be important to Lady Elizabeth. The Balistair family was rumored to be having financial difficulties.

I had little time to think on that though, my turn had come. Lady Rose stepped out of her carriage and greeted the ducal couple warmly, and then she turned to me. I offered my arm as I had seen done, and she slipped her gloved hand across it. Truthfully she was one of the most beautiful women I could recall, with long dark tresses and warm blue eyes. Well, she might not be quite as pretty as Penny, certainly her figure was a bit slighter, but she had a definite presence. Her father, Lord Hightower was the nominal head of the royal guard and commander of the garrison in Albamarl. Reputedly their family name came from the tall bailey their family occupied in the capitol.

We walked up the steps carefully. I felt awkward walking next to such a graceful lady, but I did my best to cover it. "Lady Rose I understand this is not your first trip to Lancaster?" I said. You would never guess I had a note card hidden in my pocket with a list of similar conversational phrases, thanks to Ariadne. Marc's sister was very thoughtful.

"Oh! Yes, yes I have visited twice before, when my father came to discuss matters with the Duke." She seemed distracted, her eyes scanning the crowd when I asked my question. I wondered briefly who she might be looking for.

"I hope your previous stays were pleasant. Did you make any friends of note while you were here?" That question wasn't on my list of approved topics, but I figured I could improvise.

She looked at me carefully and I could see a sharp intelligence behind her blue eyes, "Why yes I did. I was just a girl at the time but I was quite charmed with young Ariadne." Her eyes slipped away from me, and it seemed as if they lit upon Dorian for a moment as he stood duty by the front doors. It might have been my imagination though, for she returned her glance to me but a second later. “How long have you lived in Lancaster, Master Eldridge?” she asked.

‘All my life’ I nearly said, but I caught myself, “Not long, but I’ve visited many times before.” She was no longer looking directly at me but it felt as if she was staring at me intently regardless. As we passed through the doorway I gave Dorian a quick wink to let him know things were going well, but he didn’t notice. His attention seemed fixed on my companion. My curiosity was definitely piqued.

“Her grace introduced you to me as a scholar Master Eldridge… might I inquire what it is that you study?” she queried. I thought I could detect a subtle undercurrent of humor in her question. Worse I had let too much time lapse and she had turned the questioning back upon me. I was definitely getting into murky waters here.

“Mathematics, Lady Rose, although I fear the term ‘scholar’ does me too much credit. I still feel myself a novice compared to the great mathematicians of old.” See I can be quite erudite when I try.

"You do not seem old enough to be so learned," she remarked.

"In faith I am young my lady. It is a fact which has done me no good service. I shall be glad when at last can display grey hair as proof of wisdom." I was rather proud of that one, I might be a natural.

"You do not think we should revere the wisdom of the aged?" Ouch, she had neatly turned that one back against me.

"That was not my intention at all. I merely imply that in matters of mathematics advanced years are no guarantee of wisdom, nor does youth necessitate its lack." We had reached the sun room and I felt relieved that I might escape. I was beginning to doubt my ability to keep up with Lady Rose in the dueling dance of our conversation.

I started to excuse myself, but she held onto my arm for a moment, "Master Eldridge, relax. We've only just met. Let me give you some advice." I looked down and her blue eyes caught me again. "You did well for a novice. In future don't let your opponent have so much time to turn the questions to topics you would prefer to avoid."

"Opponent?" I sputtered.

# Chapter 5

"Shush" she said quietly, then she smiled, a flash of white teeth under rose petal lips. "Don't act so surprised, you'll worry your friends." She waved at Marcus for a moment. "Next time don't let your eyes give away your thoughts so readily."

Lord Thornbear came over suddenly so she let me have an easy out, "It was nice meeting you Master Eldridge, I hope we have a chance to talk more later." She turned and began speaking with Lord Thornbear, seeming for all the world as if she had completely forgotten me already.

I took my chance and began making my way across the room, looking for Marc. I found him talking with Stephen Airedale. He saw me coming and excused himself for a moment to pull me aside, "Do me a favor would you? Devon has Ariadne cornered over there and I'm sure she could use a break, would you mind distracting him for a moment?" Me? It seemed that my friend was unaware of my status as a novice in the art of conversation, at least in these circles. But I couldn't leave Ariadne without support, she was his sister after all, although she'd been a pain when we were younger.

I headed back the other way and spotted Ariadne. Sure enough she was deep in conversation with Devon. I took a moment to remember the proper address, by which I mean I consulted the note card Ariadne had made for me earlier. *Lord Devon* it read. Although he wasn't the Duke of Tremont yet he had been granted a baronet already. Since 'Tremont' could be used to refer to the Duke of Tremont, his father, the usual way to call him was by his given name rather than his surname, hence, Lord Devon.

"Ariadne," I called to her. She looked at me gratefully. I faced Devon, "Please pardon my intrusion Lord Devon, her grace asked me to see if she could be found, to assist with some arrangements."

"Certainly," he replied with a genial smile. Despite his friendly attitude the aura around him still made me uncomfortable. Hopefully the books we had found would help me to better understand these things. "I didn't catch your name when we arrived..." he let the statement trail off, making it an obvious question.

"Ah my fault, I should have introduced myself directly to you, Mordecai Eldridge your lordship." That pretty well exhausted the topics I was prepared to discuss with the future Duke of Tremont.

"Mordecai, what an unusual name, are you originally from Lothion? The name sounds foreign." Wonderful, I didn't even know the answer to that question, my father had found the name embroidered on the blanket I was wrapped in.

"Honestly I'm not even sure where the name comes from either, my mother had a love of foreign romances so she might have picked it up from one of her books. I was raised near Lancaster though, so I consider myself a true son of Lothion in any case." Practice was honing my skills in the art of dissembling. Lady Rose's advice came to mind so I attempted to retake the initiative, "My life must seem very boring to a man such as yourself, tell me about your family. Do you have any siblings?"

Devon's eyes narrowed for a moment, "A brother, Eric, but he was lost in an unfortunate accident a year ago." I have a knack for uncomfortable topics.

"Forgive me, I didn't mean to remind you of such a delicate subject," I replied.

"No harm done, he and I never got along, and there was nothing delicate about his death either. Passed out drunk in a bath and drowned." Devon spoke casually, but I could feel him watching my reactions carefully.

"Was there any suspicion of foul play?" I asked.

Devon's face never moved, but I saw the purplish aura around him flash for a moment, "No, there was no cause for concern in that regard. Eric was well loved by all, and the girl who found him attested to the fact he had been drinking heavily before entering the bath, a few of the other women in the 'establishment' confirmed her story."

"Establishment?" I was confused.

"He died in a brothel." Lord Devon answered. "Now if you'll excuse me I need to refill my glass."

"I would be happy to get that for you," I said, glad to have something else to do. He proffered his glass and I started looking for the fellow with the bottle. When I returned I found him standing with Marc.

"We were just discussing you Mordecai!" My friend said this enthusiastically but his eyes were full of warning.

"Yes, Marcus was telling me that you're a student of mathematics and philosophy." Devon added.

"I try, but I fear I will always be an humble scholar, rather than one of the pathfinders of reason." I replied.

## Chapter 5

"You sound as though you might be well suited as a poet. Tell me what you think of Ramanujan and his work with the Riemann Zeta Function, I get so little interesting conversation at home." The aura around him had gotten darker again, which made his smile ominous.

"I think no one took him seriously at first, but that was his own fault." I said.

"How so?"

"He presented his ideas in a such a way as to deliberately elicit a contrary reaction from others. If he had been open about his methods, the fact he was using the Zeta function to arrive at his conclusions from the beginning there would have been a lot less controversy." I could almost feel Devon's disappointment. There was a very good reason we had chosen mathematics as my scholarly cover. It had become something of a hobby of mine as a result of my time studying with Marc. My parents thought it was useless abstraction of course, as did Marc, but I had found great enjoyment in the subject. Consequently I had spent a lot of time absorbing material from the Duke's library that most folk would never have even heard of.

"The controversy is perhaps the only reason anyone still remembers his contributions, perhaps it was necessary to preserve his work," Devon countered.

"I'm sure he is not the first person to *hide* his methods," I was starting to get annoyed so I probably emphasized that phrase too much. "He doubtless won't be the last, but his motive was not controversy."

"Do explain," his teeth flashed as he spoke and I found myself reminded of a fox.

"He kept his methods secret to embarrass his contemporaries. If they admitted they could not follow his work it made them look ignorant, if they argued he was wrong he revealed his methodology to make them look like fools. In essence he was an egotistical ass." Perhaps I was a bit too passionate about my subject, I might have insulted Devon, but I hadn't intended to, at least not consciously. The purplish light around him was pulsing now.

"Pardon me your lordship, no offense was intended." I added.

"None taken," he replied, although it was clear he felt otherwise, "you are passionate about your subject, a commendable quality in a scholar. If you'll excuse me I should mingle some more with the other guests." I was relieved to watch him go.

Marc stepped closer to me and took me by the elbow, "Let's retire for a moment, I need to get some air." He steered me to the balcony which was currently empty. Once there he spoke softly, between clenched teeth, "What the hell was that?"

"I'm not sure what you mean," I replied sipping my wine casually.

"Could you have chosen anyone in the world to make your enemy, that man is probably the worst you could have picked." Marc seemed genuinely worried. "What did you say to get his attention so firmly fixed on you?" He was referring to my short conversation before Marc had joined us.

"Well I did stumble into an embarrassing topic quite by accident, I asked him about his siblings." I quickly related the story of Devon's brother and how he had died. "He didn't seem particularly upset about it though." I concluded.

"Of all the things you could have asked that was the worst. His elder brother's death has been the subject of many rumors. Quite a few suspect Devon of having a hand in it."

I could see the problem but not my own relevance, "Surely he must know I wasn't intentionally trying to upset him."

Marc sighed, running his hands through his thick hair, "He knows nothing of the sort. You have to understand how people like him work. Let me give you a lesson in the aristocracy. First, he assumes that because he's so important, everyone else must be nearly as knowledgeable about his affairs as he is. Second, if he *did* have something to do with his brother's death he would have to be incredibly paranoid about it. Third, a complete stranger approaches him and starts questioning him about his brother's 'unfortunate' demise. He will naturally assume that you are either trying to send him a message or embarrass him. In either case he will take it as a challenge."

"Oh," I answered adroitly. "Well thankfully I live here rather than in Tremont."

"Idiot, like that matters to someone like him," my friend was angry now.

"What do you mean?"

"The only person who can safely insult one of the greater peers is someone of equal rank or greater, such as my father, or someone from the royal family," he explained it as if I were a child.

"Thankfully my best friend is his equal in rank." I smiled thinking that would make him feel a bi better.

"That only makes it worse, look over there." he glanced behind me.

Turning so I could casually glance back into the room I saw Devon looking our way, he raised his glass and nodded at me as if in greeting. "So what does that mean?" I asked.

"He's already caught on that we're friends, and he probably thinks I put you up to the questions about his brother. We were friendly before, but now he'll mark me as his enemy. Rather than shielding you, that puts you in danger Mort."

"I'm not sure I follow," I said.

"He can't strike at me directly, so his obvious targets for retaliation will be my allies, particularly those who have limited resources of their own." Marc looked at me intently as I finally understood what he had been trying to get across to me.

"But I don't even know him! I certainly never intended to make an enemy of him." How could things have gone so terribly wrong?

"In these circles, intentions don't matter," Marc answered glumly.

"So what do I do?" I was appropriately worried now.

"Avoid him if possible and pray he doesn't discover much about your family and friends. Let's go back in, we're only making him more suspicious chatting out here by ourselves." Marc stepped back inside. I followed a moment after and made my separate way around the room.

I wound up trapped in conversation with Stephen Airedale who was self absorbed enough to refrain from asking me anything about myself. I got bored quickly though since I had absolutely no interest in spice trading, or how much money he had made investing in it. I was about to excuse myself to visit the privies when I saw Penny enter the parlor with a tray of hors d'oeuvres. She met my eye for a moment and then looked away uncomfortably.

I made my way to the privies with a sinking feeling in the pit of my stomach. In the course of one short day I had managed to become a political liability to my best friend while at the same time convincing another friend I was in league with the powers of darkness. At least I hadn't caused Dorian any trouble yet, but Marc's comments had me worrying that he might become another of Devon's targets if he learned of our friendship.

The rest of the afternoon passed slowly and I finally managed to retire to my room without causing any more problems. I tried to take a nap as the social maneuverings earlier had left me tired, but I was restless. Instead I spent my time practicing the little bit I had learned. After a while I got fairly proficient at controlling the amount of light I produced. I had begun to get a feel for the flow of aythar as I created the light ball. 'Aythar' I had learned was the proper name for the force mages use to produce magical effects.

There weren't any handy subjects to practice my sleep spell on, and the hawk had made me cautious, I still felt a little bad about that. I resolved to retrieve that third book as soon as dinner was over. I couldn't make much more headway with Vestrius' journal without a better understanding of the Lycian language.

Eventually Benchley came to tell me that it was time to eat. Apparently Penny had arranged to have him handle me to avoid any more difficulties. As dark as my mood was I couldn't blame her. I wasn't feeling up to facing more political intrigue so I begged him for mercy, claiming a sudden illness. Benchley had been a valet for many years and he understood immediately.

"Say no more sir, I'll make your excuses for you," he promptly left.

After an hour a knock at the door interrupted my thoughts and for a moment I was hopeful that perhaps Penny had forgiven me for frightening her. Opening the door I found Dorian outside with a tray of food. "I thought you might be hungry," he said.

The sight of fresh bread and cheese reminded me that I had missed breakfast. My stomach rumbled. "Dorian come in, I could use a friend about now." I put my depression aside and put on my broadest smile for him.

I ate everything he had brought and soon found myself collecting the crumbs from the plate. Now that my belly was relatively more at ease I felt more able to talk, so I spent some time describing my woes to Dorian. He was suitably impressed with the depths of my folly. "You sure don't do things by halves Mort," he remarked.

## Chapter 5

I had to agree.

"At least you got to escort Lady Rose to the parlor," my friend has always been easy to read.

"Ok let's hear it, I saw you watching her as we came in. Do you know her somehow?"

He looked embarrassed, "You remember when I was fostered out last year?" It was a common practice for the sons and daughters of nobility to live for a year or two at another lord's estate. It helped them learn more about the handling of the kingdom, gave them a broader experience of the world, and forged ties with other members of the ruling class.

"I do, someplace in Albamarl wasn't it?" Then I remembered, Highcastle's home was in the capitol. "Ohhh...," I articulated. I have a remarkable vocabulary when I put my mind to it. Finally a concise sentence came to me. "You were smitten huh?"

"Basically," he replied. "We didn't speak very much though, so I doubt she even remembers me."

"You might be wrong there," I said, remembering her glancing at him earlier, but I didn't say anything more about it. We talked for a while longer before he left. But neither of us had any decent ideas regarding my problem with Devon Tremont.

Once he had gone I headed to the library to retrieve the third book, *A Grammar of Lycian.*

# Chapter 6

*Rarest of all are those born with both a high emittance and a high capacitance. How many are born so is uncertain, probably no more than one among thousands, and few of those survive past adolescence. The reason for this is that their talents are extremely dangerous, more so to themselves than others. A good analogy for this would be a child given a razor blade or other dangerous implement; they are more likely to harm themselves than learn to use it properly. Those few that do survive to adulthood find themselves alone with little guidance in the proper use of their gifts unless they are lucky enough to be found by someone of knowledge. Due to these unfortunate facts truly gifted mages, or wizards as they are often called, are quite rare, and usually solitary, except in some very populous cities.*

*~Marcus the Heretic,*
*On the Nature of Faith and Magic*

It was late as Penelope Cooper walked down the hallway. Her duties had kept her overlong and she was tired. All she could think of was getting to her quarters and finding some much deserved rest. As chance would have it she passed through the same corridor that led to the library. Had she passed through only five minutes earlier she would have encountered Mordecai and things might have gone very differently.

As it was she was alone in the hallway and wrapped in her thoughts. She felt guilty for her behavior earlier. She knew Mort hadn't meant to frighten her, but she had been completely unprepared when that fiercely brilliant ball of light had blinded her in his room. That had *not* been what she had expected when he had her draw the curtains and sit on the bed next to him. Truthfully she was not certain how she would have reacted if he had made a pass at her, she had much less experience with men than he seemed to believe.

The subsequent darkness followed by Marcus' abrupt appearance had thoroughly unnerved her and thrown her into a panic. Her reaction had left her abashed and she hadn't known how to respond when he had looked at her in the sun room earlier, which made her feel worse.

She was interrupted in her reverie by a door opening as she passed.

"Miss, would you mind helping me for a moment?" Lord Devon stood in the doorway looking upset and anxious. Terrific, she was exhausted already and now it seemed her sleep would be delayed even longer.

"Certainly your lordship, how may I be of service?" she responded in her pleasantest tone. She took pride in her job and wouldn't let something like fatigue spoil her performance.

"Did you clean my room earlier? After my bags were delivered?" he asked.

"No your lordship, I cleaned and aired all the rooms this morning before you and the other guests arrived." She hoped this wasn't leading up to some petulant insistence that the pillows or sheets weren't fresh enough.

"Perhaps you could help me then, I seem to have lost something, would you help me look?" Despite his reputation among the castle staff he seemed exceptionally polite.

"I really shouldn't be entering your chambers this time of night, sir," she replied. He seemed harmless enough but that sort of rumor could ruin a girl at her age.

"I understand. I'll leave the door open if you prefer. It's just that I've lost a necklace and I'm beside myself trying to find it, it's an heirloom you see." He turned his back to her and went inside, leaving the door open.

With an inward sigh she followed him. He began searching through the drawers of the dressing table. "Would you check the wardrobe for me? It's dark in there and I can't see very well." She had no sooner opened the wardrobe and leaned in to look when she heard the door shut, followed by the sound of a key in the lock.

She whirled around. Devon was putting the key into his pocket. A cold shiver ran down her spine as she saw the look on his face. She had heard stories of maids abused by young lords before, but things like this had never happened within the walls of Lancaster Castle. Such was the Duke's reputation that no one had dared affront his hospitality before.

"Sir if you think to spoil me, I'll scream. The good duke won't stand for treating the staff like this," she tried to keep her voice level but she could feel panic setting in. Devon had at least fifty pounds on her and while she was no shrinking violet she had little doubt he could overpower her. Her eyes scanned the room frantically, looking for anything she could use as a weapon to keep him at bay. It occurred to her that if she injured a peer of the realm, she might be put to death at worst, beaten and dismissed at best.

He chuckled, "Go ahead. Scream if you like. Who will take your word over mine? I found you rifling through my possessions when I returned to my room." As he said this he idly reached over and knocked a jewelry case from the top of the dressing table. Rings and jewels worth more than she'd ever earned were scattered across the floor. "Looks like you were startled when I found you."

Despair crashed over Penny in a dark wave. There was no escape left to her now, in an instant she knew her life was over, her dreams dashed by this pompous and spoiled lordling. The thought made her angry and she determined to scream anyway. If she was to be driven into the mud she would make sure as much dirt rubbed off on the bastard who had done it as possible. She took a deep breath.

"Relax. I have no intention of harming you my dear, or deflowering you either, if that is what you fear. I simply want the answers to a few questions." He was smiling reassuringly at her.

"What questions?" she asked, for a second hope lit within her, and she was ashamed at how easily he had manipulated her.

"Tell me about your friend, Master Eldridge." That confused her utterly. *Why is he interested in Mort?* she thought to herself. As far as she knew Mordecai should be completely beneath the notice of someone like Devon Tremont.

"Pardon sir, I don't know him at all, he only recently arrived here and..." she started, but Devon stepped forward. She paused. He stood only inches from her now.

"What was your name girl?"

"Penelope sir, but folks here call me Penny," she hated how servile she sounded.

"Well, Penelope who goes by Penny, let me explain something. Are you listening?" He still sounded calm but she could hear his breath coming more hoarsely now. She didn't trust herself to speak but she managed to nod. If you've ever been confronted by a large wild animal when you were a child you might understand how she felt. The menace was rolling off of him in waves.

"I absolutely abhor being lied to Penny. I hate it. And I think you're lying to me now. I know it, because I saw you watching him earlier." Penny's heart was beating so rapidly she felt it would surely burst from her chest. "Do you think me a fool Penny?" She kept her head down, to avoid his eyes, but he was having none of it. "Look at me Penny." He lifted her chin up. Large tears welled up and ran down her cheeks, betraying her fear.

"Do you know Master Eldridge?"

"I told you sir, I don't. I only watched him because he seemed handsome..." her head whipped back from a stinging slap; strong enough to hurt like hell, soft enough to avoid bruising. Something snapped and her fear turned to rage, she brought her hand up to strike him in return. So furious was she, that if it had connected, *he* most surely would have taken a bruise. He was ready for her though, strong and quick he caught her by the wrist and abruptly twisted her arm, spinning her around and pinning it behind her. Her arm felt near to breaking as he applied a steadily increasing pressure. Helpless now, he pressed her face first onto the mattress.

"Now you're starting to piss me off. Which is too bad for you Penny. I had wanted to keep this a nice friendly chat, but you just don't seem to want to cooperate." He was lying across her, using his weight to keep her pinned, and worse she felt a disturbing bulge behind her. His voice was coarse and husky in her ear as he continued, "Nothing excites me more than a girl with a fiery disposition. I've learned to break girls like you. Just like a young mare, sometimes you have to ride them hard to tame them to the bit and bridle. I'm sure your husband will thank me someday." His hand was under her skirt now, relentlessly moving up her leg.

Desperation robbed her of reason for a moment, "No wait, wait, I'll tell you. Please stop! He's the blacksmith's son. He's not important, please you can't do this!" She was crying now, her voice thick with fear. His hand had reached the top of her thigh now and when she felt his fingers touch her she lost control. A primal scream of rage, and terror ripped out of her throat, seeking to deny the injustice being done to her.

The sound of it was so great that for a moment he drew back, shocked at the volume of sound coming from such a young woman. *"Grethak"* he barked in a tone of command and abruptly her scream was cut off, every muscle in her body locked rigidly in place. Devon let go of her arm and rolled her over on the bed so he could see her face.

"You really are something special aren't you my dear? I don't believe I have ever heard a maiden scream as loudly as you just did." He smiled at her,

## Chapter 6

"But then you won't be a maiden for much longer will you?" Devon's face was rapt with pleasure as he stared down at her. He reached out and began calmly trying to unlace her bodice, which soon proved to be too difficult. Taking hold of her neckline he ripped it wide, exposing her breasts.

Penny couldn't breathe; her lungs were paralyzed just as surely as the rest of her muscles. The only movement left to her was that of her eyes, which rolled wildly as she looked for some means of escape. Her head was pounding in time with her heart as she fought to draw breath. Devon leaned down and slowly licked her face, leaving a trail of spittle from her neck to her lips. "I don't believe I've ever seen such a lovely shade of purple," he mocked. *"Keltis"* he spoke and touched her throat, before running his hand down to pinch her nipple rudely. Her throat opened and she was suddenly able to draw breath. She drew air into her lungs, her breath coming in great heaving sobs. She prepared to scream again, but he put his finger to his lips, warning her. Fear stopped her.

"Now now, lets be a good girl. If you scream again I might not let you have air next time. Besides, isn't it so much nicer when you have some complicity in this? The knowledge that you *could* have screamed but didn't? Sometimes it takes something like that to teach someone just how important life is, certainly it's worth more than your maidenhead." He leered as he began sliding her skirt up, exposing her nakedness to the light.

Penny closed her eyes, the awful reality of it being too much to look upon any longer. Then blessed unconsciousness overtook her and she knew no more.

# Chapter 7

*The skilled use of aythar by a wizard relies on the last of the three important characteristics, called simply enough, 'control'. Of the three attributes it is the only one that is able to change significantly with practice or training. Mages that survive puberty generally learn to channel their aythar using some method of symbolism and ritual, generally through the use of one or more dead languages. Although aythar may be used without language or symbols, as it often is in the young, it is quite dangerous to do so. Wizards learn the use of a language or system of rituals in order to control not merely 'how' their power is released, but also 'when'. An untrained mage whose power lies purely in his thoughts is dangerous indeed, as his power may come to the fore at any moment and lend deadly puissance to unbidden thoughts.*

*~Marcus the Heretic,*
*On the Nature of Faith and Magic*

I got to the library without meeting anyone in the corridors, which was a relief. After the day I had had I wasn't really looking forward to seeing people. Once inside I retrieved the book and took a moment to weigh it in my hands. It was an impressive tome weighing several pounds and covered with arcane words and symbols that glowed in my sight. Having already read a substantial part of Vestrius' journal I felt sure it would make the remainder much easier to understand. Mastery of the Lycian tongue was quite literally the most important knowledge I could gain, it being the means for me to control my incipient abilities.

Feeling a little better I tucked it under my arm and headed back toward my room. My life might be a mess in most respects but here at least was a problem I could solve through honest application of effort. Wrapped in my own thoughts I barely noticed the voices coming from one of the rooms along the hallway. I kept walking, wondering how late I could stay up studying and still be able to rise at the proper time in the morning, when a shrill scream cut through my ruminations. It was a sound I'll never forget. A raw expression of fear and terror, the sort of scream you sometimes imagine but never hope to hear. The sort of sound someone might make falling to their death. It stopped abruptly, cut off before it could be completed.

I looked around anxiously, unsure which direction it had come from. The book distracted me so I set it down against the wall to free my hands and walked back the way I had come. There. I could hear someone talking behind a door. I checked the doors on both sides before I found the correct one and leaning in

## Chapter 7

I thought I could hear Devon's voice, speaking calmly to someone else. I almost moved on at that point, surely the person that had given that blood curdling yell couldn't be inside, not with Devon talking in such a composed manner.

I pulled my head back from the door frame, and then I felt a sudden release of power. My practice over the last few days had made me quite familiar with the sensation. That held my attention. I pressed my ear firmly to the door, straining to hear his voice through the thick wood. The words that finally came chilled my blood, *"Sometimes it takes something like that to teach someone just how important life is, certainly it's worth more than your maidenhead."* I couldn't be sure who Devon was speaking to, but it was clear that whoever it was, they were in terrible trouble.

Unsure what to do I drew a deep breath and used the only spell I knew that might help, *"Shibal,"* I intoned quietly with as much power as I had, directing my will beyond the door. I listened again, I wasn't sure but I thought I heard someone slump to the floor, and Devon was no longer talking. Satisfied I tried the door handle.

It was locked, of course. I had no knowledge that would get me past locked doors, and the doors in

Castle Lancaster were so sturdily constructed it would take two men and a ram to batter one down. I stared at the door, angry at my own ignorance; surely if I were better educated there would be a simple way to bypass the lock. Thinking of the state the poor girl must be in gave urgency to my anger. Placing my hand on the door I closed my eyes and bowed my head. I took a deep breath and drew my power up as I filled my lungs, pulling in ever more, till it felt as if it would be a race to see which burst first, my mind or my chest. I had never tried to do something like this before but I knew that without proper words it would take a lot of strength. Then I began to exhale slowly, building pressure in my hand as it pressed against the door. As my breath emptied I began to feel the door give way and I blew the rest of the air from my lungs in an explosive rush. The result was an explosion of wood and splinters as the door disintegrated, slivers of wood flying in every direction.

The vision I found within was one that still gives me nightmares. Devon lay slumped on the floor on the opposite side of bed, but I had no attention to spare for him. The figure on the bed riveted me in place. It was Penny, her long dark hair had come loose from the bun she usually kept it in when working, and it lay scattered about her head in dark ringlets. Her uniform was ripped open, from her neck to her belly, exposing flesh that I had previously imagined but never hoped to see. Her skirt was shoved up above her hips and her legs were spread, one folded awkwardly under her, the while the other was stretched out, her foot touching the floor. She looked dead. A long splinter stood out from her right thigh, blood dripping down onto the linen sheets. If I could describe the emotion that filled me then I would, but there were no words, the world went white, as if all the color had been leached from it, leaving a horror of stark white and black contrasts.

I was numb with horror and shock while at the same time filled with a cold heartless rage. Walking over I bent down to pull the dagger from Devon Tremont's belt, which was already partly undone. From the looks of things he hadn't had time to bring his crime to fruition. It hardly mattered, Penny was dead. Her virginity or lack thereof would not bring her back to life, would not make her smile at me again. I knelt beside the bed, and though I cannot remember feeling anything but a cold numbness, tears ran down my face.

Carefully, I brought the dagger to bear, directly over the bastard's still beating heart, careful not to prick him with the point lest it wake him before I made the final plunge. I held it there for a timeless moment. My only worry was that it was too clean a death, better than he deserved. That momentary debate was all that saved his life.

A sudden sound broke my train of thought, an incongruous noise, too improbable to belong there. Penny was snoring. If it had been a light snore I might have missed it, but this was no delicate thing, it was a deep rumbling vibration. The sort a fat farmer might make after having too much ale and passing out in his bed. It led me out of the dark place that had replaced my heart, and improbably I began to laugh.

It was an awful laugh as such things go; when it started it was a terrible sound, a wretched gibbering sound, the kind of laugh to make townsfolk shutter their windows and lock their doors. As it stretched on though my stomach relaxed and I began to laugh more naturally, a deep belly laugh, interspersed with gasps as I struggled to catch my breath. Eventually the laughter faded into tears and I cried quietly till I got control of myself.

Easing myself up from the floor I began to think. Carefully I drew the splinter from Penny's leg, which caused it to start bleeding again. I watched her face to see if she might waken, but I had put a lot of power into the spell and she hardly stirred. Reaching down I cut a long strip from the bed sheet and used it to bind her wound. Then I straightened up and surveyed the room.

It was a mess to say the least. Jewelry lay scattered on the floor, interspersed with oaken shards. The sheets were stained where Penny had bled upon them, and two people lay sleeping in varying degrees of disarray. It was too much to deal with all at once, so I did the most important thing first. Bending down, I slipped my arms underneath Penelope, easing one arm behind her shoulders and the other beneath her knees. It was not the best angle to stand up from and I staggered for a moment, nearly stepping on Devon's head. *Aww, that would have been a shame to ruin those pretty features.* I thought sarcastically. I couldn't risk waking him though. Penny was not a slight girl, she was nearly as tall as me and hard work had given her plenty of muscle, yet she felt light as a feather in my arms. Adrenaline I suppose, but I didn't bother to think about it.

I walked out into the hallway and made my way to my room as quickly as I could. Hers might have been better but I had no idea where she kept her quarters. Gently I laid her upon my bed, taking a moment to cover her with the blankets. I returned to the hall and recovered the book where I had left it leaning against the wall and went back to stow it safely with the others in my room. Each trip took several minutes and I worried constantly that I might meet someone in the halls. It was past midnight and my luck held; the corridors were deserted. I still had several problems.

I needed help and there was only one person I could trust at this hour. Fifteen minutes later I was standing outside the door of the Thornbear household. Lord Thornbear was the seneschal for Castle Lancaster and accordingly his family lived in the large bailey overlooking the main gate. The night air was damp and a light rain had begun so I was a little wet when I got to their door, which suited my mood just fine. A sleepy servant opened the door, a man I knew from my previous stays with the Thornbear family. I'm not sure if he had a surname as I had only ever heard him addressed as 'Remy'.

"Mort, what in the name of the gods are you doing out here at this hour?" He kept his voice lowered to keep from waking the family.

"Remy, I know this seems odd, but I want you to wake Dorian for me, quietly if you can, I need to speak with him." I tried to put as much sincerity in my voice as possible.

# Chapter 7

"Fine fine, let me see..." he turned and promptly ran into the door frame. "Damn!" he cursed quietly, "Nobody cares if Remy gets any sleep now do they? No of course they don't, Remy don't need no sleep do he?" He was muttering to himself as he stumbled back into the Thornbear family rooms.

I waited anxiously for several minutes before Dorian appeared at the door. "Mort, I don't mean to be rude, but it is really late..." he started. Then he saw my face. Something there must have tipped him to my desperation. "Hang on, let me get my cloak."

A moment later we were hurrying back across the courtyard to the castle proper. I should mention that Dorian is one of those rare individuals that sleeps wearing a long stocking cap. He had forgotten to remove it in his haste and I didn't have the heart to remind him. Some things are better left unsaid, and I needed all the humor I could find that dark night.

As we went I tried to explain to him what had happened, but I don't think it sank in properly till he saw Penny sleeping in my bed. With the covers drawn she looked like an angel lying there.

"Do you know where her chamber is? I need to get her back to her own room before she wakes." I told him.

"Sure but I doubt we can get her in there without waking the other maids," he replied.

"Leave that to me." I moved over to stand at the side of the bed, preparing myself to pick her up again.

"Do you need me to carry her?" he asked. I considered his offer for a moment, but something inside of me snarled at the thought of anyone else touching her. Something had broken inside when I found her in that room and I didn't yet even know to mourn for my lost innocence.

"No, no, I have her. If you could just help with the doors and lead the way." I drew back the covers and lifted her up from the bed. This time I could feel the strain in my back, exhaustion and lack of sleep were beginning to take their toll.

The air hissed between Dorian's teeth as he drew a sharp breath, seeing her state. The torn dress, the blood, I couldn't blame him. I felt much the same. I cradled her in my arms and looked into his gaze. Fury dwelled within him, and I wondered what we might do once we had put her safely to her bed. "Who did this Mordecai?" His voice held dark intent.

"Not yet Dorian, we have to take care of Penny first." I prayed he could keep his calm.

## Chapter 7

"I said, who did this Mordecai!" he wasn't in a mood to wait.

"Listen Dorian," I started to say, but he interrupted me.

"No you listen! I want to know who did this and I want to know now!" he was shouting.

"Goddammit!" I yelled back, "Shut the fuck up and think for a second!" I believe that was the first time I had ever raised my voice to him. He closed his mouth, startled, so I went on, "What do you think will happen to Penny if someone sees her like this? She'll be ruined! Her father is destitute, she has no dowry; she'd never be able to get married. No one would take her! Whether she's been 'spoiled' or not won't matter once the rumors start flying." I took a deep breath and calmed down. Looking at Dorian I could see he was still listening.

"Now are you going to help me get her to her room or do I have to do it by myself?" I started toward the door. Dorian was there before me and got it open.

He led me down several flights of stairs to the lowest floor of the keep; staying ahead of me the entire way, checking each doorway to see if anyone was up and about. We got to the maid's quarters without incident, yet when he opened the door someone stirred. It was fairly dark, but a woman's nervous voice called out, "Who's there?" Dorian ducked back from the entryway quickly and I didn't waste any time.

*"Shibal"* I put as much strength into it as I could still muster, not bothering to focus it in any particular direction. Again I noticed that Dorian was completely unfazed. I would really have to look into that one of these days, but now was not the time. I stepped inside and looked around.

It was too dark to see, so Dorian lit a lamp after I assured him none of the occupants would be waking up anytime soon. The room contained five small beds, all but one held sleeping women. Dorian drew the sheets back while I placed her carefully down. Then I began the difficult process of getting her clothes off.

"What are you doing?" Dorian hissed at me.

"Turn around if it bothers you, I've got to get rid of the evidence. In fact, turn around anyway, it bothers *me*." When had I developed this jealous streak?

I wasn't having any luck with her dress, so I drew my knife and began cutting it away. It was already spoiled, so it didn't matter. Once I had it off I couldn't help but look at her for a moment. Say what you will, but I'd like to see you pretend not to notice the most beautiful woman in the world lying naked in front of you. If you said you hadn't stared, even for a moment, I'd call you a damn liar.

Regardless, I was very focused on making sure Penny was safe. I drew the covers over her and stood back up. Glancing around I noticed a plain nightdress neatly folded under her bedside table. I quickly dismissed the thought of dressing her in it. I didn't see how I could manage it properly so she would just have to figure that part out in the morning. I also took a moment to make sure she had a second uniform. It turns out she had three, well two now. That was one thing less to worry about at least.

I balled up her ruined outfit and rummaged about the room for a moment till I found a scrap of parchment and a charcoal pencil. I hastily penned a note.

*Say nothing. We'll talk later.*

*~Mort*

I tucked the note under her nightdress and hoped she would find it in the morning. Then we went, leaving the room much as we had found it. It was near three in the morning now and I worried that Devon might have woken up while we were about our business. I needn't have worried though, he was still sleeping like a babe when we got back to his room, the bastard.

I turned to find Dorian staring at the scene, "Where's the door Mort?" He looked at the splintered wood on the ground and then saw the look in my eyes. I had never seen fear in my stalwart friend's face before, but I saw it flicker there now. It made me feel old and tired; a strange sensation to have at sixteen. "Did you?" he motioned at the shattered wood with his hand.

"Yeah," I answered. What else was I going to say? Then I heard Devon stir, as if he might wake. *"Shibal"* I put as much strength as remained to me into it. A wave of dizziness swept over me and I nearly fainted then, but Dorian caught my shoulder as I swayed and helped me sit down on the bed.

I looked at the floor for a moment, trying to think, when I heard the sound of steel being drawn. Dorian was moving toward Devon now, cold murder on his face. "Wait!" I said.

"Why?" he asked in return.

# Chapter 7

"Honestly I don't know, but if we kill him now we're both dead men, and I don't think that would make Penny very happy. If we're going to give this bastard his comeuppance we'll have to find another way, but not now, not tonight. We're too tired to think straight," I said. That sounded entirely too logical to be coming out of my mouth. Someone else must have been talking when I wasn't looking.

Dorian struggled with himself for a moment before finally sheathing his sword, "Alright," he said, "what do we do about the door?"

"Well there's no way to fix it," I replied. "Would one of the other doors fit?"

"Wait here," Dorian looked like he knew what he was doing, so I laid back on the bed and waited. I must have dozed off for a bit, because it seemed like only a moment before he returned carrying another door. He had a hammer and a couple of other tools tucked into his belt.

He soon had the new door on the hinges, and I had to admit it looked a lot like the original. I wasn't sure if anyone would notice the difference but I was too tired to care. Dorian went off again and came back with a broom. I swear he was getting positively domestic. He cleaned the floor without my help, but I like to think I supervised. He got all the wood up he could find, being careful to leave the jewelry where it lay; then in a stroke of pure genius, he plucked up a bottle of red wine from the credenza.

"Wha?" I asked intelligently, as he smashed it on the floor next to Devon's head.

"Maybe the fool will think she brained him with it. At the very least his clothes will be ruined, he should count himself lucky." He helped me up and half carried me to my own room. You can never have enough friends like Dorian, but I was grateful to have him. I never could have finished our night's deception without him.

I sank slowly into the soft feather bed, but as I drifted off I couldn't help but wonder, what would Devon think when he discovered his key no longer fit the lock on his chamber door? That made me chuckle for a second, then I was asleep.

# Chapter 8

*For the same reason mages eschew purely mental methods for channeling their abilities, use of the common tongue for that purpose is generally avoided. The best tool for controlling aythar is usually considered to be a dead language, one acquired by deliberate learning after reaching puberty. It is also believed that languages which have been used for this purpose over many generations serve best, as the words and phrases gain a certain amount of power in their own right. Because of this, even individuals with a moderate to low emittance are sometimes able to effect minor spells by using language and symbols that have absorbed some inherent power due to long use by mages past.*

*~Marcus the Heretic,*
*On the Nature of Faith and Magic*

Devon woke early the next morning, only two hours after Mordecai had at last fallen asleep. He was careful not to move at first, uncertain what had happened. He was lying on the floor, fragments of glass scattered about around him. He listened for several minutes before deciding he must be alone, so he sat up and assessed himself.

It didn't look good. His clothes were beyond saving, soaked through with dark stains. For a moment he thought he had been stabbed, till he realized it was wine rather than blood on his clothes. The door was closed, but the girl was gone. He was fairly sure he hadn't finished his business with her... unless he had some memory loss. Had someone hit him with the wine bottle? Was it her, or someone else? Either possibility was disturbing.

He stripped his clothes and used some water from the pitcher to clean himself up before donning fresh attire. If someone else had struck him, then that meant he had an unknown enemy, one who had managed to get into his room while he was unaware. If the girl had done it then he had a gap in his memory, for she had been quite beyond such things at his last recollection. It must have been someone else; he would not have been so incompetent as to let that slip of a girl get away so easily.

The door... he checked his pocket, the key was still there. If she had used his key she had replaced it, *unlikely,* he thought. Her fear had been too great, she would have run, and kept the key. Devon Tremont knew a lot about fear and its effects. He checked the door, and sure enough it was unlocked.

## Chapter 8

"Someone's been interfering," he said to himself. The real question was who? What would they do with the knowledge they had? *Nothing.* If they were planning to use last night against him they would have done so already, bringing guards and witnesses while he lay unconscious. If anyone accused him now he could easily deny it. Why? That's what he would have done. Whoever it was had sacrificed a large advantage. They took nothing, his money and possessions were intact, only the girl was missing.

The girl, that was it. The only reason to hide last night's crime would be to protect her reputation. *But she was a common maid,* he thought. No one would care about her. Almost everyone within the castle would be more concerned with justice; only a select few would care more for her than destroying him. What had she said last night? *He's the blacksmith's son.* "He's also a mage," muttered Devon. He had seen a strong golden aura about the man each time they had met. It was the first thing that had piqued his interest.

She had held out against fear for a remarkably long time, and still had told him little. She must have strong reasons to protect him; likely enough she was in love with him. "And his room is only a short walk from here... and one corridor over." he said to himself.

Devon Tremont had always been decisive, he did not waver now. Rising he buckled on his sword and left the room and locked the door behind himself. At least he tried to... the key would not turn in the lock. *Another mystery,* he thought. He shook his head and headed for Mordecai's room at a casual pace.

When he reached his destination he was dismayed to see a large guard standing outside the room. *What is his connection to the Lancasters?* Nothing made sense. They were clearly complicit in his deception. The man was a commoner, yet they had given him a room fit for a king. Marcus was obviously quite attached to him. *And he is a mage,* he thought. That was the lynch pin, the key everything revolved around. The Lancaster family needed a mage. Did that mean they knew something regarding his plans for the future? If so the Lancasters might well be seeking magical power to bolster their position.

He kept walking, nodding at the guard as he passed. Deep in thought he began to carefully consider his next step.

***

# Chapter 8

Much lower in the castle Penny awoke. She had worked very late so Miri, the head maid, had let her sleep in. Normally all the staff were up before dawn. Penny's eyes snapped open, something was wrong. She had slept well, but now she was wide awake. Looking around the room she was beset with confusion.

*How did I get here?* she thought. "What happened?" she said. Suddenly she remembered, and her chest tightened with emotion. Fear, shame and rage fought within her for dominance. A surging storm rose up within, the fear and helpless terror of the night before washed over her, threatening her sanity. *Mother, what should I do?* That thought brought her nearly to tears, the helpless sorrow of a child who knows she can never go back, never go home. Her mother was dead and her father was almost an invalid, unable to work. Caring for him had become her purpose; he was why she had taken this job.

Now it was gone, along with her hopes for the future. She doubted she could keep her job once her shame became public knowledge. The room was empty so she drew the sheets back, afraid of what she might find.

She was naked, every stitch of clothing gone. There was blood on her thighs and a bandage around her right leg. The blood was to be expected, but she didn't recall hurting her leg. He must have done that after I passed out. A vivid image rose in her mind, an ugly image of what had been done to her. The only mercy was that she had been unconscious; at least she wouldn't have to remember that. *Except in my nightmares,* she added mentally.

She got up and mechanically began putting on one of her spare uniforms. Her leg was stiff where it had been injured but she felt alright otherwise. There was no soreness, no pain... down there, which seemed a bit unusual. She knew some girls had little pain, but she suspected Devon had not been gentle. "I guess I should count my blessings," she said, and then it was too much, she began crying. The tears poured out of her and her body heaved with great wracking sobs. She hadn't cried like this since she was a child.

Her mother had comforted her then, but there was no one now. After what seemed like hours, she ran out of tears. She was exhausted, too tired to care, too numb to feel anything. She finished dressing and decided she might as well report for duty. Before she left she tidied up the bed and put her spare clothes away. A small slip of parchment fell behind the bedside table unnoticed as she picked up the nightgown.

## Chapter 8

She found Miri and told her she was ready for work, hoping that the head maid wouldn't be too angry with how late she had slept.

"No problem lass, you did well yesterday and we had you running till well after everyone else was snug a'bed." The older woman seemed genuinely grateful, "If you'll run down to the laundry and give them a hand there for a bit I'd be glad of it." Miri's orders always sounded like requests, as superiors went she was nicer than most.

Penny was glad to do it, anything to keep herself busy. She kept herself moving, working the rest of the day in a mad rush, desperate not to remember. No matter how she worked though, her mind kept going back to it every time she let it stray. The worst came that afternoon, she had to take fresh sheets up to the guests' rooms. Every step filled her with dread and she prayed that one particular occupant would be absent.

As luck would have it he was not in the room. She changed the sheets as quickly as possible yet she could not help but notice the blood on them, as well as a torn section that must match her bandage. She was out of the room in less than five minutes and her heart was still pounding when she reached the stairs.

Thinking herself safe at last she almost ran headlong into Devon as he came up the stairs.

She came close to dropping everything and bolting, but Penny was made of sterner mettle than that. She clenched her fists, gripping the bundle of linens and made her face a mask of indifference. She had already passed him on the stair when she heard his voice, "Penny." She stopped, refusing to turn back toward him.

"Don't think matters are finished between us," Devon's voice was like ice. "Last night was just the beginning. I'll see your blacksmith's son cold and dead before this is over. You have my word on that." She could feel his eyes on her back, and fear held her heart in an iron grip. In her mind she saw Mordecai lying in a field, his body broken, blood running from his nose and mouth, as he struggled to breath. Devon stood over him smiling, murder in his eyes. The vision was so powerful it made her gasp, and she knew instinctively that it would come to pass. Rage built in her, a raw animal fury, without thought she whirled, throwing the bundled laundry ahead of her. Perhaps it would distract him for a second. A second was all she needed, she would pull him down. If the fall didn't kill him she would finish the job herself.

## Chapter 8

"Hey now! There's no call for that!" Devon was already gone and standing where he had been was Marcus, looking surprised. The sheets had struck him full in the face and now lay scattered across the stairs. The anger that had filled her with strength drained away as speedily as it had appeared, leaving her empty. She almost lost her balance then, but Marc's hand caught her shoulder steadying her balance. "Are you ok Penny?" His voice sounded concerned.

"Yes, yes I'm fine. I'm just not myself today." Words were inadequate to describe just how *not* herself today she truly was.

"I won't ask about the laundry, then, I can guess who made you so angry," he jerked his head in the direction that Devon must have left in. "I wanted to talk to you anyway Penny. There are some things you need to know."

She looked at his face, surprised at the seriousness she found there. Marc was normally the most easy going of her friends. "What is it?"

Marc took a few minutes to describe what had happened at the reception the day before. Detailing the trouble he felt was facing Mordecai. She nodded dumbly, it all made sense. He continued, "Penny you have to understand how dangerous that man is... he doesn't understand jokes and he doesn't tolerate insubordination. If he had been standing where I was when that laundry came flying at me, things would have gone ill for you. Worse, if he finds out you are associated with me or Mordecai he will try to use you to get at us. Do you understand?"

*He's already used me Marcus. Used me and tossed me away,* she thought. "What can I do to help?" she said instead.

"Nothing Penny, I couldn't bear it if something happened to you. Just keep your head and above all else don't let him find out about our friendship, as long as he doesn't think you are connected to me or Mort you should be safe." His earnestness almost brought her to tears again.

"Sure, I'll try to avoid talking to you or Mort." she answered.

"It'll only be a few more days, then he'll be on his way," Marc tried to reassure her. He could see there were some deep emotions behind her face. He had probably offended her, but it would have to wait. He would apologize later, once Devon Tremont was safely away from Lancaster. Then they could all relax.

# Chapter 8

***

I woke early, well... in the early afternoon. I hadn't gone to sleep til almost dawn and I had completely exhausted my body's reserves, both mental and physical. Thankful for not being awakened early I sat up and stretched. Sleep had done much to repair my condition, although I still had a lingering ache in my lower back. It could have been worse I supposed.

A knock at the door gave me an idea as to what had roused me from my slumber. Crossing the room I opened it and looked out, wondering if I might find a hallway full of guards with Lord Devon behind them. Benchley stood there patiently.

"May I come in sir?" he said in his best 'I may be a servant but I'm still better than you' tone. It's amazing how much information some people can convey with simple inflections. I might ask him for lessons later. I stepped back so he could enter.

"I don't suppose you have any food on you?" I asked, raising my eyebrows.

"Lunch is already over sir, but if you dress now you might persuade cook to let you have some leftovers." he answered with a hint of a smile. The bastard knew full well what the cook thought of people who missed mealtimes. I wasn't falling for it.

"Since you mentioned dressing, would you mind assisting me?" My native intelligence was working overtime.

"I believe that is what young Marcus intended when he asked me to check on you sir," he replied. Fifteen minutes later I was dressed again. Benchley's hands were surer than Penny's when it came to doublet laces, but then I guess he had more experience dressing men. I also made note that he didn't stand behind and reach around me to do up the laces. That should have told me something but I was too preoccupied to think on it.

Once he was finished with me Benchley left, and frankly I was relieved to be alone. I needed to think. The valet had been his usual imperturbable self, so I inferred that no hue and cry had gone up this morning. Most likely his lordship Devon Tremont was lying low wondering who had caught him with his pants down and whether retribution would be coming. I was naive to think that, but I knew little of aristocrats.

Since I thought it might be safe I ventured out to look for Penny, and perhaps steal some food if any happened to be lying about unattended. I had no luck finding Penny, or Marcus, or Dorian for that matter. Everyone seemed to have found better things to do than wait for me to get out of bed. Fortune was more kind when it came to food, I stumbled across young Timothy clearing tables in the great hall and he let me take large piece of roast pheasant that someone had left behind. I wrapped it in a piece of cloth and added partial loaf of bread from another plate. Timothy gave me one of his gap-toothed grins. I winked at him, and spoils in hand I retreated to my room to plot my next move.

Once I had eaten I decided to make use of my free time to study some more. I delved into '*A Grammar of Lycian'*. Two hours later and my head was spinning. I have a knack for languages but Lycian seemed designed to twist a man's tongues in knots. The verb tenses were also confusing, why anyone needed a 'past progressive' or a 'simple future perfect' tense eluded me. I decided to focus on memorizing vocabulary since I thought it might be more useful to start there. Another hour and I had had enough, so I switched to Vestrius' journal. With my slightly less ignorant grasp of Lycian I began to comprehend a bit more of what he had learned in his first few weeks of training.

Most of it was not particularly pertinent to disposing of evil sons of rival dukedoms, but one piece did catch my eye as fairly useful. My use of the sleep spell on Devon the night before had made me acutely aware of how easily someone could be rendered helpless. I was more than a little worried that he might be able to do something similar to me in the future, since I half suspected him of being a wizard himself. I wasn't the first mage to have such thoughts apparently. A lot of attention was given to the methods which could be used to shield a mage's mind and body from harmful outside influences, or in some cases the results of his own mistakes.

The simplest method was to shutter the mind. Some men I learned were born with no ability to manipulate aythar at all. They were known as 'stoics' and I recognized the type in my friend Dorian. A mage could, with some practice, mimic their ability, or rather their lack of ability, and gain the same benefits. To do so would temporarily rob me of my 'sight' while shielding my mind from external influences. Because of its disadvantages it was primarily used at night to protect oneself while sleeping since it required no active effort.

The hardest part of mastering it was finding a way to tell if I had successfully 'shut' my mind.

# Chapter 8

Eventually I hit on the idea of staring at the book on Lycian. Since normal folk couldn't see its glow I could use it to tell when I had properly closed myself off. It didn't take long for me to manage it after that. The sensation was akin to shutting your eyes, and it unsettled me more than I thought it would. Without being aware of it I had already begun to rely on subtle cues my magesight allowed me. Closing it off made me feel blind. I decided that I agreed with the mages of yore, sleep would be the best time for it.

The second method was to create a shield of aythar. The technique could be used in several ways depending on how much and what type of protection was desired. The least tiring was to create an internal shield that protected only the practitioner's mind. The result was similar to the other method with the exception that you could still use your 'sight' and abilities without impairment. Slightly more involved was the creation of a shield covering the entire body to protect one from physical as well as magical assaults. According to the legends in Vestrius' journal some great wizards were able to manage this during all their waking hours. The legends made it clear that not only were the great wizards paranoid, but they were well justified in their paranoia. Sometimes even that protection was not enough to save them.

Lastly, in times of need, some wizards had been able to create shields extending much farther from their bodies, to protect friends and sometimes even buildings. It was considered risky, since the effort could exhaust the caster and a particularly strong assault might even kill them if it used up more power than they had to give.

I practiced with both types, first trying to protect just my mind. Without someone to test it for me I couldn't be sure I had done it properly, but the amount of energy it required was negligible. Producing a large shield to protect my entire body was easier, though it required more effort. Since it extended just beyond my body I could actually see the energy as it enveloped me. It was nearly imperceptible, even to my sight, but by modifying the spell slightly I found I could color it with visible light, making it easier to see.

I found these exercises tiring but they left me feeling better about my ability to protect myself. Still it was a relief when a knock interrupted me. I had shielded the divan (as a stand in for another person) and I was attempting to beat it to death with the chair. I failed to stop myself in time and Marc opened the door just as I struck it for the final time. This was my third swing at it, and this time instead of simply rebounding the chair had splintered with a resounding 'crack'.

# Chapter 8

"If you are that upset with the room's appointments I could have let you trade apartments with someone else," he said in a droll tone.

"Ah... this isn't what it looks like." I said, giving him a sheepish look.

"If this was the first time you had said that to me I might doubt you, but knowing you I honestly believe it," he said with a laugh. "Seriously though, why are you hell bent on smashing up the furniture?"

I thought for a moment before I smiled, "Second law of magic."

We had been bantering since we were kids so he played along, "Which is?"

"Try new spells on the furniture before you risk other people or pets," I rattled off.

He laughed, "So what's the first law?"

I took a professorial pose and lifted my hand in an imperious manner, "Try new spells on other people or pets before you risk yourself."

We laughed a bit, and it felt good. Things had been so tense lately it was nice to be reminded of our younger days. "So why have you come in search of me young supplicant? Love potions? A cure for the piles? All things are within the power of the great Mordecai."

"I thought you might want to take in the fireworks tonight. Father hired the illuminator's guild to put on a show for our guests tonight," he replied.

I was impressed, fireworks were expensive and I had only seen them once before when we were younger. The illuminator's guild was a secretive organization that guarded the secrets of producing pyrotechnics. They were often mistaken for magicians because of the dazzling nature of their shows, but their devices were made with the help of science and chemistry. Everyone within ten miles of Lancaster would show up to see it.

We talked about the impending show for several minutes before I got serious. "Have you spoken to Dorian or Penny yet today?"

His expression changed, "I haven't seen Dorian, but I ran into Penny earlier."

I immediately pressed him for the details of their exchange. After he had described their meeting I found myself more disturbed than ever. "What's wrong?" he said. "You look angry."

## Chapter 8

It was difficult, but starting slowly I related the events of the previous night to him. His face grew dark and by the end he was swearing under his breath. "That explains a bit anyway," he said.

"What?"

"The reason Dorian pressed his father to put a guard on your door this morning. I never ran into him, but he talked Thornbear into setting a guard in the hall till you woke up this afternoon," he explained. I was surprised. Dorian was more protective than I had thought.

"Do you think he told his father?" I asked.

"No, if he had told him Thornbear would have raised hell with my father."

"You think so?"

"Most assuredly, and with Lord Thornbear pressing the case Father would have been forced to act, probably to expel Devon from his demesne," he grimaced.

"What would that do?" I wondered aloud.

"Start a lot of trouble. Tremont would be honor bound to complain to the king. The Lancasters would have to present evidence at the king's court to support our insult to Tremont." He looked at me.

"And?"

"And we couldn't prove anything. At the least we would be fined to satisfy Tremont's honor, at the worst it would mean war." Marc sat on the divan and put his head in his hands. He thought for a while, "Why didn't you just expose the villain when you caught him red handed? The evidence would have been on our side then."

"Penny," I said simply. I gave him a stare that spoke volumes about how I felt that he had even suggested it.

He apologized, "I'm sorry, you're right Mort, it was selfish of me to think that."

In the end we came up with no good ideas, but made ourselves feel better by suggesting bad ones, mostly involving hot irons and blunt instruments. An hour later it was time to get moving, the fireworks were about to start. As we stepped into the corridor I waved at him to wait a second. Muttering a short incantation I set a shield around my body, no time like the present to start good habits.

## Chapter 8

"What did you do?" he eyed me quizzically.

"My latest trick," I said and, since he couldn't see it I added a few words to show off my new shield in a vivid blue.

"Holy!..." he started and took a step back. "That looks formidable."

I spoke again and the shield faded into invisibility.

"You should leave it blue," he remarked.

"Why?" I didn't like being so conspicuous.

"It might scare the crap out of Devon."

I liked the sound of that but discretion seemed wiser.

# Chapter 9

*The greatest mystery may lie in the nature of aythar itself. Although it is present in much greater concentrations in living beings it is also present in small amounts within all inanimate objects. The amount of aythar present seems to vary in direct proportion to the level of awareness possessed by the object. Sentient beings possess it in large quantity, relative to inanimate things, such as rocks. Animals possess varying amounts in proportion to their level of intelligence. Plants contain less, yet still more than non-living things. Since aythar is present within everything, so far as we can tell, it may well be a fundamental property, or even a necessity for existence. Because self-awareness is directly proportional to the amount of aythar within something scholars conclude that even inanimate matter has some minimal level of awareness.*

*~Marcus the Heretic,*
*On the Nature of Faith and Magic*

The fireworks were every bit as spectacular as I had expected. We stood along the eastern parapet, looking across the lake that dominated the view on that side. Originally the lake had been separate but when the castle was built it had been expanded to fill the moat which surrounded the castle walls, but the main body still lay to the east. It made for a spectacular view with the pageantry of the fireworks reflected in its still surface. I found myself wishing Penny were watching with me, but I had been unable to spot her in the crowd.

I was sure she had to be here somewhere; even the servants had been given leave to lay aside their burdens and enjoy the display. The crowd was large, so it was unsurprising that I couldn't find her. After a short time I was separated from Marc as well, he had been drawn aside by a conversation with Gregory Pern. Not really wanting to be involved I had kept moving, truthfully I was looking for Penny. We still had not spoken since the incident of the previous night and I was growing anxious, unsure what she might think about what had happened.

Moving through the crowd I saw Rose Hightower engaged in discourse with Stephen Airedale. He seemed very earnest about whatever he was telling her so I kept my distance and tried to avoid distracting them. I passed by and she called my name, "Master Eldridge! I had hoped to see you again before now." She spoke with more excitement than I would have thought necessary.

## Chapter 9

"My apologies Lady Rose, if I had known please be sure wild horses could not have kept me from your side." I was in a good mood, so I figured I would play the game of words. Stephen seemed disappointed at my arrival, which made sense once I understood his intentions. Most likely he had been trying to woo the lady, and as everyone knows, wooing is not a game for three. "If I am interrupting I can bother someone else," I said, giving Stephen a sympathetic glance.

Lady Rose wouldn't have that, obviously she wanted a rescue, "Nonsense, we would be charmed to have you join us." She put her hand on Stephen's shoulder in a move that had to be calculated.

"Of course," he assured me, "unfortunately I need to excuse myself. You understand I'm sure." Indeed I did, so I refrained from smiling, no need to rub salt in the wound.

He left graciously and Rose gave me a look of gratitude, "Thank you, I was having trouble finding polite ways to deter him, any longer and I might have been unforgivably rude."

"Your beauty drives reason even from men of culture. Do not hold yourself to account for it. I have little doubt that you would eventually have turned him aside without injury to his pride." I gave her a slight bow, intending to take leave myself. My part had already been played.

"Wait, I would speak with you," she put her hand on my forearm. She was a woman who spoke with her hands and gestures as well as her eyes and words. Despite the restrictions and limitations of her class Rose Hightower was powerfully expressive, a natural communicator.

"Surely you have no need of my small words," I answered her.

"Perhaps you have need of mine," her eyes were full of hidden meaning.

Uncertain I paused, "I'm sure I will be richer for hearing them."

"Then we must agree to a trade, first answer my question and I will share what knowledge I have with you." She made it sound like a game, but something in her face hinted at more.

"We have a deal then, what would you know?" I replied.

"Who were you looking for just now?" her eyes twinkled with amusement.

# Chapter 9

"A friend, no one of importance."

"That is no answer at all," she frowned and removed her hand from my arm, conveying her disapproval.

"Penelope Cooper, a childhood friend and one of the maids here. Is that satisfactory?" I was a little annoyed at having to disclose that, lately Penny had become more important to me and I found myself embarrassed to discuss her.

"A lady friend, how interesting. Well enough, you should know that you made your first enemy at the reception the other day." She gauged my reaction.

"I knew that, but there is no remedy for it." If I got any better at wordy dialogue I'd be teaching classes in circumlocution soon.

"You are wise to accept that so readily. Your friend Marcus is lucky to have you, but his friendship puts you in grave danger."

I knew that as well, but I wondered at her opinion, "How so?"

"A building's strength lies in its foundation. Your enemy seeks to bring down the House of

Lancaster. He will do so by undermining the foundation first, and you stand out as a key target in that pursuit." I had heard this before, but I didn't want to offend her.

"Lady Rose, I think you greatly overestimate my value." Maybe she wasn't as smart as I had initially thought.

"That may be, but I find it more likely that you underestimate yourself." I could have argued, but didn't bother. She would have gotten the last word anyway. A few more pointless exchanges and I pardoned myself to continue my search. This time she let me go without comment.

I wandered for a while, hunting for a woman with dark hair and eyes that could drink the moon. Lady luck didn't see fit to help me though, damn her. Penny was elusive, like a dream you can't remember on waking. Finally I gave up and devoted myself to enjoying the last of the show. A particularly impressive red bloom lit the sky above the lake, accompanied by a thundering boom. An idea struck me. Pure genius. I couldn't wait to try it out.

Forgetting the light show I hurried back to my room to search for the words I needed in the

'Grammar'. If I wasn't able to find Penny at least I could prepare myself better for whatever lay ahead.

***

Penny stood in an embrasure, shadowed by a tall merlon. She was all but invisible there, which suited her just fine. She watched the colorful lights bursting overhead but she found no joy in them. When Mordecai came striding by, she almost stepped out. He had a look of concentration on his face and he walked with purpose. She had seen that look before, and she loved him for it. His mind was constantly in motion, and she could tell something had inspired him. The wind caught his hair, tossing it back, giving him the look of a hawk stooping to find its prey. She wanted to catch him, but her heart quailed at the thought, she couldn't face him now. It was too soon.

She stood still, till he was past. Then she turned back to watch the last of the show, a forgotten tear slowly tracing the line of her cheek. There were people everywhere but she had never been so alone. A touch on her shoulder startled her and she nearly screamed thinking Devon had found her.

"Oh my! I'm so sorry, I didn't mean to frighten you my dear." Rose Hightower was there, with a concerned look.

"Forgive me milady, I was caught up in my thoughts." Penny self-consciously wiped away the tears that stained her cheeks. "Is there ought that you need of me?"

"Don't apologize. Not all nobles are so heartless as Lord Devon," Rose said this with a small grin, hoping to elicit a smile from the troubled maid. To her chagrin Penny began to cry, shoulders quaking with silent sobs.

Rose Hightower had been a lady and a peer of the realm since birth. She had addressed kings and been courted by every eligible bachelor in the realm, but she was much more than that. She was a woman of character and compassion first, without a thought she stepped forward and embraced Penny, "There there, it's ok."

At first Penny tried to pull away, certain that her weakness would lead to even more trouble for herself. "No, no, don't worry, I'm a friend," Rose said, and she meant it. She held onto Penny until the girl relaxed, smoothing her hair and speaking softly to calm her.

# Chapter 9

Penny hadn't had anyone to hold her when she cried since her mother died. Even though Rose was nearly her age she was reminded a bit of those days, days when she had felt safe. Eventually she calmed herself and pulled back. "I'm so sorry. Please don't tell anyone about this... I don't know what would..."

"Hush girl. I am not so cruel as that. What happened here is between us, and if you'll let me I will help you as I am able," Rose's eyes were sympathetic. "Now tell me why you're up here weeping while Mordecai searches high and low for you."

"What? How do you know that..." Penny was startled.

"I spoke to him just a bit ago, he was looking for you and he seemed worried about you." He hadn't actually told her that but she had read it in his voice when he had answered her question; very little escaped Rose Hightower's keen ears.

"I wasn't hiding from Mort; honestly, I just didn't want to encounter Lord Dev..." Penny stopped, "He's been making a lot of demands of the staff. I meant no disrespect milady."

Rose's eyes narrowed, "None taken, I know all too well how unpleasant that putrescent man can be."

Rose stared at Penny for a moment, her mind working, she had heard rumors of Devon Tremont's misdeeds before and she had an idea of what sorts of things he was capable of. "Penelope, do you trust me?"

"I hardly know you milady." That remark could be construed as an insult, but she was in fact beginning to feel comfortable with Lady Rose.

"Fair enough. Listen to me, I know you are close friends with Dorian Thornbear, do you trust him?" Penny nodded. Dorian was one of the most honorable men she knew, not to mention their childhood friendship.

"I would trust him with anything milady. He's a true gentleman," she replied.

"Then accept me in his stead. I would trust Dorian with my life. If I can aid him, by helping you, I would count myself happy." Rose looked steadily into Penny's eyes.

"Why are you telling me this?" Penny could sense the other woman's sincerity but she couldn't fathom the reason behind it.

## Chapter 9

"Because I want to help you and before I can do that you have to answer me honestly, as one woman to another." Rose paused.

"I don't understand, but if you're a true friend of Dorian's I will answer you, if I am able." Penelope felt silly answering like that, but Lady Rose seemed deadly serious.

"You mentioned Devon Tremont was hard on the staff, but I suspect you meant something more personal." There was no easy way for Rose to broach the subject, but the look on Penny's face answered her more quickly than words could have done. "Have you been ill-used Penny? Please tell me true, and if he has I will do all in my power to see that tyrant pay for his crimes."

"No please, you can't tell anyone, if anyone finds out he'll..." Her words were confirmation enough.

"Relax. I won't go shouting it from the rooftops. I don't know what I can do, but I'll make sure he can't hurt you again. And eventually, I'll make sure that man pays three times over for what he has done, or I am not a Hightower." Her voice held a cold steel that made Penny shiver for a moment, yet it gave her hope as well.

"He's the son of a duke; what can women do to such a man?" Penny was more interested in hope now than dissuading Rose.

"He's the *younger* son of a duke, and his late brother Eric, was my friend." Rose took her by the hand and began walking toward the stairs leading to the courtyard. "And you would be surprised what *women* can do." The look in her eye would have given pause to even a king.

# Chapter 10
## The Dark God

*At heart, the gods as we have come to know them are merely powerful sentient and incredibly dense concentrations of aythar. It is thought that many of them formed originally as the result of mankind's innate need to worship a higher power, but this theory is unproven as some of the gods currently known certainly predate the existence of humanity. Whether they arose as a result of a prior sentient race similar to humankind is uncertain, they might well have developed from some purely natural phenomenon, independent of believers. The real question lies in what their ultimate goals are regarding mortal beings. Some have proven definitively malignant while others still seem benign.*

*~Marcus the Heretic,*
*On the Nature of Faith and Magic*

The fireworks were of benefit to more than just the spectators. It proved to be a perfect distraction for Devon Tremont to do a little research. The puzzling events in his room the night before had left him troubled. Someone had made a fool of him, and given the circumstances there was only one man that could possibly have done it.

He had shoved the furniture to one side, clearing the center of the room. Using a stick of charcoal he drew two black circles on the floor, one within the other. In the space between the two he traced a row of strange symbols. They glowed subtly as he finished and began his incantation. The summoning took several minutes, and during the invocation he repeated one name at regular intervals. As he finished the light in the room dimmed and shadows began to move strangely within the circle.

A dark form solidified within the center, a shape that moved and twisted like smoke trapped in a jar. "What do you seek of me little wizard? You have not yet paid what you owe." The voice was deep and coarse, rumbling like thunder in a winter storm.

Devon kept his aspect calm, showing fear here would be a grave mistake, "You will get your payment when I am king. The Lancasters are but the first of many rewards you will receive."

"You would do well to leave me undisturbed if you have no gift of blood, I am not some petty demon to be trifled with." A black maw of twisted teeth appeared in the smoke for a moment before vanishing again.

# Chapter 10 – The Dark God

"Perhaps if your information had been complete I would be more likely to provide such gifts, Mal'goroth." A bead of sweat ran down Devon's brow, he was taking a risk here.

"You imply I have violated our pact?" The voice was curious.

"You told me that there were no living wizards," he replied.

"All the ancient bloodlines have been severed and the knowledge they kept is broken and scattered, there are none left. Do you dispute this?" Mal'goroth's words were heavy with implicit threat.

"There is a wizard here, in the House of Lancaster, I would not think such a thing would escape your notice," Devon answered.

Mal'goroth spoke, "The talent arises from time to time, you yourself are proof of this. This mage can be no threat, without knowledge he is helpless, there are no more wizards."

"His name is Mordecai, how would you explain that? A random mage appearing here among the Lancasters; bearing a name from the line of Illenial?" Devon felt surer of himself now.

"Lies! The line of Illenial is no more, the last of them died sixteen years ago at the hands of the Shaddoth Krys." Mal'goroth had become still within the circle.

"Then the Shadow-Blades failed, even the Shaddoth Krys can make mistakes it would seem. Your information was flawed, like their mission." Devon was baiting Mal'goroth now, he hoped to get more from their bargain.

After a long pause Mal'goroth answered, "Yes."

"Then you must redress that mistake. I will require more assistance." This was going better than Devon had hoped.

"The Shaddoth Krys are too far, it would be better if you allow me to help you directly." Mal'goroth sounded eager.

"I am no fool, I will not bridge the gulf for you," Devon snapped.

"I would not suggest that, merely let me join with you, my power could make your task simple." The dark god's voice was almost friendly now. It was suggesting Devon open his mind to it, channeling the evil god's power. The thought was tempting but Devon shivered at the thought of letting the being into his mind. There was no surety he would ever be able to get it out again.

"That is unacceptable. What of your followers?" he was referring to the cult of Mal'goroth, a secret society worshipping in the shadows, hidden from the eyes of saner men.

"They could not reach here soon enough wizard, unless you open a way for them. Are you capable of such a thing?" Mal'goroth sneered audibly.

"I can manage it, *without* need for your power," Devon said. "How soon can they be ready?"

The dark form of Mal'goroth shifted in the circle, "Four nights from now. They will be waiting."

Devon smiled, creating a path to transport them would be difficult, but the result would be worth it. His original plan had been subtler, but sometimes bold strokes created a masterpiece. The Lancasters would be removed, they and their retainers would feed the dark god and their absence would destabilize the kingdom, a necessary first step. He finished his discussion with Mal'goroth and ended the summoning spell. Once he was sure the creature had gone, he broke the circle and began planning.

First he would remove the blacksmith's son. He represented a significant threat to the completion of his scheme. After that he would see the House of Lancaster expunged and their retainers brought to ruin. The House of Tremont would not benefit in the short term, but in the years to come, when the royal family suffered a great tragedy there would be no rivals to contend for the throne. Tremont would be the only possible choice.

There was yet more to do, so Devon left his room and went below. He needed a quiet isolated location within the keep, a place where something as conspicuous as a large transportation glyph would go unnoticed. Now would be the best time to find a place for it, while everyone was still watching the pyrotechnics he would be free to roam the cellars and tunnels beneath the keep.

# Chapter 11
## Return Home

*Regarding the differences in power between a mage and a channeler, otherwise known as a 'saint'. A mage is, in most cases a free agent, given that his power comes from within, while a channeler is beholden to the source of his power. Although both achieve their effects through the use of aythar a mage must rely upon his own control and his own reserves. A channeler is partly controlled by his deity, therefore his control is provided in large degree by his god and his reserves are much less limited. The channeler is largely restricted by two other factors: his credos, for he may not act against the wishes of his god, and his human frailty, a factor scholars refer to as 'burnout'. If too much power is channeled one may destroy one's health and possibly the ability to channel as well. A wizard's own power is rarely great enough for burnout to be a possibility although some exceptions have been known.*

*~Marcus the Heretic,*
*On the Nature of Faith and Magic*

I rose early for a change and for the first time in days I felt as if my mind and body were in harmony. I have lived according to a dawn to dusk schedule for most of my life, so the late nights had really thrown my body out of whack. I also had a plan, things to be a'doing. The feeling of purpose gave me renewed vigor.

I hadn't told anyone yet but I had decided the night before to return home today. I had already begun to feel some homesickness. After all I was just the son of a humble blacksmith. The politics and intrigue of court life wore on my nerves. I had no stamina for it. I wasn't going to spend the night however; I intended to ride back before nightfall. The idea that I had the night before required a lot of wide open space, and I wanted a place where I wouldn't create a panic with my experiment.

My home suited that purpose perfectly, out in the country we had no close neighbors and if anyone did happen to be in the vicinity, the smithy was often the source of odd noises. I would have to explain matters to my parents beforehand though. Even had I not planned my 'test' I needed to do that. My sudden departure had left my parents in the dark.

I borrowed a horse from Dorian's father, there being fewer questions that way, and began riding home. It took me close to an hour but the weather was nice and the palfrey I was riding had a smooth gait. I was in a fine mood by the time I got there. My only worry was how my parents would react to my new abilities. I'm pretty sure that it's not every day your son comes home to tell you he's developed a knack for magic. I guessed my mom would have the most trouble, she has difficulty with surprises. Dad would probably ask me if it would help with the metal somehow. He was very practical that way.

I found my father hard at work. He saw me come in and nodded at me, directing me to the bellows with a glance. I got to pumping. Half an hour later he set the piece he was working on aside to cool slowly. Annealing it was called, to take the temper out. "I didn't think you were supposed to be back for a few more days," he said.

"A lot has happened, I'm going back this evening, but I need to talk to you and mom," I replied.

"She's in the house I think, let me wash up and we'll go in. She'll probably want to feed you some of our leftovers." His face was still but his voice had a smile in it.

A while later, after some bacon and hash-browns; we sat at the table together. Slowly I began to tell them of the things that had happened to me. It took more time than I thought, even with me leaving out the parts about Penny. I didn't feel it was my place to discuss what had happened to her. Throughout all of it my father sat quietly, his stern face deep in thought. Mother looked as though she might interrupt a few times but he shushed her and she held her peace. When I finished she got up, "I have to hang the wash out. I'll be back in a bit." Her tone was tense.

"What's wrong with mom?" I asked.

"She's just having trouble facing the future, she'll be ok in a little while," he answered me. "Go on and do your 'test'. Just make sure its far enough away from the cows that you don't sour their milk."

"I'll try."

He thumped me on the back, "Go on, I'll talk to your mother. We'll have more to say when you get back. We just need some time to chew on all this." I had to love him. He might be quiet and taciturn, but it would take a lot more than learning his son was a mage to make my Dad lose his calm demeanor.

I walked away from the house and when I looked back I could see them talking. Their discussion looked rather heated, at least for Mom. I kept walking, I'd find out what was wrong when I came back. Once I had gone a long way I checked around to make sure our few cows were elsewhere. After I had reassured myself of that I thought about what I planned to do.

The fireworks had given me the idea. I would combine the spell for light with something to produce a loud noise. I thought of it as a 'flashbang'. Some people tell me I'm terrible with names. I checked myself to make sure I was still shielded. Then I started.

I focused on a point about thirty yards away and gathered my will, *"Lyet ni Bierek!"* I used my will like a whip, snapping quickly at the point I had chosen. The result surprised me.

A flash of light blinded me, accompanied with a sound like a cannon, a deep cracking boom so loud and sudden that it made me stumble back. *Dad was right to worry about the cows,* I thought to myself. What I had accomplished was creating an effect similar to an explosion, but without the damage. I repeated my experiment, this time placing it close to the ground, to see if it made any impression on the earth. It didn't. I continued, making them further away each time, since my ears were already ringing. It seemed I could place them a great distance away. Possibly over a hundred yards or more, although it became more of a strain the further out I put them.

After an hour I had thoroughly scared all the wildlife into finding more peaceful areas to relocate to. I returned to the house, wondering what Mom might think of my war against the quiet of the countryside. I found them sitting in the house, back at the table. It didn't look good.

My mother was flushed and her eyes were puffy. She had been crying. Dad looked tired, his eyes focused on a small box on the kitchen table. "Is everything ok?" I asked.

I expected Dad to answer, given how Mom looked but she spoke instead, "No. It isn't ok, but your Father has convinced me that it is time to show you this." Her eyes looked at the box.

"Does this have something to do with my new abilities?" I was worried, whatever was in that box had upset my mother in a way that I had never seen anything else do. Whatever it was might change everything.

"Well sort of..." my father started.

"Hush Royce! She gave this to me. You may have decided for all of us, but it's *my* responsibility!" Mom was in tears but she gave me a direct look, "Mordecai, this is from your mother, your real mother.

She trusted this to me to give to you when you were older, when you needed to know. She and I both hoped you would be grown before you saw it." She glared at my father as if he had sprouted horns.

"What's in it?" I asked uncertainly.

"A letter, from her to you. She wrote it here, in this room when you were just a baby. It's the last thing she did before she died. It's yours." Her voice sounded as if the world were ending.

I reached for the box and my father put his hand over mine, "Son, what you'll find in that box is your mother's love for a son she couldn't raise. You will also find her pain." He uncovered my hand and looked away. I had never seen my father cry, but his eyes were wet when he told me that.

I lifted the wooden lid. It was attached by two delicate hinges, my father's work. Inside the box was lined with velvet and a heavy surcoat lay folded neatly. It was a dark maroon color, with golden trim and a golden hawk spreading its wings in the center. Later I would come to know that its posture was called, 'rampant'.

"It's your mother's tabard," said Mom. "She was a daughter of the House of Cameron."

I nodded dumbly and pulled it out, letting it unfold. I tried to imagine the woman who had been wearing it.

"She was tall," said my father. "Nearly as tall as I am, and strong limbed; she had blond hair and blue eyes. Eyes like yours son, though I guess you get your hair from your father."

Underneath it was a folded piece of parchment. I lifted it carefully and unfolded it. Then I began to read:

*My Son,*

*It pains me that these will be the only words you ever receive from me. Trust me when I tell you that your father and loved you dearly and told you so often when you were yet a babe. I am entrusting you to Meredith Eldridge as I will not survive more than a few days at most. She is a good woman and I have come to respect her while she has cared for me here. I hope that you grow loving her as I have loved you, as I still love you.*

*My name is Elena di'Cameron and I was married to a great man, your father, Tyndal*

*Ardeth'Illeniel. He was the last and best wizard of his line. Given your parentage you may well inherit his powers, but he will not be there to guide you. What knowledge he might have shared is gone now, lost in the fire that consumed Castle Cameron, my childhood home.*

*The household was poisoned, and assassins came in the night, the Children of Mal'goroth if I am right. A fanatical cult obsessed with one of the dark gods. Your father and I fought to preserve you that night, but we failed in protecting ourselves. I failed. I was bound by oath and bond to protect your father. I was Anath'Meridum, one of the special guards that have guarded the old lines of mageblood over the generations. That is how I met him, but our love could not be contained in a simple bond, and so we married. You are the result.*

*At your father's request I forsook my vows and left him that night, taking you to safety, or so I hope. There is so much more to say, but I have not the strength to write it all. I told Miri as much as I could in the time I have had. I have also informed the Duke of Lancaster so that he might look over you from afar. Now that you have read this you may wish to seek him out, he will know more than I could possibly write here.*

*Above all, do not be angry with Miri. I begged her not to tell you these things until you were older. None of this has been her fault. She and Royce were simply kind enough to care for a stranger, thinking nothing of the risk they put themselves into. They are good people, the salt of the earth, the sort of folk your father always sought to protect. Now they protect you, and for that I am eternally grateful.*

*All my love,*

*Elena di'Cameron*

I stared into space. My world was coming apart and being reformed in ways that I could not recognize. There was much more in Elena's letter than I ever hoped for, and much less. I cannot describe the emotions running through me at that time. I don't even have names for them. "Is that it?" I asked finally.

"No Mordecai, there's more." My mother spoke now, "Your mother had very little time with us but she told us of the night she sought to escape with you," and she proceeded to tell me. Her words faltered a time or two as there were things in them that were hard to say. It isn't easy to tell someone of the death of their parents, even if they never knew them.

As she went on I began to ask questions. We talked until late in the afternoon. At last there was nothing more she could tell me. Meredith Eldridge looked at me with red-rimmed eyes, unsure how I might view her now.

My feelings were such that I didn't know how to express them, but a few things hadn't changed. Meredith and Royce Eldridge were still my parents. "Mom, stop looking at me like that. I still love you. You will always be my mother. I just have an extra one now." I looked at my father, "and I am still the blacksmith's son." There was a lot of hugging after that. My Dad, who is normally very reserved, put his arms around both of us.

"I need to go." I said.

"What will you do," asked my father.

"Nothing for now, I will talk to the Duke and see what he can add. I am not going to go mad seeking revenge if that's what you're afraid of, I wouldn't even know where to start." *Yet,* I added mentally. I put the letter back in the box, but I kept the tabard. I had plans for that. I went outside and started saddling the horse I had borrowed. My father walked behind me and as I started to mount he put his hand on my shoulder.

"Wait, I have something for you," he said, and he led me to the smithy.

"Your mother had a sword with her when I found her. She told me it was the blade of one of the men who slew your father. She wanted nothing to do with it, her own sword was gone, but I kept it." He walked to the back and drew out a long iron bound box.

"I am not a sword smith, but even I could tell the blade was poorly made. I took the metal and melted it down for bar stock." That surprised me. Normally my father bought his stock iron from the foundries in Albamarl. It was difficult and expensive for a small smithy like ours to do its own smelting. He had taken a lot of trouble to do this. "I did not have the skills, so it took me years, but I thought you might want something like this one day."

He opened the box and nestled inside was a sword. It was a simple thing, straight and true, the edges finely honed. The guard was plain but the steel pommel was inset with the Cameron arms. The base of the blade carried the maker's mark of Royce Eldridge. As far as I knew it was the only weapon he had ever crafted aside from knives and similar tools. He was not fond of violence.

"I did not make this for your vengeance. I did this to show that even from the ashes of wickedness and tragedy something of beauty can arise. I made this hoping the same for you. Use it for yourself; use it for defending those who cannot protect themselves, as your true father would have. Do not shame either of us." Then he hugged me, again. Twice in one day, surely he must be getting senile. I didn't complain though.

He sheathed it with a scabbard that had been stored alongside it in the box and gave it to me. I buckled it on, feeling awkward for I had never worn a sword, much less learned to use one. Then at last I got mounted and began to ride slowly away. Before I crossed the rise that would block the view of our house from my sight I looked back. He still stood there in the yard, watching me. Royce Eldridge is a blacksmith, and his work had made him strong, but at that moment he seemed old to me.

I rode on to Lancaster with the twilight casting deep shadows about me.

Mordecai

# Chapter 12
## The Blacksmith's Son

*Gods and wizards have historically been primarily antithetical, given that they usually embody opposite philosophies, those being 'submission' and 'free-will' respectively. Wizards rarely have much to do with deities and higher powers, having little interest in sacrificing their own goals. The reverse is not true however; the gods have always had a strong interest in wizards, for their ability to provide something which no channeler can. The gods are restrained by the fact that they reside upon a different plane of existence. Although a channeler may provide them an outlet into our material world he cannot offer them entry. The act of creating a portal through which the planes may be connected requires a great deal of power from both sides of the gulf between worlds. The only known case in which a wizard willfully conspired with a god to effect such a thing led to the destruction historians call the Sundering. The dark god Balinthor was allowed to cross and his actions here nearly destroyed our world. It is not clear how the ancients eventually stopped him nor how he was forcibly banished to his proper plane.*

*~Marcus the Heretic,*
*On the Nature of Faith and Magic*

I reached Lancaster with very little light to spare, but as chance would have it Marc and some of the guests came riding in at the same time. They had gone hawking that afternoon after I had left, which suited me just fine. I had enjoyed enough of 'polite' society already and the day with my parents had been a welcome respite. I was wrapped in my thoughts, still digesting what I had learned about my 'other' parents, so I gave them a casual wave and went to return Lord Thornbear's horse.

As I came out of the stables I encountered them again in the yard. Marc had a proud falcon on his arm, and he looked every inch the young nobleman in his hunting leathers. Stephen Airedale, Devon, and Elizabeth Balistair were still with him. I suppose the others had left their horses with the grooms already and gone to wash up.

"Ho! Mordecai! Come and see my catch!" As always he retained the exuberance of youth. I couldn't help but find his enthusiasm catching. I walked over and let him show me the contents of his game bag. He had quite a collection of small birds and gazing at the lethal beauty of the falcon he carried I wasn't surprised. Seeing that, I felt somewhat better about my accidental hawk 'murder' the other day. Birds everywhere rejoice! Mordecai the hawk slayer works to even the scales on your behalf.

"Where did you get off to today Mordecai? I couldn't find you earlier," my friend asked.

"My apologies, I felt a sudden need for fresh air and borrowed a horse from Lord Thornbear," I replied innocently.

Devon chose then to make his presence felt, "Off to visit the blacksmith, Master Eldridge?"

That took me off-guard, "In fact, I did ride that way. Why do you ask?"

"No reason," he replied with an audible sneer. "How was your father? Well, I trust?"

Stunned I had no reply. Artful words would not suffice; it was lie or admit my deception. Marc didn't suffer from my hesitation, "Where's this coming from Devon? Or are you just practicing at being a rude jackass as usual?"

Devon ignored the insult, "I was simply curious. I heard that our Master Eldridge here was actually the blacksmith's son, I thought I'd see if it were true or not."

Marc's cheeks were flushed red, "I don't appreciate your treatment of my guests *Tremont*." He put emphasis on the name, to remind Devon of the political implications of insulting him I would guess.

Elizabeth Balistair tried to break the tension, "Devon you shouldn't pay heed to servant's gossip, it demeans you. Where did you hear such a thing?"

"From one of the serving girls, Penelope I believe she said her name was." He stared directly at me as he said this.

"Why would she tell you this?" Stephen asked.

"In my experience a woman on her back will tell you anything you want to know," Devon said with a leer. The man had no shame.

I was overcome with rage. The world turned red and all I could see was Devon Tremont bloodied and torn beneath me. I raised my fists and advanced on him, ready to make my vision a reality. I heard a whisper of steel and felt a razor edge at my throat, stopping me cold in my tracks.

"I see you wear a sword, blacksmith. Why don't you try that instead?" Devon's eyes glittered triumphantly. The man had trained with the sword since childhood, whereas I had never held a blade in my life. There could be only one outcome.

"Planning to add murder to your list of sins Devon? You know he cannot beat you with the sword," Marc spoke now, his voice calm and sure. "Only a coward provokes a fight he cannot lose. Why don't you try something more interesting."

Devon's sword never moved but his confidence wavered, "What do you suggest?"

Marc smiled, "Since you have challenged him, let Mordecai choose the contest."

Devon considered for a moment, then answered, "What would you choose boy?" He glared at me. I had the distinct impression that if I chose a sport he could not win he would find an excuse to use the sword anyway.

"Chess," I said. I could feel cold sweat dripping down my back, but my face was defiant.

"You think you can beat me at a gentleman's game?"

"I think you are no gentleman," I answered, but my more sensible side was screaming at me to shut up.

Normally you don't provoke a man holding a sharp instrument to your throat.

"Very well," and he sheathed his sword in a graceful motion. "But if there is no blood, honor cannot be satisfied. Why don't we put a wager on the game?"

"What do you want to wager?" I said.

"A hundred gold marks," he replied with a grin, "and if you cannot pay the debt I will take you as my bond servant."

I was in deep now, that was more money than I would see if I worked ten lifetimes, even a nobleman would fear to lose such a sum.

"No," came a deep voice, "If he loses I will pay his wager." James, the Duke of Lancaster stood unnoticed behind us. "And if he wins you *will* pay, I will make sure of that."

Devon found his manners and gave a shallow bow, "It shall be as you say your grace." He did not dare insult his host at this point.

After that we repaired to the sun room parlor, there were tables a plenty there. The Duke walked beside me as we went. "I trust you will teach that dog a lesson, Mordecai," he said in a tone meant just for us. I looked at him and for the first time I considered how much he had done for me. As a boy I had never questioned the fact that Marc's family wanted me to spend time with their son. Now, knowing what I did about my origins, it made more sense. I resolved to make sure I won.

What Devon could not have known, was that I was perhaps the best chess player in Lancaster. Marc had planned on it when he suggested I choose the game. The biggest unknown was Devon's own skills, which I suspected might not be insignificant. "I will do my best your grace," I answered him. "I would also ask that you grant me a private audience afterward."

"No need to be so formal Mordecai, you are much like a son to me yourself, no matter your birth," he answered courteously.

"It is about my birth that I would speak to you," I said, and he looked at me with raised brows. Then he nodded.

"I expected this day would come," he replied, "but let us see to the matter at hand first." Marc had gotten closer and looked at me with questioningly. I shook my head in a way that told him this wasn't the time.

Minutes later I was seated at a small table across from Devon Tremont. "Why don't you set up the pieces, blacksmith?" he sneered, as if to suggest I might not know their proper placement. Without comment I obliged him.

"It appears you are a piece short, or don't you know where the last piece goes?" he said when I had finished.

"I thought we might make this more interesting," I replied. Honestly I'm not sure what had come over me. His condescending attitude had gotten under my skin. "I'll offer a handicap of one of my rooks."

"You insult me. Taking such a handicap puts you at a disadvantage. I would rather beat you with an even board, that none can claim your foolishness gave me the win." He was no longer sneering, his mind working to decide if I was being clever or a fool.

"Let's sweeten the wager then, since my handicap might cheapen your victory." A cold rage was on me now and I wanted to see this petty lord-ling sweat. "Say two hundred marks? And I will be your bond-servant, even if the duke pays my debt."

Devon almost flinched at the number, "You seek to bet with money not your own, perhaps the good Duke has his own thoughts on your reckless disregard with his purse." He glanced at James, "Your grace?" he waited for a reply.

"My money is as safe as if it were in the king's own storeroom. I have no objection," his words were calculated to make Devon unsure. He gave no sign of worry.

"Very well then, I accept your offer," Devon replied calmly, but I could see the purple aura around him wavering with uncertainty. Over the past few days my ability to sense things had become more acute. He opened with his queen pawn.

The next few minutes were quiet as we played, and I became aware that my opponent was quite skilled. The knowledge threatened to undo my concentration but the anger within pushed my doubts aside. He offered a pawn sacrifice, a subtle gambit, but one that would cost him little given I was already down a major piece. If I took it I would find myself pressed hard on the side of the board where I was already weak.

I refused to take it and spent the next few moves improving my control of the center board. Then I offered a gambit of my own, placing a pawn in a seemingly indefensible position. He took time studying the position and while I waited I noticed the room had filled with people. Every notable staying with the Lancasters was there, along with the Thornbears and her grace, the duke's wife.

Eventually Devon decided to ignore my gambit and I smiled at him. His uncertainty had led him to believe it was a trap. A pawn sacrifice usually is, but I had counted on his fear, my gambit had been a bluff. If he had taken it I would have been even further behind and at risk of losing completely. As it was, my pawn unbalanced his position and allowed me to take his defense apart.

He hadn't seen it coming, but several moves later it became clear his position was fast becoming untenable. Sweat stood out on his brow and he glared at the board, seeking some way to salvage the situation. I had pinned his king's knight and he was left with a choice of what piece to sacrifice. He responded by moving his bishop to put me in check, but the move exposed him further as I calmly countered, bringing up a pawn to defend my king. He was forced into an exchange of pieces that ended with my taking the knight. I was still behind in material on the board, but his position was scattered and indefensible.

A quarter of an hour later it was over. I slid my remaining rook into position and it was check and mate. I smiled at him graciously. I would have sworn he was ready to spit nails, but he held his tongue. "I must concede," he said.

"Then it is time to settle accounts," Duke James spoke now.

Devon stood, "I'll write a letter of credit on my accounts in Albamarl."

"You'll pay him in hard coin. You made no mention of papers and clerks when making your wager!" James was angry, but it was calculated. He had already known it to be highly improbable even Lord Devon would carry so much gold while traveling.

"I don't have that much with me! What man carries a strongbox while traveling?" Devon Tremont was flustered now.

"Then you'll pay what you have and write the letter of credit to me. Your banks and clerks would just as easily cheat another man, but they will pay when I call your account due!" Then he turned to me, "You'll get your reward Mordecai, I will not see a man insulted and then cheated to boot."

Devon was red faced now, "You dare imply my writ is no good?!"

James Lancaster stared him down, and I was reminded of two mastiff's squaring off for a fight, "I have no love for bankers. If you come to Lancaster again and seek a quarrel, bring your strongbox with you, you will have need of it." And then he laughed. It was a deep laugh, the sort that starts in the belly and makes its way all the way up. I'm not sure how he managed it, given how hot the emotions were running, but it worked.

Soon enough everyone in the room was laughing with him. Devon didn't laugh though, not at first. He had been thoroughly humbled. Yet he was smart enough to see a way out when it was offered. He joined in at last, and a bitter laugh it was; it was not enough to cover his bruised pride. Devon left quickly after that, and I wondered who would suffer for his anger this time.

I found myself beset with people who wanted to clap me upon the back, and within a half an hour I felt I was near to being thumped to death. Devon wasn't popular it seemed. Marc's father finally rescued me, "Let the boy be! He's had enough for one day." He cleared a path for us through the crowd and got me into the hallway. "I'll see you in my chambers in an hour, Mordecai. Try not to be late this time," he joked.

I winced at the reminder of my previous blunder, "Yes your grace." He strode off down the hall and I decided I'd best go to my room and get my head on straight. Since leaving that morning I had had nothing but one surprise after another. I could still hear them laughing and carrying on in the room as I walked away. "Did you see Devon's face!" "Two hundred gold marks!"

I ran across Timothy on my way back. "Evenin' sir!" he said to me with his usual energy. "I heard you gave that Lord Devon a fine trouncing!" Word spread quickly; doubtless a crowd of the servants had been hovering outside the parlor while we played.

"Not as much as he deserves," I replied, "but let's keep that between us." I gave him a conspiratorial grin.

"Don't worry sir, Tim here would never sell out his friends!" he gestured to himself with his thumb.

"I would be honored to be counted among your friends Master Timothy," I said with mock exaggeration. That pleased him I think, even though he knew I was teasing him. For such a young lad he was remarkably sharp. "Would you do me a favor Timothy?"

"Sure sir!" he answered.

"Keep an eye out, and if you or someone you know sees Devon Tremont doing anything odd or suspicious, come find me. Can you do that?" I might have only a few friends among the nobility but perhaps I could turn the staff to my advantage.

"Glad to sir. It's nice to see one o' them get their comeuppance at last. Meanin' no disrespect to our own good Duke o' course!" he said.

"If you run into Penny let her know I need to see her, I've had a devil of a time finding her the past two days," I added. He assured me he would and then we had reached my door. I said goodbye and stepped inside. The cool dark room was a welcome relief. I must be getting accustomed to the comforts of privacy and a feather bed.

That thought made me pause, the rooms I had been given were easily the size of my parent's entire house. I felt lucky to have my own tiny room and bed there. What would happen when I spoke with the Duke? Would I be living like this from now on? What of my parents? Even aside from any possible largesse I might receive as part of my heritage, I was already rich. Two hundred gold marks would be enough to buy my parents anything they could conceive of.

What would that sort of money do to me? Or them? I didn't want to wind up like Devon Tremont, arrogant and uncaring. The Lancaster family was kind though, so perhaps nobility would not inevitably turn me into a pompous ass. I became aware that I was pacing the room, making a circle around the sitting chair and the divan.

In the dark. I stopped and stood still. The room was pitch black. I could hardly see my own hand if held it an inch from my nose. Yet I had been navigating easily around the furniture a moment before. I realized I could feel where everything in the room was, a sensation similar to seeing, but more visceral, like touching everything around me with feather soft fingers. Curious I closed myself to my power, as I had recently learned to do before sleeping. The sensation ceased and I found myself trapped in the cloying dark. It felt as if the world was closing around me and for a moment I was claustrophobic.

I hastily opened my mind and I could see again. Just not with my eyes. It was such a subtle thing I had not noticed it when I could see normally. I lit a lamp and sat on the bed. I had a lot to learn and without a proper teacher I had no idea what to expect. I wished Penny were there to talk to, but then again, the last time I had seen her she had been frightened senseless by my newborn power.

It was time to see the Duke, so I pulled out my mother's surcoat, emblazoned with the Cameron arms. It was a loose garment, open at the sides so I was able to put it on, even though it was clear that I was a bit larger than Elena had been. She had been a tall woman, so it was only an inch or two shorter on me than it should have been. I belted it around the waist and went out to find James Lancaster.

I found him in his rooms, with Genevieve beside him. They had the look of two people who had been sharing secrets. James gestured for me to close the door behind me. After I had done so I stood facing them.

"I am here at my mother's request." I said.

Genevieve burst into tears. It was so sudden and unexpected I had no idea how to react. She leapt up from her seat to throw her arms around me. In the sixteen years I had been alive, and the eleven or so I could actually remember, I had never seen Marc's mother lose her composure. Laugh yes, angry occasionally, sorrowful perhaps... but I had never known her to weep like this. Worse she was clinging to me in a manner that should have been reserved for her own children or her husband.

Nervously I put my arms around her and patted her lightly on the back; looking to her husband to guide me. He merely nodded, as if to tell me it was alright. After a moment, Genevieve released me and returned to her seat. She was still sniffing and her face was a mess, red and puffy.

"I was certain when I saw you walk in here wearing that," James said. "I have not seen her in over sixteen years, but you look much like your mother, although your coloring is your father's."

"You knew them?" I asked.

"I did. I met your father several times in Albamarl while he served the King. I knew your mother even better as she grew up in Castle Cameron not twenty miles from here. I met Ginny there," he looked affectionately at Genevieve.

That confused me and I guess my face said as much. Genevieve answered my unspoken question, "I was there to visit my sister, Sarah, your grandmother." Her eyes were still wet. I took a moment to work out what that meant. If she was my grandmother's sister, that made Genevieve my mother's aunt, and my grandaunt. She was *family*!

"But that means..."

"Your mother was my niece, and you are my great-nephew." I guess her hugging me wasn't such a breach of protocol after all. Then another thought struck me.

"So Marc is my..." I have never been very clear on the rules for calculating the various degrees of cousin-hood. Fortunately I was in a room full of amateur genealogists; the nobility learn this stuff from the time they're old enough to talk.

"Your first cousin, once removed," she finished for me. It would take me some time to sort out the connections in my own mind. At first I wondered if this meant I was a relation of the Lancaster family, but that was not the case. I was related to Marcus through his mother, who had been a Drake before she married James.

"How well did you know my mother?" I asked, once we had gotten back on topic.

Genevieve answered, "Very well, she was my only niece. When she announced her intention to return to her family's home for a visit I wanted to go as well, but James and I were required to be in Albamarl that week. I would have liked to have seen you... with her," she almost broke down again, but taking a deep breath she regained her composure. "She was very young and full of life. When she decided to devote herself to the line of Illeniel and take the vow I thought her father might go mad; so angry he was."

"He didn't want her to marry a wizard?" I had no idea what sort of issues being a wizard entailed in the circles of high society.

"No dear, that was later, I mean when she decided to become Anath'Meridum," she replied. "Your mother was mad for fairy tales and adventure, that and her athletic nature led her to seek your father out."

Now I was more confused, "What does Anath'Meridum mean?"

Genevieve explained as best she could, with occasional help from James. Neither of them understood it, but apparently certain wizards were bonded to a guardian, a warrior that would watch them, stay with them, and eventually die with them. At least that is what the legends implied, but I got the impression that James didn't really believe their lives were linked in the physical sense.

"Why would a wizard allow himself to be bound in such a way that if his guardian died he would die also? That never made sense to me, not that I don't believe it is possible. I just don't think they would set things up to work like that," said the Duke.

Genevieve nodded, "In any case, her father was none to pleased about it. She was his heir and the vow precluded her from inheriting. I don't think he was too keen on passing the estate to her younger sister."

"When did she marry my father, Tyndal?" Genevieve was proving to be a wealth of information and the past was coming to life before my eyes.

"About a year after that she and Tyndal were engaged. It was supposedly rare for a woman to become Anath'Meridum, but those that do frequently fall in love. I guess it is to be expected when a woman and man are forced to spend every day together," she said.

# Chapter 12 – The Blacksmith's Son

"How many Anath'Meridum are there?" I asked.

"None now, I would assume. There was only one for each wizard, and the Illenial family was the last of the recorded lines. You have to understand, I don't know much about the traditions, only what Elena told us," she seemed apologetic.

"So my name is Mordecai Ardeth'Illenial, or should I call myself di'Cameron?"

James spoke up, "Properly your name is Mordecai Illenial, although you could choose to carry your matrilineal name as well, Mordecai di'Cameron Illenial in that case. Ardeth is a term added for a wizard that has been bound."

I had no idea if I would or could be bound as Tyndal had. It sounded extremely awkward. Of course I had no understanding of the true reasons for it at that time. We continued talking for a while, till the conversation turned to the future. A subject I was understandably nervous about.

James broke the topic, "Mordecai, you realize the Cameron estates are still in my hands don't you?"

As a matter of fact I didn't. I was so ignorant of the workings of the upper class I wasn't even sure what he meant. "No sir," I said uncertainly.

"After the fire, the murders, none of the Camerons were left, other than some distant third cousins. I might have passed the estate to one of them, but your mother's note made me aware of your survival, so I have held them in trust," he paused, "for you."

He had to explain a bit more to me then, but it seemed that the lands of the Cameron family were held by the Lancasters, and through them by the King. In other words, the Count of Cameron had been his vassal and the Duke of Lancaster had the freedom of deciding to whom he would bestow the title and estate to, if he chose not to keep it for himself. In short, he was offering the lands to me.

"If you intended all along to pass the land to me, why did you wait till now?" I had done nothing but ask questions since I came in.

"Your mother, and I as well, felt you would not be safe," he said simply.

"Wouldn't I have had guards and a castle?"

"They were not enough for your parents. Almost everyone in Castle Cameron died that night. I had no way to prevent something similar from occurring again. Even now I worry that you might fall prey to a similar fate, but you cannot remain as you are anymore." For a moment I wished that I could remain a simple blacksmith's son, the world he described was too big, too dangerous. Mort Eldridge didn't belong in a place like that.

"Why not?" I wished aloud.

James responded, "Your only protection until now, has been anonymity, and anonymity is no longer enough. You now have an enemy who will someday be one of the most powerful peers of the realm, rivaled only by myself and superseded only by the king. Your only protection now is that of rank and station."

I had to admit the logic of his words, but something else occurred to me, "You said 'almost' everyone in the castle died. Who were the survivors?"

"The only ones that lived were those who were away or didn't eat the meal that evening. Even those that didn't partake were slaughtered when the assassins came. A handful of servants hiding in the cellars survived, as well as Father Tonnsdale; who was fasting and locked himself within the chapel," he answered.

"Who was the poisoner?"

"We never found out. There was nothing left to discover. The fire gutted the castle and the few that survived didn't work in the kitchens," he said. The lack of evidence obviously bothered him as much as it did me.

"What about the assassins? Surely something must be known about them, or who sent them..." I asked.

"We believe they were the Children of Mal'goroth, a cult to one of the dark gods. They overran the Kingdom of Gododdin many years before you were born, we thought they had plans to repeat their actions here, but there has been little sign of them in Lothion since that night. The few we found were already dead," he sighed. "We won't uncover the secrets of sixteen years ago tonight, and we have other things to accomplish."

"Such as your grace?" I was curious now.

"You reached your majority last year, I believe...," he looked at his wife.

"Mordecai is sixteen and will turn seventeen in almost two weeks," she answered. Genevieve was possessed of an excellent memory regarding birthdays apparently. The age of majority in Lothion was sixteen.

"Very good, Mordecai I will confer your title and land upon you tomorrow evening, followed immediately by your commendation ceremony." He smiled at me.

"I am overwhelmed your grace." I said, stunned. Who could have thought he would move so quickly?

"Please, call me James when we are in private. Now, you should go and get some rest. Marcus is planning a boar hunt in the morning and you'll want all your wits about you for that." He clapped me upon the back and led me to the door. He leaned out and shouted, "Benchley! Fetch the scribes. We'll be working late tonight!"

"Thank you your gra... James," I stumbled. He nodded at me and I found myself walking back to my rooms in a state of profound shock. I was barely aware of my surroundings and nearly walked into Penny as I rounded a corner. She was accompanied by Rose Hightower.

Penny let out a most unladylike yelp when she saw me. At first it seemed she didn't even want to meet my eyes. I had never known her to be shy before, but she had been through a lot lately, so I figured it might be understandable. "Penny! Thank the gods! I've been looking everywhere for you!" I grabbed her hands with a sense of relief. "I need to talk to you." I gave her my most serious look.

A slight cough caught my attention and I realized my mistake, "Forgive me Lady Rose, I forgot myself. I hope you are well this evening."

"No need to apologize, I cannot blame a gentleman so taken with the sight of his lady-fair." She gave me a knowing smile and I started to protest but she continued, "What is this?" She was looking at my surcoat. Penny took notice as well.

"Mort?" she made my name a question.

"It's complicated, and one more reason I need to talk to you, but not the most important one," I was having trouble getting her attention. She looked to Rose.

"Unless I am mistaken those are the arms of the family Cameron, long thought defunct. It would seem that Master Eldridge has a surprise in store for us. You just left the Duke did you not?" Fantastic, Lady Rose was an expert in heraldry as well. She would have made a fine detective.

"Lady please, I beg of you, keep this to yourself for now." Surely she could see my desperation; I think she enjoyed tormenting men.

"Until the day of revelation I suppose?" She pursed her lips in a mock pout. The woman was entirely too perceptive.

"Indeed," I replied. "If you will allow me a moment alone, I truly need to talk to Penny." I tugged at Penelope's hands and Lady Rose nodded her approval. We walked a short way down the hall. "Penny I've been trying to find you for two days, it's about the other night..."

She flinched when I said that, "Whatever you heard is probably true Mort. I'd rather not be reminded."

"No that's not what I meant," I was puzzled. "Did you get my note?"

"The one where you told me that you are a nobleman in hiding, biding his time to reclaim his ancestral home, or the one where you told me that you're a wizard with the powers of light and darkness at his command?" She had gone from curious to upset rather quickly.

"I tried to explain that to you the other day but you ran off before I could finish!" My own frustration was bubbling up.

"And how long have you known about your illustrious heritage?" she countered.

"I just found out this afternoon when I went to see my parents, that's where I got this tabard." I held the fabric out as if it would support my tale.

"And yet within just hours of finding out you manage to challenge one of the most powerful men in the realm to a chess match and clean him out." She said in a tone that implied she was not as mad as I thought.

"Yes, well he said something about you that I couldn't forgive, and things just sort of went downhill from there." I replied.

Penelope's face went white and her entire demeanor changed, "I appreciate you defending my honor Mort, but you don't understand."

"I wasn't defending your honor exactly... he said some things about my parents, and then he mentioned how he had learned them; which is why I need to talk to you about the other night. When you were in his room; I know what happened and I wanted..." I tried to say, *I wanted to tell you what happened after you went to sleep*, but I never got there.

Her hand struck me solidly across the cheek and left a ringing in my ears. "So you were upset that he insulted your parentage! Never mind that you think I'm a whore, that's completely understandable. You are the world's second biggest ass! And what did you say you wanted? Were you going to ask if you could pay for an evening as well? Now that you're about to be a high and mighty lord yourself. Go to hell Mordecai!"

She was walking away now, as I stood there trying to figure out where I had gone wrong, "Wait Penny...you've misunderstood me, and I *still* haven't told you the full story yet!" I yelled after her.

She didn't stop and I didn't chase her. After a minute Rose walked over to me, "You certainly handled that well."

"Do you ever say anything helpful? Anything sincere, to actually help someone? Or do you just sit there on your high society horse and play games with everyone?" I was mad and Rose was near at hand.

"That actually stung. Despite what you believe I care a lot. That girl of yours has been through a lot and if you love her you'll be patient," she actually looked sincere as she said this, her usual sly smile was gone.

"She's not *my* girl," I answered. "And she's been through a lot more than you know. If she would talk to me I could help her."

"I know more than you realize, and I'm telling you to be patient. Simply put, you may think you know what she's been through but you haven't the faintest clue. Keep barging around and you'll only drive her away." Rose Hightower had drawn herself up to her full height and she radiated a warning aura. I had well and truly pissed her off. "Good evening to you," she finished and turned to head the same direction that Penny had stalked off in. I might have said she 'flounced' away, but a woman as high bred and well mannered as Rose Hightower never flounced.

# Chapter 13
## The Hunt

*After the near destruction of the world by the dark god Balinthor, the ancients established a system to prevent such an event from ever occurring again. All the known bloodlines that had produced powerful wizards were catalogued and their heirs were carefully watched. Any mage born with sufficient power to create a world bridge was given a 'protector'; although I use that term loosely. They were required to form a bond with someone, usually a trusted friend. The person bonded came to be referred to as Anath'Meridum, which meant 'Final Pact' in the old tongue. This guardian's true purpose was to ensure that the mage they were bonded to would never forsake humanity and create a bridge to allow one of the gods to cross over, whether by choice or under duress. Wizards powerful enough to require bonding were called 'Ardeth'.*

*The bond between a mage and their Anath'Meridum is poorly understood but it is known to link the lives of both individuals, such that if one were to die the other would immediately follow. Anath'Meridum were trained to kill their charges if they should be corrupted by the enemy or betray their oaths. Failing that, they would kill themselves, thus ensuring the safety of all.*

*~Marcus the Heretic,*
*On the Nature of Faith and Magic*

Getting into a fight with someone is an excellent way to ensure that you will get the worst possible sleep. Someone was knocking on the door. In my head I could hear a voice saying, please please go away and let me sleep. Unfortunately reason reared its ugly head and explained to that voice in no uncertain terms that I would have to get up, since they would not go away. Reason is a bitch sometimes. "Alright, hang on!" I shouted at the door.

Benchley stood outside, "If you had left the door unbarred I could have woken you a bit more carefully sir."

"People like *you* are exactly why I barred the door to begin with," I grumbled to myself.

"Master Marcus told me to get you ready for the hunt this morning." He had a set of riding leathers draped over one arm. I decided then and there, that if there were ever to be hunting on the Cameron estates it would have to be an afternoon affair. The idea had merit. I should probably issue a proclamation requiring all the animals to stay in bed till noon as well, to even the playing field. I tried to explain my idea to Benchley but he seemed to be related to the voice of reason that had made me answer the door in the first place. Both of them ignored me.

A quarter of an hour later I was dressed and more or less awake. Benchley had a lot of experience at this sort of thing and had come prepared. Black tea, hard bread and a bit of sausage followed him in the door, carried by Timothy. “Breakfast for you sir!” Timothy still had that gap toothed grin that always cheered me up.

Soon enough I was down at the stables where everyone was gathering. I had never been on a boar hunt, so I didn’t realize what a large production it was. The good duke had a large kennel with a variety of hunting dogs, and there were two particular kinds that would be used today. The ‘bay’ dogs would find the boar and alert us to their location. The ‘catch’ dogs would attempt to hold the boar in place, a dangerous task. Apparently it was not uncommon for one of the large mastiffs to be killed.

The Duke's master of the hunt was a man named William Doyle, who also happened to be my friend Timothy's father. As I came up he was explaining the lay of the land, where the boars were to be found that morning. I found out later that it was customary for him to go out before every major hunt, a 'quest' it was called, to find the game before the hunters rode out. I guessed he must be a masochist, since he had been up several hours before the rest of us.

Sir Kelton, the marshal was out as well and he had the grooms running back and forth, fetching horses for the participants. As was usual, we were all to be mounted on coursers, their speed being preferred for the hunt. I found myself on a dun horse and carrying a boar spear. The spear itself was interesting. The ash shaft was about six foot in length and terminated with a long leaf shaped blade that probably added another foot or so to the overall length. A small crosspiece behind the blade was there to protect the hunter. I checked the head and found my father's mark impressed on the steel there.

Marc rode up beside me, his face flushed with excitement, "You know what to do right?!"

# Chapter 13

I shook my head, "Not a damn clue." Apparently my remark was funny because someone behind me started laughing. Dorian had ridden up.

"I can sympathize with you my friend, I never got a taste for these sorts of adventures either," said Dorian. "I always feel sorry for the poor boar." Despite his position and training as a warrior Dorian had always been a gentle boy as we grew up. He often played peacemaker when others lost their temper and he had a great affection for animals.

"Just listen for the hounds Mort! When you hear the baying start you know they've found one, so ride quickly or you'll be late for the kill." My experience with killing was limited to chickens and considering how enjoyable that was I didn't really know if I *wanted* to be the first to find the boar anyway.

We set out riding across the fields around Castle Lancaster, spreading out as we cantered along. Dorian and I took a position on the right hand side and soon we were more than a hundred yards from the nearest riders on either side of us. We reached the edge of the forest and then we were among the trees. The ground was dappled with spots of sunshine coming through the leaves, and a light breeze kept everything in motion.

The air was sweet with the smells of spring and green things growing. Despite my early morning crankiness I had to admit that the idyllic scenery around me worked a subtle magic. The wind ruffled my hair as the powerful horse beneath me walked easily along. Dorian and I spread apart as well, and soon even he was lost to sight. Closing my eyes I could feel the forest around me, tasting it with my mind in a way that was almost spiritual.

I relaxed and soon forgot the hunt. If I heard the hounds I decided I would ignore them, the day was too beautiful to spoil with blood. Or maybe I was just lazy. I continued to expand my awareness, startled at how much life there was around me. Things unnoticed by the eye, the badger in his lair beneath an oak thirty yards away, the finches fluttering in their nests high above, mice and small creatures filtering through the grass, searching for seeds. These were things I had never known before, not in such an intimate way. Reaching further I felt Dorian more than a hundred yards to my left, fighting to get through a thick patch of brambles. I couldn't 'see' him, but somehow I knew it was Dorian, it felt like him.

## Chapter 13

I laughed thinking of his predicament, for I knew he was in no serious trouble. Then I felt it behind me, a tight knot of hatred, a man and horse, emanating that sickening purple aura. Devon Tremont was following me cautiously. He was still at a distance, but he was closing steadily, so I picked up speed. I would rather not encounter that unpleasant man on such a fine day.

Within a minute I knew he had sped up as well, he must be at a full gallop in fact, since he was closing quickly. *Lets see how he handles this then,* I thought to myself, and I switched directions, heading to my left. That would put me across Dorian's path eventually. Assuming that Devon wasn't able to track me he would wind up quite some distance from me very quickly. As a precaution I made sure I had myself completely shielded, I had forgotten to do so that morning.

Sure enough Devon turned to follow... he must be able to sense me, in much the same way I could sense him. *Does that mean he's a mage also?* I had been wondering that since seeing his purplish aura the first time, this seemed to make it even more likely. I kicked my horse, breaking into a full gallop now, if he wanted to catch me I would lead him a merry chase through the woods. I smiled to myself as the trees raced by... the wind was in my face and I could not help but laugh.

Glancing over my shoulder I saw Devon come into sight through the trees, he was bent low over his mount and pressing it for all the speed his horse could muster. He looked serious, which only made me laugh harder, so I gave him a cavalier wave. "Ho Devon, it seems you want to race!" I shouted back, although I have no clue whether he could make out my words as the wind and trees whipped by me.

Then I felt something. Something against my shield, pressing, trying to reach my mind. After a moment it was gone and I laughed even harder knowing that he had failed at whatever he planned. Have I mentioned that I sometimes lack all common sense? Finding his target unreachable, Devon did something I should have expected, if I had been thinking rather than laughing at him.

My courser, the beautiful horse that was galloping beneath me, froze. I don't have a better way to describe it. One moment we were racing the wind, the next every muscle in the poor beast's body locked up. It went down immediately, legs snapping as it struck the earth like thunder, twisting and rolling. I might have felt sorry for it, but my own problems were nearly as great. Still laughing I suddenly felt as if a giant hand had plucked me from my seat. As the horse went down I sailed forward, like some great misshapen bird flying headlong into the trees. I probably would have flown a great distance but for a large oak tree that stopped my forward progress.

I woke on the ground. Something wet was running down my face, making it hard to see, so I reached up to wipe it off and my hand came away covered in blood. I could hardly breathe; each shuddering breath came with stabbing pains in my side. Some of my ribs must have been cracked. Miraculously both arms and legs seemed functional, but I could not help but think that if it hadn't been for my shield I would be dead already. *He tried to kill me!* That thought ran through my mind and it seemed extremely important, although I was having trouble remembering why.

A shadow fell over me and I looked up, Devon stood over me with a smile so evil I knew he had not *tried* to kill me. He was there to finish the job. *"Grethak!"* he spoke and my body went rigid. I was beginning to understand what my poor horse had gone through and perhaps Penny as well, but I didn't have time to worry about that. "Poor Mordecai, you really shouldn't have been riding so fast!" he said.

In his hands he held a large leather pouch, "And here I was just trying to catch up with you, to give you the money I owe!" I was struggling internally now, my lungs were locked and I could not breathe. Imagine drowning, tied and unable to move and you'll be close to the sensation I was experiencing. Nothing worked and my heart was beating faster and faster, pounding in my ears as my body starved for air. Within my mind I could feel his magic, wrapped like a snake about my brain, paralyzing my movement centers. I tried to pull it loose, but it was difficult, more so because I had no way to speak. Even so, I could eventually have gotten free, with or without words, but I didn't have that much time.

Devon was standing over me, gloating, but I could no longer hear his words over the pounding of my heart in my ears. I felt a fool as I stared up at him with my eyes bulging. My vision grew dim and then I could not see at all. Trapped in darkness I wondered if the next life would be better, this one had been nothing but trouble. At last the darkness left me and I sank into oblivion.

# Chapter 14

*Frequently misunderstood are the gifts of those who are sometimes called prophets, or seers. They are thought to be similar in nature to channelers in that they do not possess a large amount of native aythar, in many cases they also show little emmittance as well. The visions that frequently haunt them seem to be largely unintentional in nature. Possibly they possess some sort of subconscious sensitivity similar to magesight, but below the threshold of awareness.*

*~Marcus the Heretic,*
*On the Nature of Faith and Magic*

Penelope's shoulders moved steadily, the muscles tensing and relaxing as her arms swept the floors. She was young and healthy, long practice had given her ample stamina for the task so that she hardly broke a sweat as she worked her way down the long corridor. It was one of those jobs that never seemed to end. By the time you had finished sweeping the entire labyrinth of Lancaster Castle the floors were dirty again back where you had started. Consequently the maids had someone sweeping almost constantly as Genevieve Lancaster would not tolerate dirty floors.

Penny didn't mind though, the work was steady and unlike most of her other tasks she was able to think or daydream without interruption while she swept. Today she was thinking about Mordecai. She had watched him that morning as he had ridden out with the hunting party. Tall and slim, the riding leathers had looked uncommonly good on him, accented by his dark hair and bright eyes. *To be so good looking and so stupid at the same time,* she thought to herself. Their conversation the night before had upset her, and she was still angry with him. She kept telling herself that, but she just didn't feel it. In all honesty as she thought back, she was more ashamed and embarrassed than anything else.

*When he said he knew what had happened... I just couldn't bear it,* she realized. Obviously Devon had been bragging, and so bold that he had even told Mort. And he was upset that Devon had called him a *blacksmith!* She knew Mordecai wasn't so insensitive as that, he hadn't meant it that way. Yet to tell her he knew what had been done to her, and then say something else was more important? "What the hell could he have wanted to tell me then?" she said aloud to herself. Now that she had slept and her mind was clear she could see that something had been bothering him, something important.

## Chapter 14

She kept sweeping, letting the rhythmic movement of her body relax her mind. She drifted, daydreaming as she worked, but Mordecai kept returning to her mind, until finally she saw him, as he must be now. He was riding hard, driving his horse through sparse woods and past large oaks. The sun was shining on his face, lighting his eyes up like sapphires while he laughed and rode on. He looked over his shoulder to see something, and then he was flying. The horse fell and she could see that it would never recover from such a fall. Mort flew from the courser's back at the speed of a full gallop and flew head first into the trunk of a large oak.

The force had been so great his head had sheared the bark from the tree where it struck; while his body lay on the ground, blood running from his nose and mouth. He must surely be dead, yet even at that thought new hope arose. His eyes fluttered and she could see his chest heaving as he fought to draw air. The wind had been knocked out of him, or perhaps his ribs were broken, in either case it was a miracle he was alive. No one should survive such a blow, no one *could* survive such a blow. *Magic!* she thought, and she knew it had to be true.

Then she saw Devon Tremont approaching. He had dismounted and was walking up with a sinister gleam in his eye. He stopped when he reached Mordecai and she saw him speak, gloating over his fallen foe. Mordecai went rigid and his face began to turn red, while in the background Penny could hear a woman screaming, a raw ragged sound. The voice of someone beyond hope, someone with nothing left but one long note of despair rising up from the depths of their soul. Finally she realized it was her own voice.

Someone was shaking her, "Snap out of it! Penny! What's wrong?!" Her eyes focused on the face of Ariadne Lancaster. She was staring at her with a worried look.

"He's dead, he's dead, oh god I saw this before! Why? Why didn't I tell him?" Penny was beyond distraught now. "Devon's killed Mordecai." The words fell from her mouth like dead leaves in autumn, dry and empty.

"Penny you're dreaming... you're in the hall. Mordecai isn't here... he's out hunting, everything is fine." Ariadne tried to calm her down.

## Chapter 14

"I have to go... do you know where Lady Rose is? She'll know what to do, please Ariadne you have to help me." Something in her eyes must have gotten through to the younger woman because she answered her without further questions.

"She was in the parlor just a moment ago, taking tea with mother and Elizabeth," she replied. "I don't understand what's wrong though..."

Penny was already running, and she reached the Duchess' parlor well ahead of the younger girl. Without pausing to knock she burst in, something she normally would not have dared to do. Inside she found Lady Rose sipping tea with Genevieve Lancaster and Elizabeth Balistair. They looked up in alarm at her sudden intrusion. The Duchess spoke first, "Penny you really should knock before you come bursting in..."

Rose laid a hand on her arm, "Wait Genevieve, something is wrong."

Penny shook her head, "Yes, yes, your grace, might I have a word with Lady Rose?"

Genevieve nodded, clearly annoyed but she kept her peace. Rose stepped out into the hallway with

Penny. "What's the matter dear?" She sounded calm but she could sense Penny's desperation. Sparing few words Penny described what she had seen, including the fact that this was not her first vision of the event.

"You don't think this could be a dream? Or a moment's fancy?" Rose asked.

"No it's real. I can't explain how I know, I just do. It's happening right now!" Penny was close to tears.

"Come then, there isn't any time." One remarkable thing about Rose Hightower was her ability to judge people, and she knew beyond doubt that what might be happening was deadly serious. She hurried down the corridors with Penny, all thought of stately manners forgotten, until shockingly, she hiked up her dress like a common maid and ran, long legs moving with surprising speed. Penny was hard pressed to keep up with her and she considered herself a fair runner.

They reached the stables in record time and scared one of the young grooms half to death when they threw the doors open. "Pardon milady!" he cried, unsure what to think.

# Chapter 14

"I need two horses now." Rose said in a tone that brooked no argument. One could hardly tell she had but a moment before been running like a dairy maid late to milk the cows.

"Certainly ma'am," he promptly answered and headed for where the palfreys were in their stalls.

"Not some placid mare, dolt! I need fast horses, are any of the coursers left?" Rose barely raised her voice but she sounded as if she were shouting all the same. Long minutes later, they were riding out the gate. Rose pulled up for a moment and looked at Penny, "Which way?"

Without thinking Penny pointed, "That way, almost a mile off..." At this point she didn't even care how she knew; she just needed to find him.

Some distance from them Dorian Thornbear was riding through the trees. He had heard a loud noise and now there was the sound of a horse screaming in fear and pain. He nudged his mount to a faster pace and soon came into sight of the dying animal. It was lying on its side, feebly kicking with broken legs. He looked for the rider and spotted Devon Tremont nearby, standing over the fallen rider. He looked positively ominous. *That was Mort's horse!* he thought to himself.

Kicking his horse into a gallop, he reached the spot in less than a minute. He might almost have thought Devon was there to help his fallen friend but the man was standing quietly without moving to do anything. Then Devon noticed him and his face twisted into a grimace, angry at being interrupted. Dorian could see Mort on the ground, his face red as he slowly strangled. Without a second thought Dorian drew his sword and leapt from his horse before it had even come to a stop.

Devon Tremont looked at him and lifted his hand, *"Grethak,"* he said, in some language Dorian did not recognize, but the warrior paid him no heed. Dorian came at him like a berserker from the legends, his face terrible to behold, and the young lord knew fear, for his spell had completely failed. He might have tried another, something more potent, but Dorian was on him already, sword sweeping out to remove his head. Quick as he was, Devon had his own sword out and stopped the stroke before it ended his life.

The exchange that followed was brief. Dorian pressed him back, raining blows upon him with a speed and fury that Devon had never encountered. Despairing he threw up his hands, “Wait! If you kill me he will die!” Lightning quick, Dorian struck the sword from his hand and had his blade against the other man’s throat.

“If he dies you will follow,” the words grated from his throat like gravel, the sword pressing so hard against Devon’s neck that blood sprang up from the wounded skin.

“I was only trying to help. Let me try something and it may save him!” Devon’s eyes were wide with fear, he could see his death in the other man’s eyes.

Dorian’s sword never moved, instead he moved closer and grabbing the young lord by the neck he forced him to his knees alongside Mordecai’s now still form. “Save him now or your head will join his upon the ground.” Without raising his voice he radiated such violent intent that it would have chilled the heart of a hardened killer.

Devon reached out to Mordecai but Dorian jerked his head back roughly, “Betray me now and you won’t live past your next breath.”

"I need to touch him, to get him breathing." Devon was desperate with fear now, for he knew time was short and the man holding him would kill him if Mordecai failed to recover.

Dorian nodded and Devon reached out again, *"Keltis,"* he said, and Mordecai's body went limp, yet still he did not breathe.

"What did you do?!" Dorian kicked the other man sending him sprawling. Raising his sword he made ready to cleave the traitor's head from his shoulders.

"Dorian no!" it was a woman's voice, but Dorian didn't care. He would have blood for his friend's life. A small hand reached for his arm, to stay his strike. Without thought he swatted the hand away, backhanding the one who sought to stop him, and then his eyes saw Rose Hightower falling back. That stopped him, and he saw her reach up to wipe the blood from her lip. His rage left him, as shock at what he had done brought him to himself.

## Chapter 14

"I was trying to help him... and this idiot brute attacked me!" Devon never managed to stay silent for long; even now he was regaining his feet.

Rose spat at him, "Silence fool! You think your lies will be heard here? Count yourself lucky I stopped this man; else your head would be parted from your shoulders. Even so I would not have saved you if I did not fear a good and honest man might hang for your murder." Rose Hightower drew herself up and looked at Dorian.

"Gods! Rose! I'm so sorry. I never meant to hurt you. Never! Not for the world!" Dorian's eyes were wild with grief and he saw Penny kneeling next to his fallen friend. "He's dead Penny, he's dead, and that bastard did it, I swear!" He raised his sword again, pointing it toward Devon Tremont, a growl rising in his throat.

Rose Hightower was having none of it, and she flung herself at Dorian, a flurry of skirts and hair whipping around her. "Stop it you stupid stupid man! Goddammit Dorian, I won't let you throw your life aside like some cheap token." She was a tall woman, but Dorian Thornbear was a mountain of a man, still she climbed him like a furious cat, striking him with her fists.

Astonished Dorian stopped, during his year in Albamarl he had never touched Rose, and their only words had been the measured speech of polite society. Now she was hanging from him like some maddened wild creature, a more absurd picture he could not have imagined. He had a sudden urge to kiss her, but suppressed it immediately. "Lady, I think perhaps we are both overwrought," he said, as he began to disentangle himself. He managed to get her back on her feet, but Rose steadfastly refused to let go of him, and he didn't have the strength to force her.

Penny was on the ground, her hands on Mordecai's chest, gripping his shirt, "Live damn you! You can't be dead. We still have too much to say," her tears left wet spots on the cloth of his shirt. The pain and sorrow were too much for her and without pausing to consider she leaned down to kiss him, ignoring the blood staining his face. She laid her head on his chest while her world unraveled, the only man she had ever cared for lay dead, and she was to blame. Then she heard his heart, beating slowly. "He's alive!"

# Chapter 14

Silence reigned for a moment as everyone took in what she had said. "He's alive I said! Someone get help, we need to get him back to the keep!" Her eyes flashed, "You!" She pointed at Devon, "Get someone, get everyone... go!"

"I'll go," said Rose, but Penny forestalled her with a raised hand.

"No, I need you here, and I don't trust him without Dorian here," she replied. Soon enough Devon was on his horse, angry at being ordered about but fearful of Dorian's response should he balk at her commands. He rode off quickly and headed for Lancaster Castle.

The rest of the afternoon was a frenzied blur as they got him to the castle. Penny refused to leave his side during the entire affair, not trusting him out of her sight. Once Marc arrived things got much more organized and they soon had him in his own bed. The Duke's own physician, Sean Townsend was sent to examine him.

The room was full of people and the doctor quickly waved everyone out, "I'll need some privacy to examine him." Most of them went. "Miss you will have to go, it's hardly proper for me to examine the young man with a woman present, I'll have to undress him."

Penny didn't move, "I won't leave him. So you might as well get to it."

The physician looked at her for a moment before appealing to the Duke, "Your grace if you don't mind, I can't have women in here while I work."

James walked over, reaching out to take her hand but she stepped away, "Try it, you'll draw back a nub next time...," she glared at him, "Your grace." She added belatedly.

The Duke of Lancaster stared at her for a long moment, considering, then spoke, "Very well, doctor you'll just have to work with a lady present."

"I have to remove his clothes your grace, you can't mean to let..." he started.

"I won't repeat myself sir, be about your work," without another word the Duke left the room. The physician was huffy at first but when he saw that she had no intention of giving in to him after having faced down a duke he relented.

His first move was to remove Mordecai's clothing which proved to be difficult, till Penny began assisting him. He gave her an odd look at first but said nothing. Once that was accomplished he carefully went over Mordecai, checking his neck and chest, feeling his head and looking into his eyes and mouth. Eventually he sighed and stood up. "He's got several cracked ribs and I think one of them may have pierced his left lung. In addition he certainly has a concussion from the blow to his head. From the description of his fall I'm surprised his neck wasn't snapped, but something protected his neck. He should be dead already."

"Well he's not dead, so what do you plan to do?" Penny asked.

"There's not much to be done, bleeding him might help a bit though. Let me get my case..." he headed toward the black leather bag he had left by the door.

The doctors had bled her mother till she was too weak to survive the illness that claimed her life. "You're not bleeding him. He's bled enough already, if that's the best you have to offer you can leave," she said, standing between the doctor and the bed.

"Fine, you already seem to think you're a doctor." Sean Townsend was annoyed, he had dealt with troublesome family members before but this woman was beyond frustrating. "If he wakes, try not to let him go back to sleep, he might not wake again. Don't get your hopes up though; he probably won't make it through the night." With that pronouncement he left. She could hear him muttering about stubborn women as he walked out the door.

Some of those who had been waiting outside filtered back in, anxious to hear what the doctor had said. Penelope related the physician's words to them. There was quite a bit of discussion over that, but eventually most of them left, and finally only Marc, Dorian and Rose were still there.

"You should go, get some rest Penny; fretting over him won't help," Marc said.

"I'll leave when he's dead," she replied frankly. "Take your own advice. I'm sick of people telling me what to do."

# Chapter 14

He started to argue but Rose got his attention, "Let it go Marcus, she's not leaving, and I don't blame her. If you want to help, try to keep the rest of them out of here."

"I can manage that," Dorian said, "I'll be outside, making sure his lordship doesn't come back to finish the job. In the end only Rose remained, sitting with Penny through the long evening and into the night.

"You need some rest Penny," she said at last, when midnight was approaching.

"I'll sleep here," Penny replied.

"There's only one bed, and it has a naked man in it," Rose raised her eyebrow.

"Everyone knows I'm a ruined woman anyway, what more can they say about me? Leave me be, I'll lie with him till it's over," she never took her eyes off Mordecai. Rose nodded then stood, without a word she left.

Once she was alone Penny barred the door and removed her dress, she hadn't brought her nightclothes but she hardly cared. She eased under the covers and lay beside him, watching him breathe till the candles burned down and darkness covered the room. In the dark she still kept her hand on his chest, feeling it rise and fall, listening to the wet sound of his breathing. She never meant to sleep, but at last she did anyway.

# Chapter 15

*Theologians generally divide the gods into two categories, the Dark Gods and those believed benign to humanity, the Shining Gods. Yet the ancients had other theories. They thought the nature and motivations of each particular deity must be related to its origins. The Dark Gods were thought to predate the Shining Gods, having arisen from the beliefs of some long dead race. The loss of their people may have driven them mad, for their relationship with mankind is anything but beneficial. While the Shining Gods derive their power from faith, in a mutualistic bond, the Dark Gods take their sustenance forcibly. Even those who worship them willingly are often subject to sacrifice and dark rituals.*

*~Marcus the Heretic,*
*On the Nature of Faith and Magic*

I dreamt restlessly. I was swimming in a deep lake, one that held no light. I was drowning, choking on the water as I sought uselessly to breathe. The dream seemed endless yet I never quite finished drowning, until at last, I woke. Reality was not much better though. My lungs felt full of liquid, and each time I drew breath a burning pain shot through my chest. Everything hurt.

The pain was so great that it was a while before I realized I wasn't alone in the bed. The first sign was soft hair, tickling my nose when I turned my head to the side. In the dark I couldn't see whose hair it was, but the scent told me. It was Penny, curled gently beside me. Her hand rested lightly on my chest but she had been careful to avoid placing any weight on me. If everything hadn't hurt so damned badly I might have been excited, but the pain drove all such thoughts from my mind.

*What the hell happened to me?* I thought. A moment later I remembered. The hunt, the chase, my folly, I had been a fool. *Next time shield your horse too.* If there was a next time, at the moment I was none too sure about that. I didn't want to move and disturb Penny, and just shifting my weight immediately told me I wouldn't be moving anyway. The slightest motion caused a stabbing pain in my chest, great enough to make me aware that the previous pains had just been playful warnings.

I lay there for a long time, aching. The worst part was the constant sensation of drowning. My lungs weren't working properly, and they felt heavy, full. A short cough blinded me with pain, and I resolved not to do that again. I tried to distract myself by examining the room with my special 'sight', feeling the room with my mind. Then a thought struck me, perhaps I could do the same with myself.

Turning my mind inward I slowly explored my body. My task was made difficult by my ignorance, so much of what I found was strange. A few things were easy to recognize, such as my heart, which was steadily beating. I worked out from there, finding my lungs and ribs. One lung was very different, filled with blood, unable to work at all. A sharp piece of one rib had pierced it and torn arteries were still pushing more blood into it and the space around it. I almost panicked then, as I could tell I was dying. Slowly but surely, the blood was filling the other lung, drowning me. Worse, while I thought my abilities might be able to fix some of it, I didn't know the words to use.

Ignorance left me helpless. Still I decided to try anyway, I already knew magic could be done without words; it was simply much harder, requiring perfect focus. I sent my attention to the rib that had pierced the lung and imagined it sliding away, back to its normal location, meeting the other part of itself. At first I wasn't sure if anything was happening, but then it began to move, sending waves of pain through me. I clenched my teeth, fighting a scream, but then I didn't have enough air to scream anyway. I nearly passed out by the time it was back in its place, and then I was horrified to feel it sliding back as soon as I took my attention from it. Fighting against fear I held on grimly and tried to envision it joining the other bone, becoming whole again. At last it stayed, and I slowly relaxed, letting go of it.

Next I tackled the problem of my punctured lung. It took me long minutes but finally I felt that the hole in it was sealed, though that still left me with a lot of blood to deal with. Unsure how to get rid of the blood I decided to seal off the arteries still leaking blood into my chest cavity, that was easier. That done, I considered my lung again, and I tried using the aythar to inflate it a bit. That sent me into painful spasms as my body began to cough, heaving to try and get the blood out. The other ribs were splintered and sent stabbing pains throughout my body.

*Ok, ribs first then,* I thought. One by one I eased my other ribs back into place, trying to fuse each with its estranged parts. The agony was excruciating and I could feel my strength fading. At last I thought I had them all in place and began to consider the task of coughing up the blood that still choked me. *There should be a chamber pot under the edge of the bed.* I wondered if I would reach it in time.

Steeling myself I sat up and got out of bed. Well that's what was supposed to happen, when I sat up my head made its own issues known. The room reeled about me like a drunken sailor after a three day binge. My attempt to get out of the bed ended with me falling to the floor, still tangled in the sheets. The coughing started the moment I sat up, not having the consideration to wait for me to be prepared, and blood was everywhere.

Naturally enough Penny woke up to find me lying on the floor; coughing and bringing up volumes of... well you get the idea. It wasn't pretty, and the coughing was bad enough I thought it might be enough to finish me off. I felt her hands on my shoulders as the spasms shook me. Long minutes passed while I sputtered and choked, before at last I was able to stop. Each breath threatened to send me back to coughing but I held myself still.

Lying there I looked up to see Penny crouched over me, stroking my hair and shoulders. Her nakedness surprised me, but I didn't care, all that mattered were her hands on my skin. Finally I managed to choke out a few words, "You look awful," I said. The words caught her attention and her eyes snapped to my face. Until then I think she must have thought I was dead, or nearly so. A sudden involuntary laugh started from her then turned into a sob.

"I thought you were gone already." she said in a small voice. Something about the way she had her head positioned told me she couldn't see me, and I realized the room was black. Someone was pounding on the door.

"You'd better answer that, before Dorian breaks the door down," well I would have said that, but it was still too hard to speak, I managed to croak, 'the door' and I think she understood me. Soft lips touched my shoulder, then she was gone.

Penny opened the door to find a wild eyed Dorian standing outside. She could see Rose standing beside him. As the light from the hallway spilled over her Dorian stepped back and turned his head aside. "It sounded like you needed help," he said, seeming bashful of a sudden. The light spilling from the hallway had revealed Penelope's state of undress.

## Chapter 15

She was embarrassed but had no time to indulge her modesty so she merely stepped behind the door. “He’s coughing up blood. Rose would you mind fetching towels and water? Dorian you can stay outside.”

Dorian was already facing away when Rose answered, “I’ll have them brought up immediately. Dorian will make sure no one enters so leave the door unbarred for me.” Then she was gone.

Closing the door Penny stepped to the side table and lit the lamp sitting there, the candles were gone, burnt to nubs earlier. In the warm light she could see Mordecai, still lying on the floor, dark splotches of blood dotting the floor around him. He was pale and his face was the image of death itself but his breathing seemed easier. Crouching next to him she tried to move him away from the mess on the floor, then she straightened the sheets, replacing them on the bed. By some miracle they were largely unstained.

Rose entered a few minutes later, carrying a bucket and several large towels, Dorian stood at the door holding an assortment of rags and a second bucket. He kept his eyes averted until Rose had emptied his arms and then he shut the door. Together the two women eased Mordecai onto his side, placing a small pillow under his head so that he could breathe easier. Then they cleaned the blood from the floor as much as possible.

At one point the two women shared a glance and Penny was overcome with a feeling of gratitude. *This is what true nobility looks like,* she thought, looking upon Rose Hightower. She had never known a noblewoman of such resolve and kindness. "I will not forget what you have done for me," she said. She knew not what else to say.

"You've got blood all over you," Rose answered, lifting a towel to daub a spot away from Penny's face. "Do you need my help cleaning him up?"

"No, thank you, I can handle it," Penny answered her.

Once Rose had left the room she took the second bucket and some of the rags that were still clean and began carefully sponging Mordecai's body to remove the stains on his skin. It took a while and throughout it all he kept his eyes shut, too weak to protest. After he was as clean as she could manage she went to the mirror and began working on herself.

A few hours later I woke, lying on the cold floor with a small blanket over me. I might have shivered from the cold but Penny was pressed against my back and her warmth had kept the chill from me. I tried to sit up again and the world swayed around me. Another cough started, but I managed to reach the chamber pot this time and avoided making more of a mess.

A warm hand fell upon my arm, "Let me help you back into the bed." I thought I could manage on my own, but that proved false. Penny wound up lifting me by main force, with her arms under mine. Agony ran through me as my ribs took some of the strain and it gave me strength to help her with my legs. Finally I was in the bed and she drew the covers over me.

"Penny you don't have to do all this for me." I spoke to her as she leaned over me, her dark hair falling about her face in a shower of curls. My power of speech amazed even myself. She looked at me oddly then, eyes wide, her face close to mine. Time stopped for a moment then, held in its course by a power I could not understand, till at last she brought her face to mine and kissed me softly.

"I will do as I please Mordecai Eldridge, and neither death, nor dukes, nor doctors will keep me from you." I might have cried then, but I was far too weak and my body was dry. A thousand responses ran through my mind, but I had neither time nor strength to say them.

"Thank you," I answered simply, and I closed my eyes again as she slipped into the bed behind me. I wanted to talk to her, to explain many things but instead I fell asleep, safe within her embrace.

I awoke hours later, near dawn. I had somehow managed to roll onto my side, which must have been painful but I didn't remember doing so. I could feel Penny breathing softly against my neck. *Of all my childhood fantasies to think this would happen and I am completely unable to take advantage of it,* I thought to myself. I shifted a tiny amount, just enough to give me a better feel of her against me. I'll admit it, even near dying I'm a dirty dirty man.

After a while I became aware of her looking at me. She had woken quietly and was avoiding moving. *She must think I'm still asleep,* I realized. "I'm still alive," I said.

# Chapter 15

"I know," she whispered into my ear. Half dead as I was it still sent electric tingles down my spine. She kept her arms around me, and for my part I didn't complain. Thirty minutes went by and I found I had to ruin the moment.

"Penny..."

"Yes?" she replied.

"I need water, my throat is so dry I can hardly swallow, and then I think I need some privacy for a moment." My bladder was finally making its demands known, despite loss of blood and lack of fluids. She brought water and I drank an amount that was probably unwise given the state of my stomach. Then she looked at me.

"So how are we going to do this?" she said.

I knew what she meant, "We? I may be an invalid but I'll be damned before I let you do that with me." That led to an argument, which I lost, but we finally worked out a compromise. I draped a sheet over myself and stood near the window, leaning against the wall for support. She stayed a few feet behind me, ready to catch me if I started to fall.

Several embarrassing minutes later I was back in the bed. I thought surely at this point she would dress and leave. She still had a job after all. I was wrong; she slid back under the covers next to me. I thought of her kiss the night before and wished dearly I was in better health. The wish fairy ignored me.

We didn't sleep then, instead we rested, wide awake. Well I did anyway. I'm not sure what her reason for being in the bed was at that point. "The doctor said you would die," she told me.

"I hope he's wrong more often then," I replied. "I think I would have, but I managed to fix some of it last night." That got her attention, and I spent the next few minutes explaining what I had gone through during the night. After a bit I had a question of my own.

"I think Rose left you a night dress, I saw it on the table," I hated myself for mentioning it.

"She did." It was a statement.

## Chapter 15

"Why aren't you wearing it?" Stupid never dies, I must be getting better to have regained my idiocy so soon.

"Are you afraid you'll do more damage to my reputation?" she asked.

That made me tense up, but she still seemed relaxed, "Yes. Wait no, that's not what I mean." My general lack of eloquence that always seemed to appear around Penny was back in full force.

"He may have taken my innocence, but I will always have this time, even if only because you were too weak to escape me." Her voice measured equal parts anger and sadness.

"No he didn't Penny. I've been trying to tell you for days." I said.

"What? How would you know something like that?" she replied, starting to become angry. I worried this was about to turn into a repeat of our conversation of the previous day. If only I could *show* her, to get past all the misspoken meanings and misunderstandings. Then an idea hit me. Looking back now, if I had known of the dangers I would not have tried it, especially given my inexperience.

"Let me show you Penny. I think I know a way, do you trust me?" I gave her my most emphatic look, unsure how she would react.

"Magic?" she asked.

I nodded thinking she would surely refuse, but she didn't.

"Ok, what do I do?" she answered. I rolled over then, which made me ache all over, but I wanted to see her face. Being a complete novice in bed I hadn't thought of how our arms and legs would work in that situation. Naively I had thought she would simply scoot back a bit to give us room to face one another without having to touch, as in the innocent days of our childhood. Instead she slipped one leg beneath mine and draped her arm across my waist. Thankfully the covers were still drawn, since I was starting to feel well enough that the intimacy caused me to feel a stirring below.

I did my best to suppress those thoughts and took a deep breath. The ache that caused did an excellent job of returning my mind to business. I looked into her eyes before she said, "What next?"

"I need to touch your face for a moment, I think that will be enough." She nodded at me. I had only learned one word in Lycian regarding the mind, but I thought it might be enough to help me do what I intended. *"Mirren,"* I said, stretching my mind out to touch hers. I raised my hand to touch her face, but she didn't wait for that, and as I moved she leaned in, kissing me suddenly.

The world vanished. The sensation was similar to what had happened to me with Marc's horse but different. There was no sudden plunge as I had experienced then, and I didn't leave my own body. Instead our minds melted together, co-mingling our thoughts and feelings. I could sense her body in much the same was as my own, but it was still 'hers', unlike what had happened before. In one sense it was less complete, yet it was infinitely gentler.

Words were no longer effective, in our hearts words are merely a veil that lies thinly over the reality of our experience. Instead I relived the memory of what had happened that night, what I had done, how I had found her, and the emotions flooded through me as if it were happening again. In turn she showed me her own memories, before and after, when she had awoken. The pain she had gone through afterward made me ashamed to have done so little to find her and explain, but I felt her telling me to let go and forgive myself. Her own feelings had shifted from the panic and terror of the experience to a warm acceptance of my part in it. In particular her mind kept returning to the point at which I had laid her gently within her bed that night. She was tasting it, feeling the emotion that had run through me as I looked at her that night, lying frail and beautiful in her bed.

Vaguely I was aware that we were still kissing. Throughout the entire experience we had remained locked in that embrace, though we hardly moved, except to breath. I could feel her awareness as well, and her heart quickened. Excitement built within me, such that I almost lost my link to her, but I adjusted quickly... I didn't want to lose her yet. I could sense the changes in her and she knew mine. The stirring in me before had grown beyond my control yet she did not shrink away.

She could feel the aches in my body as surely as my emotions. Carefully she eased me over on to my back and worked her way up over me. The foolishness of what we were doing made me hesitate for a moment, but I felt her mind then, serious and intent. *I need this Mort, I need to erase the fear he left in me.* There weren't words, but that was the meaning that crossed between us.

I cast my doubts aside and what followed was both painful and joyous. Ironically I felt more pain than she did, which might have made a fine joke if there were ever anyone we could tell it to. The next hour was one I am sure neither of us will forget, for we kept our minds entwined throughout, until at last I became too tired and sleep overtook me.

# Chapter 16

*The various rulers and lords of men, kings and nobles alike have long had an uneasy affiliation with wizards and mages. They cannot easily ignore such power in the hands of an individual. Such men of power are a duel edged blade, as likely to cut the hand of the lord who wields them as to destroy their foes. Wise rulers are wary of this, for they cannot easily do without the advantages a wizard affords, yet they must always be suspicious of one with the power to kill with a word.*

*~Marcus the Heretic,*
*On the Nature of Faith and Magic*

The sun was shining through the clouds as Timothy worked, weeding the garden near the kitchen yard. It was a small garden, nowhere near large enough to serve all the people that the castle fed each day. Most of the food was brought in on carts. Instead the cook used this garden to grow herbs and spices, and small things that were best fresh. Timothy frequently got the task of making sure it was weeded properly, but the cook did all the harvesting himself, when he needed something from it.

Most of the other boys living in and around Lancaster Castle disliked weeding, but Timothy never minded the job. He had lost his mother while still a baby and only had a few friends among the children nearby, so he often had too much free time, even with the tasks he was given. The garden was full of growing things, and dirt, not to mention all manner of insects and small creatures, like frogs. He quite liked frogs. Since there was no rush for him to finish the cook never complained if he took hours to complete the task, so long as he didn't damage the plants. So he weeded, and talked to frogs, weeded some more and then got distracted by a grasshopper. Small boys are easily distracted and Timothy was no exception.

He looked up as a shadow passed over him, Father Tonnsdale stood there, smiling at him. "There you are! I've been looking high and low for you Timmy!"

"I was right here the whole time Father! Cook likes me to weed and he don' mind if it takes a while," he gave Father Tonnsdale his best smile.

# Chapter 16

The older priest tousled his hair, smiling at him, "It's alright boy, I just needed you to fetch something from town for me."

"Sure Father, I can finish this later," Timothy replied, dusting himself off.

Father Tonnsdale gave him directions to a house in town that had what he needed. He told Timothy it would be a small but heavy package, possibly jars. He was to fetch it straight away and bring it back to the chapel.

"What's in the package?" Timothy asked curiously.

The old man gave him a conspiratorial wink, "It's a secret, a surprise for Mordecai when he gets better. Something like an heirloom, he'll be glad when he gets it. Just remember, don't tell anyone till after you get back to me with it. We can tell him together tomorrow if he's better."

Excited Timothy took off at a run, full of the endless energy of youth. He liked Mordecai and had worried that he might not recover from his fall. Being given something he could do to help made him feel better.

***

The morning after the hunt Devon found himself waiting outside the Duke's chambers. He had been summoned at dawn and although he had arrived within a quarter of an hour he had been waiting for at least an hour since then. It was a sign of the good Duke's displeasure that he left him in the sitting room for so long and Devon knew it.

A man stuck his head into the room, "The Duke will see you now." Devon took a deep breath and followed, he was sure this would be unpleasant. Inside the room the Duke sat at a small table, having just finished his breakfast. There were no other chairs, although Devon was sure he had seen several there just a few days before. Another subtle hint, he would be kept standing.

"You called for me your grace?" he spoke, since James Lancaster seemed disinclined to start the conversation.

# Chapter 16

"I wanted to speak with you regarding yesterday's events," James was not one to beat about the bush once a conversation was underway, and he looked tense. Devon noticed there were two armed guardsmen within the chamber, which was close to an outright insult. Surely the Duke did not plan to arrest him?

"Ah, I expected that your grace. Young Dorian seemed most upset after we parted ways," that was an understatement, but Devon wasn't going to put words in the Duke's mouth.

"If by most upset, you mean he stormed up here and demanded your immediate arrest, trial and execution, then yes, he was considerably perturbed." The Duke's face left little doubt how he felt about the matter.

"I had not realized he seriously considered me at fault. I thought his temper might cool after hearing my explanation." Devon thought nothing of the sort, but he wouldn't be caught giving even a hint that he might consider himself at fault. He knew from long experience that once the hounds caught the scent of blood nothing would satisfy them but more.

"As he told the tale he nearly took your head from your shoulders before you did something to help Mordecai. What was done to him before, and what you did to help him were unclear. That hardly sounds like a man who might be ready to forgive and forget." The Duke's eyes never left Devon's.

"Your grace, in all honesty, I had nothing to do with the accident and I was hard pressed to think how to help him once I reached him. He had struck a tree and wasn't breathing. Dorian assumed I was at fault without proper cause. If I were not so considerate of his hot blood I might challenge him for the insult," he projected an aura of righteous indignation.

"You would be a fool to do so, he would have your guts on the ground within the first minute," James paused for a moment, "If you did nothing to cause the accident, what was it you did to save his life?"

"If I may be frank your grace, I am ashamed to admit that young Dorian had me in such a state that I did not know what to do. He seemed ready to remove my head and had me at a serious disadvantage. So I pretended I had some way to make him breathe again. In fact it was the grace of the gods themselves that

## Chapter 16

Mordecai began to recover when he did, else I am sure I would not be here now," Devon projected embarrassment.

"It is convenient no one saw the fall. My men also report no sign that the horse was injured before it threw him either. Dorian claims you are some sort of sorcerer." James was pulling no punches today.

"If I were I would not resort to such crude means, but to answer your question no, I am not. To my knowledge there are none of any noteworthy power left," half truths came as easily to Devon as breathing water did to fish, and he smiled inwardly.

"It seems there is no proof of wrongdoing then," the Duke sighed as if disappointed. "There are however, other things that have reached my ears. Things which have made me wonder at your character, Lord Devon."

"I would be happy to answer your questions your grace. It is difficult to defend oneself when one's accusers are absent and unknown." Devon replied.

The Duke stood then, and Devon noticed he wore a sword, highly unusual in his own chambers.

Clearly the Duke was prepared in case Devon might incriminate himself, "I am told that you accosted one of my staff, rudely forcing yourself upon her." James' eyes flashed as he said this.

Devon's mind raced. What did he know? What had he been told, and by whom? The crime would not be enough to do more than fine him, and possibly send him packing; his station protected him from more than that. Within a second he decided that the Duke would be unlikely to press the case, he meant to embarrass him. "Who said this, your grace? It is unfair to accuse me with what seem to be baseless rumors," he kept his face smooth.

"Baseless rumors?" James laughed, but it was a dark sound, "Think you I would put this before you with naught more than unfounded gossip? There are at least three direct witnesses to your action. Tremont's son or not, your word would not carry enough weight to deny all of them." James Lancaster did not in fact have three witnesses, but he had Dorian's word that if Mordecai awoke there would be three, should the matter come to light.

## Chapter 16

"I am not even sure who the young lady is that I am supposed to have made these advances upon," Devon answered.

The Duke's face turned red and his jaw clenched, advancing on Devon it seemed he might draw his sword before he stopped, his face inches from the young lord's, "Do not test me Tremont! Your father's reach will not protect you here if I lose my temper. If you so much as touch another of my maids it will not be a paltry fine you face, I'll string your liar's head up from the gallows and war be damned!" He spat these words as if he were chewing nails.

Devon drew back, uncertain before the Duke's fury, but he did not surrender the point, "You would do well to remember the tenets of courtesy while I am under your roof! If you seek to accuse me openly then do so, otherwise you cheapen your honor."

James was livid and he leaned forward, "You dare speak to me of hospitality!? You trespass upon my bondsmen, you abuse those I protect, and then you claim the protection of hospitality! Mark my words, if I have cause to suspect you have harmed another person in these halls again and I'll have you gelded, as your father should have been before he lay with your mother.

Get out of my sight! You have until the week's end. Once that is done I will have you gone. Save your whoring till you return to Tremont!" The Duke finished and strode away, standing with his back turned until Devon left the room.

Once he had gone, Genevieve entered the room, she had been listening. "Are you sure it is wise to risk this? His father may call you up before the assembly of lords."

"He's a fatherless son of a whore!" James was shouting now that Devon had left. It took her a few minutes to calm him down, but inwardly she agreed wholeheartedly. Her husband rarely lost his temper, and never without good cause. It was a point of pride to her that he would risk everything over an abuse to one of his people.

***

Later in the day, before the lunch hour a knock came on the door to my room. I had eaten a huge breakfast earlier and my strength seemed to be returning, but I still didn't feel like walking about to answer doors. Luckily Penny was still with me, dressed now. She had been discussing the merits of having a bath brought in to get me truly clean. I wasn't too keen on it but she seemed very attached to the idea. She rose and answered the door for me.

Father Tonnsdale stood in the hall. "May I come in?"

Penny started to turn him away, but I waved her off, I was beginning to feel like a bit of company. He came in and moved a chair to face the bed, then took a seat, "I spoke with the Duke yesterday, before your accident. And he told me that we had something in common." He gave me a meaningful look, glancing toward Penny.

"Don't worry Father, she already knows," I replied. As a result of our...linking, among other things, Penny now knew an awful lot about me. Mostly regarding recent events, our feelings, and anything we had thought about during that one blissful hour. I couldn't tell you for example what her mother's birthday was, or even what she looked like. It hadn't come up during that time.

"Ah, very good then. The Duke thought you might like to know about the events of that dreadful night," his face was a mixture of sadness and nostalgia as he said this.

"Yes, whatever you might tell me. I was only an infant, so anything that might help me to understand would be appreciated," I truly felt grateful to be in the presence, of someone, anyone who had actually *been* there.

He spent the next hour relating the events of that terrible night, which from his perspective had been pretty boring. He had been fasting in preparation for the special spring dedication to be held the next morning. It was a yearly holiday celebrated by all the adherents of Millicenth the Evening Star. The Evening Star was one of the more popular goddesses in Lothion, and had been venerated by the Cameron family as well as the Lancasters.

Because of his fast he had been in the chapel all that evening, skipping dinner, which ultimately saved his life. When the fire started in the main keep he came out to see what was going on, but once he saw the strangers in black garb he knew he had best stay hidden. Even so they beat down the door to the chapel after he locked himself in, but he had hidden himself in a secret storeroom used to keep the church's relics safe at night. He was one of only a small handful that survived the night. The rest died of poison, fire, or were butchered when the assassins found them.

After that he described my parents to me, but none of it was really new. The one thing that surprised me was the small silver star he gave me. "I helped with their burials. Another priest came to assist since we had so many, but I dressed the bodies of the Cameron family before they were buried. Your father's body was never found and your mother's was lost as well, but this belonged to your grandfather, the Count di'Cameron. I'm sure he would have wanted you to have it."

I was touched to say the least. Raising the small symbol to my lips I kissed it and put it over my neck. Like his own symbol I could see that it held a faint golden radiance, a sign of its connection with the goddess herself. I thanked him as best I could and he left shortly after.

I sat staring at the silver star for a short while, and Penny sat down beside me. "Does it make you sad to think on it?" she asked.

"A bit," I answered. "I've never met either of my grandparents, and know even less of them than I do my parents. At the same time, as of a few days ago I had no knowledge of any of them. It all feels sort of made up. Inside I'm still Mordecai Eldridge, and I feel guilty that I don't feel more for these people that are gone." Penny was a good listener and we talked for a while, till another knock came at the door.

Before Penny could reach it, Dorian opened it from without and announced, "His Grace, James, Duke of Lancaster is here." That was all the warning we got before he strode into the room. The Duke looked in good health, he moved briskly and his face was slightly flushed, as if he had been exercising. I didn't know that he had recently confronted Devon Tremont, but I would have been glad if I had known.

As it was, he seemed to be full of energy. "Mordecai!" he said, in a rather loud tone. "I am most relieved to see you awake and moving again." Rather than pull up the chair he sat on the bed with me.

"The reports of my demise were premature your grace," I answered smiling.

## Chapter 16

"I told you, call me James when we are alone," he replied. "I was planning to have your commendation ceremony and oath of fealty taken tonight, but it seems that will not happen for a few days more at least. You seem to be gaining strength quickly though."

"Thanks to Penny, she has been an angel of mercy through all of this," I smiled at her.

"Yes I have some matters to discuss with Penny as well," and he looked at her grimly.

"I cannot thank you enough for your care of my nephew," he said, "I understand that you burst in upon my lady wife and insisted Rose help you find him?"

"Yes your grace," she kept her eyes down.

"You seem to have a touch of the prophet's gift I hear. No matter. Then yesterday you stood your ground and told me in no uncertain terms that if I tried to usher you from the room I would... let's see... what was it?" He was searching for words.

"Draw back a nub, your grace," she filled in for him.

"Yes that was it. And you meant it too didn't you my dear?" He was smiling at her in a fashion that reminded me of a dog, before it bites you.

"Yes your grace, even now," she said demurely.

"You realize of course that such brazen disrespect for your lord could have dire consequences. I could have you taken to the yard and whipped for insolence," his tone was neutral, but I started up, trying to get out of the bed.

"You can't do that!" I said, but he waved me away.

"Yes your grace, this is true," she replied.

"You have not reported for work since yesterday when you left your post without notice," he continued, "and you spent the entirety of last night alone in this room with my nephew."

"Yes your grace, I would not leave him, till he were dead or sure to live," her tone held a sliver of defiance in its tone now.

## Chapter 16

"Others could have managed. It was hardly proper to have a young woman in here all night, but you don't care do you Penelope?" he asked.

"No sir," she said, "I would sooner be damned than leave him to the care of others." She was staring him in the eye now.

"Are you in love with my nephew Penelope?"

"Yes your grace." she would not hide it.

"You leave me no choice then, Penelope Cooper you are dismissed from my service; I have no need for such a disrespectful maid. One who does not know her place cannot serve me. I expect you to clean your things out of the maid's quarters within the hour," his tone was deadly serious.

Somehow Penny had not expected that response. Somehow she had thought that her good deeds would outweigh her mistakes. She stood stunned for a moment, lips parted slightly. A few seconds later she felt tears beginning to form in her eyes and she turned away, thinking to get her things before he saw her weeping.

"Don't leave Miss Cooper, I have a few things to say to Mordecai as well, and you should hear them first," James added. "Mordecai, since you are unwell I doubt you will be able to attend the dance tomorrow night. It is our last celebration before the guests return to their homes, so it should be a grand affair. Genevieve has spent quite a bit of time planning for it."

"So I am told," Mordecai was unsure where the Duke was leading the conversation.

"Genevieve wanted me to tell you that if you had a lady in mind to bring to the ball, she would be welcome, even if you were unable to attend." He looked at Penny then, with a mischievous smile. Reaching into his jacket he pulled out a scroll and tossed it onto the bed. "The oath and such will have to wait, but the lands are yours, along with the title and privileges, Count di'Cameron."

I stared at him slack jawed, "I am honored... I..." I was having problems figuring out what to say.

"As my guest, and a fellow lord, you are entitled to your own retainers and such, within reason. If you have a wife, consort, or even a simple companion, they of course may stay with you. It is not my place to judge a landed noble. Advances upon my staff would be considered a grave insult however, so I trust I don't have to fear such a breach of faith with you." He studied Penny at length during his speech. "Don't sell yourself cheaply my dear. You're worth your weight in gold, and if my nephew has sense to realize it he will be a wealthy man." Then without another word he turned and left the room.

Once the door had closed Penny and I looked at one another, "What the hell was that?" she said.

"I think he was trying to do us a favor... maybe," I replied.

"I just lost my livelihood!" She was not amused.

"Well I'm prepared to offer you a new position," I ventured.

"As what, chief concubine? Because if that's what you think of me you'd better guess again, just because last night we... That was magic, I didn't have full control of my faculties!" She was working herself into a fit. Not that I would have said as much.

Taking slow breaths I eased myself out of the bed and started walking toward her, "I would never suggest something like that Penny. The Duke was just making it clear that we could continue to stay together, under whatever relation or fiction we choose to employ."

"*'Fiction we choose to employ,'* can you hear yourself Mort? Just because you're the bloody Count di'Cameron now doesn't mean I'll happily pack my bags and come move in as your doxy!" I was almost to her now, but she was backing away. Given my delicate state I wasn't fit to chase her around the room. I tried another tactic.

"*'Companion'* doesn't necessarily mean prostitute Penny, and if you need some better title you could be my maid-servant." I gave her a lopsided grin, employing my considerable knowledge of psychology. It worked. She turned red and came at me teeth bared and claws out.

"You pompous slack-wit!" She launched herself at me with a shriek that would have made a banshee proud. I caught her wrists as she came, and struggled to subdue her. Unfortunately, as most wrestlers can tell you, a lot of your upper body strength relies upon the muscles around the rib cage, and mine were in terrible shape. I'm sure I've mentioned before how terribly smart I am.

Pain shot through me as I grappled with her, trying to get her still for a moment. In spite of the agony I managed to drag her in close and wrap her in a bear hug, whereupon she bit me. *She bit me!* I refused to let go though, and stepping back I fell onto the bed, holding her tight to me. That earned me a lot more pain as her weight fell onto me. Twisting I got myself on top and pinned her down. Have I mentioned she's as strong as a she-cat? But at last I had her caught. "I'm not making the same mistake I did the last time we argued," I said, my face inches from her own. "You're not going to escape as soon as I start talking."

She growled at me, her face flushed, but she relaxed a bit. "You're going to pay when I get loose, and you don't have the strength to keep me down for long."

"I don't need long, I need a lot more than that. Penelope Cooper, will you marry me?" The genius of my plan was such that she went stock still.

"What!?" she said.

"I asked if you would marry me," I repeated myself articulately, and with great charm I might add.

"I'm a commoner you idiot," she replied.

"So am I."

"Not anymore you're not, you're the bloody damned Count di'Cameron now," her words were pessimistic, but her face showed me a glimmer of hope.

"I could have married you before and no one would have cared, and as far as I know there's no law to prevent me from marrying anyone I choose." She wasn't fighting anymore, so I relaxed my grip.

"I don't want to marry you," she protested, "you look funny." Her eyes were wet.

I leaned down and kissed her. She kissed me back, growling a little in the back of her throat. When I came up for air she looked at me, "this has to be the stupidest way to propose to a girl I ever heard of." I kissed her again and put my best effort into it. "You don't even have a ring," she mumbled after that. I kissed her again and she quit complaining.

## Chapter 16

Some time later we lay, exhausted. Well, I was exhausted; despite my youth I was in no condition to be engaging in wrestling matches and... other things. It was worth it though. A thought occurred to me, "So was that a yes?"

She looked at me slyly, "I haven't made up my mind yet."

I smacked her with a pillow. That started a war but eventually she yielded, "Fine, fine! Yes, yes I'll marry you!" She was laughing as she said it.

Later I lay thinking, in spite of the good fortune I was currently enjoying I still had one rather large problem, Devon Tremont. He had already assaulted Penny, and now he had tried to kill me. I was also quite sure he intended to create a lot of trouble for the Lancasters. Unfortunately I had no idea what to do about any of it. Another knock came at the door.

Penny had gone down to fetch her things, so it was up to me to answer it. Life is hard sometimes. Dorian and Marc stood outside, "You really are alive!" shouted Marc. I stood back to let them in.

"To what do I owe the great honor of your visit?" I said mockingly.

"Does a man need a reason to visit his cousin?" Marc answered.

"Your father told you then?"

"Indeed! And he gave me something for you," he tossed a large pouch to me. I almost dropped it. It was very heavy.

"What's this?" I asked.

"Two hundred gold marks, Father got most of it off his lordship this morning and he made up the difference from his own purse. The two of them had the most amazing conversation I hear." He spent a few minutes catching me up on what he had heard.

"Hah!" I laughed when he finished. "That's a fine start, but the devil still has much to answer for." We all agreed on that point, and we spent a while discussing what sorts of unpleasant things might befall Lord Devon before his return home.

# Chapter 16

Since that conversation wasn't really leading anywhere productive I decided to switch topics, "Oh by the way! Have I mentioned I'm getting engaged?" That drew some stares. We talked for a long while after, and I wondered how I would resolve the question of who would be the best man. I decided to put the problem off for another day.

# Chapter 17

*In recent times mages have become much rarer. When mages were more common no lord of men dare rule without magic to back him. With the loss of most of the old bloodlines, wizards are no longer so necessary to those who wield political power, for their enemies do not have magic to use against them. As a result the last few families died out in large part due to assassination, often coming from those they served. Those mages who arise from common stock have ever more to fear, for they have none to support them.*

*~Marcus the Heretic,*
*On the Nature of Faith and Magic*

Penny was gathering her things, from the maid's quarters. It wasn't a large task, since she really didn't have much. The two uniforms she left, her replacement might need them and they didn't belong to her anyway. A few nightgowns, a homespun dress and a few sundries, putting them in a pile they seemed pitifully few. Up until now her life had been a long hard road. Perhaps now things would work out better. She sat down on the bed one last time and looked around the room, letting her mind drift back to the day she had first come to work there.

The vision took her without warning. A man was walking down a hallway, wearing a brown robe and something about him seemed familiar. In his hands he carried a large clay jar, and by the way he moved it must have been heavy, filled with something. She saw him enter the kitchen, a place so well known to her that she recognized it instantly. The cook looked up and him and went back to work without a word. The man was well known there. The kitchen scullions were out setting up the tables so the two were alone.

The hooded figure stepped up to the cook and said something but she couldn't make it out. With a nod the cook stepped out, taking the back door to fetch something from the small garden outside. Once he had gone the man drew back his hood and opened his jar. She recognized him then, and wondered why she was seeing him there. Lifting the jar he poured the contents into a large pot where the soup was simmering, and something told her it was nothing wholesome in that jar.

The vision shifted then, and she felt somehow that it was several hours later. It was the ball and people were dancing, but something was wrong. She saw herself in a long gown, dancing with Lord Devon and he was laughing, as if at some joke she had just told. Around them people began to double over, retching. Blood was on the floor and people were crying in pain. Devon leaned over to kiss her... and she screamed.

She woke then, still screaming, her face damp with sweat. *Not again!* she thought. This can't be happening. Then she remembered Father Tonnsdale's story. The night everyone had died at Cameron Castle, and she knew what she had to do. *Goddess forgive me!*

She left her things on the bed. She knew the events of her vision were still some time in the future, but she didn't think they were too far off. Slipping into the hallway she headed for where the villain lived.

It took her only a few minutes to get there. Such a short time when you know that your life is about to change forever. Just a bit ago she had been happy, looking forward to a life she could not have imagined. She should have known it was too good to be true. She took a moment to consider, she could try to warn everyone, but no one would believe her. That would only leave the killer to find some other time to work his evil. The world was not just, she knew that. *Those people learned that lesson sixteen years ago, and still their murderer goes unpunished,* she thought. But no longer, she would see to that.

She was almost to the door when she realized she needed a weapon. The man she meant to kill was too large to attack unarmed. She went back to the great hall and found one of the hard iron pokers used to manage the logs in the fireplace. The long black iron was heavy in her hand. She figured it would do nicely, so long as she could surprise him. She returned to the large double doors that led into the chapel. She opened them, and as she entered she put the hand holding the iron behind her back.

The chapel itself was empty, but she knew he was likely in the chambers behind the back of the altar. Her heart was beating wildly, but she kept her attention on her task. She found him in his study, leaning over his desk. A small form lay on top of it, quivering. The horror of it almost unmade her, but she held her resolve in an iron grip, a grip as hard as the iron in her hand.

"Shhh Timothy, just relax, it will be over soon. The goddess needs everything you can give." Father Tonnsdale kept his hand on the boy's forehead, holding him down, while the force within him drew upon the boy's spirit. Timothy was dying, but it was necessary if he was to become the tool Father Tonnsdale needed. A small noise behind drew his attention and he was startled when he saw her enter the room.

"Penny!" he said, trying to keep his calm. "Timothy has suffered a fall, would you help me hold him? I think he's having a seizure!" It was a poor lie, but he was sure she would believe it, at least long enough for him to salvage the situation. Two bodies would be almost as easy to hide as one after all.

He looked away from her, back to Timothy, hoping to draw her attention to the boy, while his eyes found the dagger that lay on the desk.

"Certainly Father, I'll be glad to help you," she stepped up behind him, and even as his hand reached for the dagger she brought the iron poker down across the back of his head. He dropped like a felled steer, sagging limply to the floor. The back of his head was crushed. She took another swing to make sure the job was done properly. Then she dropped the iron and checked to see if Timothy was alright.

He wasn't. The boy was dead, though there were no visible marks upon him. His skin was slack, drawn, as though something had been drawn from within him, leaving him empty. The sight of the boy ate at her conscience. *If only I had gotten here sooner, perhaps I could have prevented this as well,* she thought. She was still in shock, numb and unfeeling, but her mind was clear.

*I will hang for this,* and she knew it was true. There was no evidence that the good Father was anything more than he had always appeared. Timothy's body would prove nothing. There were no marks to show anything had been done to him. Even had there been, she was the one alive, she was the one who had just bludgeoned a priest to death. She double checked to make sure the priest was dead. No sense hanging for a crime unfinished.

*No one saw me enter.* That was a thought with promise. If she could hide the body she might even delay the time until the search for his killer began. She took the older man's legs in her hands and began trying to move him. "What did you eat?" she said aloud. There was no way she could move the fat bastard very far. He had to weigh in excess of two hundred and fifty pounds. At last she settled for dragging his body behind the desk, where it could not be seen from the door. She lay Timothy beside him, though she felt bad at having to leave him there with the corpse of his murderer.

Taking the keys from the priest's pockets she locked the study door behind her as she left, with luck it would be several days before they were found. There were no services for three days so it was possible they might not be missed for a while. Now she just needed to get out without being seen. For some reason she still had the iron poker with her, *I should have left it with him,* she thought. No matter, she would just replace it where she had gotten it. Trusting to luck she stepped through the double doors of the chapel and into the hallway.

Luck had apparently taken a vacation. Genevieve, the Duchess of Lancaster was passing as she exited. "Good evening your grace," Penny said with a small curtsy.

"Good evening Penny, how is Mordecai doing?" the Duchess asked.

"Very well, thank you for asking," she replied.

"Is that one of the fireplace tools?" Genevieve asked with a raised eyebrow.

"Yes your grace, I was moving the logs in the great hall, when I thought of a question for Father Tonnsdale. I forgot to put it away before I came. I'll take care of that now." *Stupid, stupid! That was the worst lie in history!* she thought.

"Did you find him? I thought I might talk with him as well..." asked the older woman.

"No, I didn't. I'm not sure where he's gotten off to, I'll have to look for him later. If I see him I'll tell him you were looking for him as well, your grace," she replied.

"I appreciate that. Well I'll let you get to what you were doing," and the Duchess moved away, down the hall.

Penny went back to the maid's quarters, along the way she stopped to throw the iron poker into one of the closets they stored cleaning supplies in. Her mind was racing despite her calm outward appearance. *The Duchess saw me,* she thought. When they found the body, hopefully in a few days, questions would be asked. Genevieve would remember seeing her, and she had noticed the iron in her hand. There would be no doubt now. It would lead straight to her. *I'm going to hang.* Her mind kept coming back to that. There was no explanation that would exonerate her. She hadn't even found the poison. *I forgot to even look for it.* She considered going back, to search, but discarded the idea immediately. She couldn't go back.

Thoughts of escape came to her. She could run, take everything she had now, and just run. But she had no money, no family to hide her, no place to go. If she told Mordecai he would probably help. That wasn't right, he would *definitely* help. But what could he do? If he ran with her it would only destroy his own life. *He's the Count di'Cameron now, he's got everything to lose,* she thought, *but I am nothing. I can only ruin it for him.*

"I'm going to die for this, nothing can change that. The only thing I can manage is who goes with me," she said aloud. She might not be able to avert the consequences of her actions, but she could choose who she took with her. Asking for help would only ruin her friends, but the other option was to take the opportunity to make what remained of her life count for more. If she had to choose one other person to spend her life on, the choice became simple. Having made the decision she felt a calm come over her, and she began to plan.

I was still talking to Marc and Dorian when Penny returned. I was glad to see her, Dorian was busy trying to convince me that beer would speed my recovery and Marc was offering to have several pitchers sent to the room. We were young and hadn't had much experience with strong drink, so the thought of drinking to excess was a new and exciting concept. But I knew I was in no shape for it. Penny's presence put the damper on their plan immediately.

"C'mon Penny, you just got engaged!" Mark suggested, using his considerable charm.

"Do you see a ring on my hand Marcus Lancaster?" she offered up the unadorned appendage for his inspection.

"Well no, but you already said yes, isn't that cause for celebration?" He grabbed her hands and led her into a short mock dance. She couldn't help but smile.

"Marc, don't you dare tell anyone about this! You too Dorian!" she yelled past Marc's shoulder.

# Chapter 17

"Penny my dear! Are you embarrassed to let people know you're going to marry this ruffian? Perhaps you should reconsider; there are other eligible bachelors still available after all." Marc puffed up his chest and brushed his fingers across the front of his jacket, a roguish grin on his face.

The conversation was causing Penny some consternation, and I could see it on her face though she tried to hide it. She glanced downward, as if shy, "Honestly, I'm not ready to announce it yet, I still have to tell my father and I'd rather not set everyone to talking till I'm ready." Something about her expression didn't ring true to me, but Marc and Dorian took her at face value.

"Let her be Marc," Dorian put in, "weddings are important to girls, we shouldn't spoil things for her."

"Fine, fine, I was only teasing," Marc answered, looking as though he had been wrongfully accused. He had been a clown since we were children.

"Dorian," Penny said, "would you mind doing a favor for me?"

"Sure," he answered.

"I need to talk to Rose, about the ball tomorrow and... other things. Would you mind taking a message for me? To see if she has time this evening?" She smiled sweetly at him. I wished she smiled at me like that more often.

They both left after that, and I made myself busy eating a tray of food that had been sent up for me. I considered asking Penny about her deception, I was sure she was hiding something, but Rose showed up before I could ask her.

"You didn't have to come up right away. I would have come to see you," Penny said.

"Nonsense, I was bored anyway," Rose replied.

They talked for a few minutes and Penny explained what she had in mind. The Duke's mention of the ball had apparently caught her fancy, something I would never have expected. She wanted Rose's advice about how to appear, and other details.

"Don't go as Mordecai's escort, since he's not going. Come as my companion," Rose suggested.

## Chapter 17

"You'll draw less attention that way, and since he's not yet known as the Count di'Cameron you'll get more respect as my friend."

"That's fine," Penny said, "It doesn't really matter to me either way. My true concern is that I don't have a dress. I never expected to attend an event like this, being what I am."

Rose smiled at her, "That won't be an issue my dear. I'm glad you called me first; I have just the thing for you. You're close to my size anyway." Rose Hightower was probably the tallest woman at Lancaster Castle, standing five foot eleven inches, but Penny was rather tall herself and stood close to her height. "Mordecai," she continued, "Penny is going to need some things if you intend to keep her."

I looked up, "What do you need?"

Rose smiled at me, "Ten gold marks should do." I choked, that was enough to buy a farm, two if you bargained hard. My father didn't make more than two or three gold marks in a year, if things went very well. She saw my expression, "Hand it over my lord, you aren't living that life anymore, and if you don't start thinking of her needs Penny is going to suffer for it."

I counted out the money and handed it over and Rose gave me a pat on the shoulder, "That's a good man. When I'm done you won't regret it. Just be glad I'm not charging you for my services."

They left then, Rose taking Penny by the arm. I swear I could hear them laughing as they walked down the hall. Once they had gotten back to the rooms Rose was staying in she proceeded to show Penny a selection of dresses. She had packed with the intention of being ready for anything.

Penny was concerned, "These are much too fine for me Rose."

"As long as you aren't better dressed than me, nothing is too good for you my sweet," Rose said with a twinkle in her eye. "We might have to have the seamstresses in to raise the hem a bit, the length is ok on you, but we need to show a bit more of your ankle for the proper impact."

"If you don't mind my asking Rose, what will we use the money for? If you're lending me one of your dresses surely that's all we need?" Penny asked.

# Chapter 17

"I'm thinking of the future, particularly yours," Rose replied. Wasting no time she sent one of the servants out to fetch a dressmaker. Once the woman had arrived she began discussing fabrics and styles. Several hours went by as Rose ordered a bewildering array of things, from blouses to garters, nightgowns and skirts. At the end she had agreed to pay the woman almost five gold marks for an impressive selection of clothes, winter and summer dresses, and even ball gowns.

"It'll take me several weeks to manage all this milady," the woman said.

"That's fine, just be sure to send along the nightgowns and house-clothes first, she'll need those as soon as possible." Rose paid her then, never thinking to consider she might be cheated. Penny realized that she wouldn't be. You don't cheat nobility, not if you want more business; not if you want to continue eating.

"What's the rest of the money for?" Penny said, and Rose gave her a sly grin, handing her the remaining money.

"I can't take this! It's not my money," she protested.

"You are a lady now, or soon will be. As a Countess you will need to know how to handle yourself with money. Even more so you must never be perceived as having to count pennies. Use it, waste it, make sure people see it, and don't ever act as though you need it." Rose gave her a serious look, "I'm not joking. Your future will rely on learning these things. As soon as you have that boy of yours wed, make sure he gives you an allowance. If people suspect he's being cheap with you they will think he's broke. If they think he's broke things will get hard for him. Never let them smell blood."

Penny could see the sense of her words, but she felt like a fraud. She had no intention of marrying Mordecai now, she would not live out the week, much less see the day those clothes Rose had ordered arrived. Yet she had to keep up the pretense. If Rose caught wind of her plan it would be all over.

They went back to the ball gowns again. "Rose, this might sound odd, but I don't feel safe going to the ball without Mordecai, do you suppose I might... carry something?" She gave the woman an uncertain glance.

## Chapter 17

Rose understood immediately, “Oh my, I would tell you that you have nothing to fear, but I know why you feel as you do.” She went back to her closet. She returned with another dress, this one had long flowing sleeves a contrast to the others which had had close fitting sleeves. “This will do the trick, though it’s a shame, you have such pretty arms.”

In truth Penny liked the other dresses better, but function would be more important tomorrow evening, “So how do the sleeves help?” she asked.

Rose gave her a feral grin, “I take it you want to carry a dagger correct?”

Penny nodded.

“And considering your feelings, something like this probably wouldn’t be enough,” she plucked a small slender knife from her bodice.

“Do you always carry that?!” Penny was a bit shocked.

“Just because I said you were safe doesn’t mean a girl shouldn’t be prepared. But if you want to carry something more serious,” she walked over to a trunk and began rummaging before standing back up, "like this." She held a double edged dagger with a seven inch blade, "You'll need sleeves, big sleeves. Here let me show you." She brought out an odd scabbard for the dagger, with several straps attached.

"So you strap it to your wrists?" Penny didn't know what to think of this noblewoman who suddenly seemed so intimately familiar with blades.

"Ordinarily yes, but not for a dance. You'll be lifting one arm up, to rest on a gentleman's shoulder and your sleeve may slide back. Plus he might feel it when he touches your wrist, so the forearm is a fashion no-no."

"Oh."

"There are two main ways for a lady to wear something as considerable as this. The first is strapped to your leg, either the calf, or the inner or outer thigh. The calf is impractical if you wish to use it quickly, and the outer thigh will spoil the lines of some dresses. The inner thigh is my preference, but it can be awkward, especially if you're dancing. Plus the dress needs to be designed for it, like this..." She slid her hand between the pleats of her skirt and brought out a dagger similar to the one she had gotten for Penny. A hidden slit in the dress allowed her to reach her leg.

"Good lord Rose, you're a walking arsenal!" Penny exclaimed.

"And don't you forget it," Rose winked at her.

"Have you ever needed one? To use?" Penny was curious.

"Not yet, usually you can discourage even the worst of them before it comes to that, but it pays to be prepared." Rose discussed the topic with a casual nonchalance that Penny could not help but envy.

"So how will I wear this one, so that I can dance?" Penny asked.

"Here," Rose pointed to the inside of her upper arm. "It won't be entirely comfortable but your partner won't feel it and if your sleeve slides back it won't be revealed. Put on the dress and I'll show you how it works." They got Penny into the dress, which took several minutes, but it fit well. "Now, we strap it to the inner side of your upper arm, with the hilt down. The sheath is built to hold it in even in that position. Show me how you will draw it if you need."

Penny thrust her right hand up the left sleeve and grabbed for the handle. "No no!" Rose remonstrated. "You do that and he'll be three feet back and calling for his mother to save him."

Penny laughed at the image, "Isn't that the point, to warn him off?"

Rose shook her head, "Not publicly, you'll wound his pride and earn yourself a bad reputation. If you *do* need it you want to have the blade against his skin before he realizes it, so you can quietly make him aware of your feelings. Once he's admitted defeat you can replace it and no one is humiliated... publicly."

The methods Rose described suited Penny's purpose perfectly, although she did not mean to use the blade for self-protection.

Rose went on, "As a woman you have to remember, if he catches on to your intentions you lose most of your advantage. He's bigger, stronger, and possibly quicker. Put your hands together, gracefully... then slide them to your elbows, as if you are thinking, or perhaps cold. From there you can easily grasp the hilt."

Penny couldn't help but wonder how she would do that while dancing, but she didn't dare ask. That question might be too direct, so she asked a different question. "Rose, do all noblewomen carry weapons?"

Rose snorted, "No, only the smart ones."

"Who taught you all this?" Penny added.

"My mother," and then she regretted it when she saw the look on Penny's face. She had already heard of Penny's own loss. "Penny, this may sound odd, but if you will have me, I already consider you a sister."

Penny's eyes misted and without thinking she hugged Rose, "I always wanted a sister," but inwardly she already felt badly about the betrayal she knew was coming. She could only hope that Rose would someday recover once she was gone.

# Chapter 18

*Little is known of the time before the Sundering, when Balinthor nearly destroyed the world. Most historians agree that mages were freer then and more common. They were not bound by the Anath'Meridum. The gods of men were still young, and too weak to threaten their power. The Dark Gods were powerful but none were foolish enough to bargain with them. In those days almost all kings were wizards themselves, but whether they were foolish or wise is not known. Poetry would suggest they were wise, but stories are like pictures, painted to show their best sides. In all likelihood they were as petty, foolish and sometimes cruel as rulers today.*

*~Marcus the Heretic,*
*On the Nature of Faith and Magic*

I was sitting up reading when Penny returned, and I was welcome for the distraction. As interesting as it was, *A Grammar of Lycian* was not the sort of book to keep you awake for long. I had been searching it and experimenting with some of the words I found there, trying to speed up my recovery. Inner exploration had shown me that while my lungs were both functioning now there was a lot of blood around one of them. I had spent considerable time trying to get the blood broken up so that my body could remove it more easily.

That turned out to be quite difficult, and I wasn't sure what effect my efforts had produced, so I also worked on making improvements to my ribs and the muscles supporting them. I really wasn't sure but I *thought* that I had them in good shape. They seemed to be aligned properly now and I had them fused better. I also experimented with some of the words I found in the book and they might in fact be stronger than normal ribs should be, but there was no good way to test the theory.

I resisted the urge to try anything with my brain. That way lay madness. I could tell however that the swelling was gone, and I did fix a small crack in one of the bones of my skull. Surely that couldn't cause any unforeseen problems.

"You're home early," I said, trying to sound domestic. I'm also quite funny in addition to being brilliant. Honestly I am, I tell myself so all the time.

"Did you take that bath?" she asked. Penny seemed to have a one track mind sometimes.

# Chapter 18

"Have I mentioned how lovely you look?" My skills in the subtle art of noble discourse had been improving lately so I thought I might try a distraction. If only Penny would cooperate with my cleverness.

She leaned in, sniffing, and wrinkled her nose, "You stink." The conversation went downhill from there and before long she had servants bringing in a large copper tub and buckets of hot water. Knowing all the staff made it terribly easy for her to find the people she wanted quickly. I would have been impressed with her efficiency if it hadn't been directed at me.

Once everyone had gone (you would be amazed at how many people it takes to draw a proper bath), she gave me a hard look. "Strip," she said. Somehow the way she said it managed to take all the sexy out of the word.

"Yes ma'am," I replied, waggling my eyebrows at her. I'll be damned it I let her take the fun out of the conversation. I was feeling quite a bit better at the moment, so I got my clothes off unaided and eased myself into the tub. The water was very warm, almost steaming.

I have to admit, it was the best bath I'd ever had up to that point in my life, especially considering I had a lovely woman to scrub my back. She even washed my hair; something I had never known could be so pleasurable. I closed my eyes and relaxed, I was in heaven. A splash caught my attention and I opened one eye, apparently one of the angels had come down to join me in the bath. Things got rather more interesting from there.

A while later we lay between cool linen sheets, recuperating. I couldn't believe the good fortune lady luck had handed me. At that point I was too happy and contented to remember that lady luck is also a brazen bitch. I would regret that later.

Despite the covers, the bed seemed cold. I pulled the blankets up further. Penny snuggled beside me. "Mort, you seem awfully hot," she said.

"That would be entirely your fault my little minx," I pulled her in for another kiss and the room spun a little. "I do feel a little woozy though," I added.

I had a fever. Not to point any fingers, but looking back I suspect it might have had something to do with my efforts to help my body reabsorb the excess blood in my chest. Messing with mother nature can be a mistake sometimes, she and lady luck are probably good friends. Penny was the very picture of concern and empathy. She pulled the sheets back, exposing me to the cold air. She must have been taking notes from mother nature and lady luck. They're all in on it together I tell you, one big female conspiracy.

"What? No, no, it's cold! Gimme those back!" I'm a skilled debater when I put my mind to it.

"You have a fever and you need to cool off." She refused to let me get the sheets past my waist. Without a doubt it's because she wanted to gaze upon my chiseled muscles.

"I bet you tell all your fiancees that." It made sense to me, but obviously I wasn't quite as clear headed as I thought. Penny draped a wet cloth across my forehead. She didn't seem too impressed with my attempts at humor.

After Penny had satisfied herself that I wasn't in imminent danger of an early demise we lay uncovered on the bed. She still wouldn't let me have the covers, but she did permit me to borrow some of her warmth. I rather liked her warmth. "Mort," she asked, "I have a question."

Even in my fevered state that set off my warning sensors. "What sort of question," I replied guardedly.

"If I ever did something bad, something really bad, that made everyone else hate me. Would you still love me?"

*What the hell kind of question is that?* I thought, but I was wise enough to frame a better reply. "I would still love you. I know you well enough to know that you would have your reasons, even if they didn't make sense to everyone else at the time. Why?"

"I just wondered, the past few days have changed so much in my life that I guess I need a little reassurance," she said.

"A few days ago I didn't even realize I loved you, so it's a little early trying to figure out ways to get rid of me," I smiled at her. Stupid never dies, looking back I can hardly believe I was so naive. I went to sleep dreaming of open skies, chasing a crazy tomboy of a girl through verdant fields. That has always been my best memory of Penelope Cooper. Even now as I look back I realize that was when I first fell in love with her. Somewhere in my heart she will always be that silly girl with grass in her hair.

***

Penelope woke early as was her habit. Mordecai still slept but his temperature had cooled so she drew a thin sheet over him. The ball was today. She looked at the dress hanging in the corner of the room. It was a beautiful combination of blue velvet and lace. She had tried it on with Rose the day before; amazed at how lovely it was when she looked in the mirror. It showed her bosom off to great advantage without being tasteless and the fabric draped gracefully down to accent her figure, exposing just a hint of her ankles. It was ironic that this would be the only day she would ever get to wear such a garment, and that Mordecai wouldn't be there to enjoy seeing her in it.

*I don't want him there,* she thought. That's not how she wanted him to remember her. Considering that, she decided that perhaps she should write a letter. She couldn't explain herself, but at least she could make sure he didn't blame himself. She checked to make sure he was still sleeping soundly before going to the writing table.

Unlike some of the maids at Lancaster Castle Penny was perfectly able to read and write, partly because of Mordecai, but in large part because she had always had a strong curiosity and a desire to learn. Unfortunately her penmanship was not the equal of her wordsmithing, but he would just have to deal with her bad handwriting. She took up pen and carefully wrote out a long letter. Several blots and misspellings forced her to start over a few times, but at last she had a letter she wouldn't be embarrassed to have him read. Except for the content of course, but there was no helping that. She folded it carefully and put it away, she wouldn't want him to see it until later.

That accomplished Penny began brushing her hair. It wasn't easy, she had a lot of curls in her long dark hair and they had a tendency to tangle. It took quite a while to get it smoothed out and when she was almost done she felt my eyes on her. I had woken half way through the process and lay quietly watching. It was fascinating to see her working the brush slowly through the long tresses. I could have watched her all day.

## Chapter 18

She smiled at me in the mirror, "Are you feeling better?"

I was. We ate breakfast and I took up my books, being ill had provided me with more time to read and I decided it would be foolish to waste it. Penny got dressed and went to see Rose again, more preparation for the ball. I really hated that I would miss it, but at least Penny wouldn't have to suffer through my imitation of dancing. There would be more balls though, and maybe I could get some lessons before I had to expose my limited dancing skills to Penny. Ariadne had offered to teach me in the past so I thought I might take her up on it, but that would be for another time.

The day went smoothly but after lunch my fever came back. Penny returned and made sure I didn't have too much in the way of covers. She obviously didn't believe in 'sweating' out a fever. At least she didn't try to bleed me, so I probably shouldn't complain about feeling a bit cold. A long nap made the afternoon more pleasant.

Around six Penny started getting ready. She was kind enough to let me watch, so I kept my lurid fantasies to myself while she dressed. The dress was stunning when combined with her curves and graceful features. I couldn't help but wonder how I had lured such an enchanting beauty into my bedroom. My careful gaze caught her strapping something odd to her left arm.

"What's that?" I asked wide-eyed.

"A dagger sheath," she answered, as if it were the most common thing in the world. She finished adjusting the straps and slid a deadly looking seven inches of steel into it.

"Are we expecting trouble or should I be concerned for when you return later?" I half-joked.

"Rose has been most helpful educating me on the matter of protecting myself. After this past week I am no longer as trusting as I once was. Plus I have an excellent man to keep myself unspoiled for..." she gave me a charming smile, batting her long lashes at me. That should have warned me, her most frequent use of feminine wiles seemed to be distracting me from important issues.

# Chapter 18

"I thought I spoiled you quite thoroughly last night," I leered at her.

"There is always more spoiling to be done," she answered, then she leaned over and gave me a long kiss. "I have to get going, I'll need Rose's help to get my hair done up properly." She stopped at the door and gave me a long look, "Don't forget I love you." Then she was gone, but for a second I could have sworn I saw a tear in her eye.

I convinced myself it was my imagination, but it took me a long while to get back to my reading. Women are never simple. I however, am as simple as they come.

***

Penny found Rose in her apartments, still getting ready, "Shouldn't we be hurrying more?" she asked.

"It won't hurt them to wait a few minutes. Besides, the best arrive last." Rose laughed. She finished what she was doing and began working on

Penny's hair. With sure hands she worked it into a delicate braided design piled on top of her head, exposing the younger woman's graceful neck. "You're going to garner a lot of looks tonight."

"None that I'm anxious for, but I suppose a little attention will be nice," Penny answered.

"Enjoy it while it lasts, we won't be young the rest of our lives," Rose remarked.

*You might not, but I probably will be,* Penny thought to herself. The two women rose and headed downstairs. The ball was already beginning.

# Chapter 19
## The Ball

*Few objects of magic still exist. They have become as rare as the men who create them, and those who remain rarely gain the knowledge necessary for their creation. From my research I have ascertained that the process is similar in function to the way in which mages create their spells. Aythar is manipulated, but rather than using words, symbols and written language play a greater part. Most who are born to magic eventually try to bind power within an object, but few succeed. The art of sealing power in such a way that it remains forever bound is lost. For this reason the only magical objects found today are wards, symbols drawn with power for specific purpose. Yet these lose their strength within a span of decades unless they are regularly renewed.*

*~Marcus the Heretic,*
*On the Nature of Faith and Magic*

The great hall had been transformed. The great trestle tables had been removed, replaced by a few long tables along the walls where refreshments were being served. A small scattering of tables and chairs provided a place for the dancers to rest, but their numbers were small enough to discourage people from spending too much time there. It was a dance after all, and the night would be wasted if too many spent their time lounging instead. The Duke's musicians occupied one end of the hall, playing endlessly to provide the music needed for a successful ball.

Penny and Rose were announced as they entered, "Lady Rose Hightower and her companion Penelope Cooper." That earned Penny a few stares, especially from the servers. Most of the staff knew her and although they had heard she had taken up with Mordecai they were still unsure what that meant for her status. Arriving with Rose made it clear that she was headed up in the world.

Marcus spotted them and came over, walking slowly to avoid outpacing his sister, Ariadne. He was escorting her for the evening although they would both be dancing with different partners before long. His sister was a picture of loveliness in a fanciful pink gown. Ariadne was only fourteen and had yet to fill out completely, but Penny was sure she would be a great beauty someday.

# Chapter 19 – The Ball

"Penny! I see you ditched that clumsy oaf and replaced him with someone better looking!" he gave a small bow in Rose's direction.

Rose gave a light tinkling laugh, "Yes she's seen fit to find better company this evening." Penny couldn't help but wonder how Rose managed it, even her laugh was perfect. Marcus asked Rose if he could have a dance and they were on the floor a moment later, leaving Penny and Ariadne alone.

"Your brother is quite the charmer," Penny ventured.

"Mother says he could charm the skin off a cat, but I know his rougher side," Ariadne answered. "Still, as brothers go, I'm rather fond of him." They chatted for a few minutes before Marc and Rose returned, then he swept Penny away for a dance as well.

"How is Mort doing?" he asked as he twirled her across the floor.

"He's doing well. He had a fever today but otherwise it's remarkable how quickly he has recovered, his ribs aren't bothering him at all now," she replied.

Marc raised an eyebrow, "More magic?"

Penny sighed, "Yes, he keeps trying different things, but so far he's done himself more good than ill."

"Don't tell him I said this, but he's really quite brilliant, always was. If anyone can figure out how to use that gift of his without a proper teacher he can. Especially with someone like you looking after him," he smiled.

"He does take a lot of managing," she laughed, wishing she could make it sound like the delicate laugh Rose used. Then she thought of her reason for coming and her face darkened.

"Are you alright?" Marc could be quite perceptive in his own way.

"Just a dark thought, has Lord Devon arrived yet?" she hadn't seen him yet.

"No, he hasn't shown his face yet. Relax Penny, I won't let him bother you." But Penny wasn't worried about being bothered, she was more worried that the young lord might not show up at all. After their dance she went back to stand with Rose, who was chatting amiably with Ariadne. Marc found Elizabeth Balistair and took her out for a whirl on the floor, he would surely dance with every lady before the evening was over, it was a duty after all.

She wasn't there long before Stephen Airedale asked her for a dance, she might be a commoner but apparently beauty trumps class, at least at dances. While they were on the floor Penny heard the announcement, Lord Devon had arrived. She moved closer to her partner and began scanning the room over his shoulders, looking for her nemesis. She failed to spot him, but she did see Dorian standing off to one side, talking to Gregory Pern. *He's too shy to dance so he talks history with the Admiral's son, typical,* she thought.

After her partner returned her to Rose and Ariadne she looked for an excuse to escape from them for a moment. "I'm going to get something to drink, I'll be right back," she said, and without waiting for a reply she headed for the table where they were serving refreshments. Rose watched her go, narrowing her eyes for a moment.

Penny was happy when she saw that the wine server was one of her fellow maids, Laura was her name. She knew her well and felt she could trust her for one final favor. She asked for red wine, but caught Laura's hand as she handed the glass to her. "I need a favor Laura, will you deliver a message for me?" Penny tried to look casual.

Laura was a bit startled, "Sure Penny, but it will have to wait till after the ball or I'll get in trouble." That was perfect so Penny nodded and handed the other girl her letter. The outside was addressed simply 'Mordecai'.

"Just take this to Mordecai after you are done here, he'll want to see it." She thanked Laura and headed back to where the other ladies were waiting, unaware of the blue eyes that followed her every move.

Standing with Ariadne and Rose she began to feel a nervous flutter in her stomach. Her resolve had kept her calm thus far, but handing over the letter made her anxious. She kept her eyes on the crowd, looking for Devon. "Penny," Rose interrupted her thoughts, "Have you seen Dorian? I intend to get a dance out of that man if I have to drag him onto the floor."

## Chapter 19 – The Ball

Penny had just spotted Devon, so the opportunity to get rid of Rose's watchful gaze was perfect. "He's standing over there, talking to Gregory Pern," she pointed. "I'm sure poor Gregory could use a rescue, you know how Dorian gets once he's talking about history and long done wars."

"I don't know him that well yet," Rose answered, "but I hope to one day." She winked and walked away. She moved gracefully in the direction that Penny had indicated. She drew near to where Dorian was standing but did not approach him, she kept moving slowly. His eyes left Gregory and she could feel him staring at her. Rose glided past him, turning her head to stare him full in the face, a twinkling gleam in her eye and a smile on her face. She kept walking, heading for the refreshments, but her eyes never left his face.

Even Dorian Thornbear could not miss that clue, dense as he so often was around women. He excused himself from Gregory Pern and followed her to the table. When he got there he found her in deep conversation with the girl serving wine.

"I need you to give me whatever Miss Cooper handed you my dear," Rose was holding two silver bits in her hand even though they weren't supposed to pay the servers.

"I'm sorry milady I don't know what you're talking about," Laura was a good friend, but holding off the formidable Rose Hightower was making her nervous.

Rose leaned in close to her ear, "We can do this one of two ways, one way ends with you being embarrassed and possibly whipped, the other you get two silver bits and do your friend an unexpected favor." She leaned back and smiled at the girl. Dorian couldn't hear all of the exchange, but the look on the girl's face made him feel badly for her. A moment later Rose had him escort her over to a small table where she could examine the letter.

It was sealed with a blob of red wax, and the outside had the word 'Mordecai' written on it. Rose considered opening it, but she wouldn't do that to Penny. Her mind worked quickly and the clues of the past few days began to come together, Penny's sudden interest in the dance, her odd questions and her occasional dark moods. She still wasn't sure what Penny might be planning, but she knew it must be serious, and it would be here, at the ball. The letter would likely complete the puzzle.

"Dorian," she said giving him her full attention, "I need you to do something a bit strange for me."

"Certainly Lady Rose," his warm eyes held hers.

"Call me Rose from now on. It's silly how you keep addressing me like that. We've been through enough now to call each other familiar." She reached over and put her small hand over his own. Dorian's eyes widened, he was on uncertain ground now. "Forgive me Dorian, I wanted a dance but this may be more important. Will you take this letter to Mordecai? He needs to read it now, the moment you find him. I would urge you to run if you would help him most."

One of the most amazing things about Dorian Thornbear was his unfailing loyalty. Where many would question or seek to delay, Dorian took the letter and stood up, "Save that dance for me Lady Rose." He moved away through the crowd, striding quickly, and once he was outside he did indeed break into a jog. Rose watched him go before rising to find Penny.

***

I was reading again when the door opened, "You could knock first," I said as I saw Dorian striding in, he was breathing hard. I guess running up stairs will do that to a man.

He ignored my comment, "Here," he said, "Read this and be quick, Rose seems to think it's urgent." I could see he was in no mood for foolishness so I took the letter from his hand. It was marked with my name and I was fairly sure the lettering was Penny's.

Opening it I started scanning the contents, then I reread them to be sure I hadn't missed anything.

*Dear Mordecai,*

*I write this now with great trepidation, not because of what I must do, but rather because it is impossible for anyone to put all their thoughts and feelings into something so limited as a simple letter. I need you to understand that you have always been my friend, and for that I am grateful. You should also know that the events resulting from my actions from this point forward are no fault of yours. I believe strongly that each person must take responsibility for their own actions, to do otherwise is to make oneself a victim in the hands of fate, and I will not be a victim.*

*Marcus has explained your situation with Devon Tremont to me fully, and for that reason I want you to know that what I plan to do is not because of you. As you know, I have good cause for hating that singularly unfortunate individual. I would that he had never been born. The fact that his removal might aid you and the Lancaster family is a great comfort to me, but it is not the cause for my actions. Please do not blame yourself. I make my own choices.*

*I will keep my reasons to myself, for they would only do you a greater hurt, one you do not deserve, for you have always been a gentle soul. I will say only that fate has conspired against me. I have done that which cannot be undone and it has left me with few options. Rather than be held a prisoner by those options I choose to act, hopefully preventing greater harm to others. I feel there is no redemption for Devon Tremont, just as there is none for me. At least my actions may lead to greater good, while his have done nothing but ill.*

*Last, and this is the most difficult part, for I fear it will cause you pain, I want to explain my feelings to you. My love for you is no recent thing, no sudden fancy. In our games as children you were always my knight in shining armor, though I doubt you realized it. Your kind heart and silly wit won me over during the endless summer days of childhood. I love you, and I always will, for whatever time is left to me. No matter what they say of me after this day do not forget that. There are others that love you though, and it is important you remember that. When I am gone do not let despair drive you to foolish choices, for you are important to a great many people, and I am least among them.*

*Yours forever,*

*Penny*

"Dammit!" I swore. "Dorian, where did you get this?"

## Chapter 19 – The Ball

"Rose got it from one of the servers," he answered.

I was already dressing. The doublet and hose would take far too long so I put on my simple breeches and tunic, the clothes I had arrived in. After a moment's thought I put my mother's surcoat over them and buckled on the sword my father had given me. Dorian's eyes registered surprise at that. "You can't wear a sword to the ball."

"I'll be damned if I don't, and you might want to collect your own, we may need it." I slipped my boots on. My fever had gone so I felt better, though I was lightheaded. I started for the door, then paused. A few quick words and I had shielded myself, I wasn't certain what might happen but I wanted to be ready.

We went as quickly as I could manage, which was nearly a run despite the soreness in my back. My ribs no longer hurt but I was still short-winded from the damage to my lung. Dorian left me when we reached the ground floor, going to fetch his own sword I think, but I didn't ask.

***

Back at the ball Penny was dancing. Rose had been a frustrating distraction, sending a variety of dancing partners her way, making it difficult for her to single out the man she sought. Lord Devon had solved the problem for her though. She had been watching him steadily while she danced with various partners and he had noticed her looks. After her dance with Gregory Pern he walked over with a curious expression.

Rose moved smoothly into his path, seeking to turn him aside, she could see he was focused on Penny, "Lord Devon, what a happy surprise to see you here tonight? I thought you might be busy tending your bruised pride." Rose needled him, hoping to draw his anger.

"Excuse me Lady Rose, I believe the lady seeks a dance," he answered with a sneer, brushing past her.

"Very perceptive of you Lord Devon," Penny said with a sly smile. "I had little hope you would notice me." She put her hands together and slid them up the sleeves till they were at her elbows.

# Chapter 19 – The Ball

"Would you care to dance?" Devon gestured at the milling dance floor.

"Certainly if my poor grace will be enough to entertain you," Penny answered. She drew her arms apart and Rose was relieved to see her hands were empty. Devon took one of her hands and placed his free hand on her waist, slightly lower than was proper, but she did not complain. Penny had her other hand on his shoulder. She had planned and practiced for this and the dagger's pommel was in her palm with the blade running up her forearm while her fingers held it still. Holding it reversed forced her to keep her wrist straight and her hand was stiff, but no one could see it, still hidden by her sleeve. Once she had her hand resting on his shoulder he would be unable to see the strange posture of her hand.

"I wonder at your motives," Devon said, "to seek a dance with me."

"I have had time to think, on our encounter a few nights ago," she gave him a smouldering look.

"A small burn would lead most to seek to avoid the fire, lest they burn themselves again," he replied.

"Some women find danger to be an aphrodisiac, once they have had time to get over their initial fear," Penny leaned closer, placing her face against his neck.

Devon had met all manner of women and he knew some were quite twisted, but he could not help but think this maid was playing a subtle joke of some sort. "What of your blacksmith?"

She leaned back to look into his eyes, "He isn't here tonight, and you my Lord... are..." she brought her lips up to meet his. She only needed to distract him for a moment while her hand moved up, letting the sleeve fall free, clearing the blade for its fatal plunge. Devon's eyes widened for a moment, but her distraction worked for he failed to notice as her hand rose.

Penny held the long blade up, point carefully aimed so that it would strike between his shoulder blades, just below his neck. She would only get one chance, *Forgive me Mort,* she thought and then she tensed to drive the blade home. A scream went up from across the room, "Penny don't!!" It was Rose Hightower, and her warning spoiled Penny's careful plan.

Chapter 19 – The Ball

Jerking her about Devon saw the blade and caught her wrist in his hand, twisting her arm violently, causing the blade to fall free and sending pain shooting up her arm, "You stupid girl!" he yelled and then he threw her to the stone dance floor. She started to rise but his boot caught her in her midsection. The air exploded from her lungs with an audible 'whoosh', leaving her choking and gasping on the ground.

"Damned whore! Did you think to slay me? Look at me you feeble minded trollop!" he screamed at her. Penny looked up and his second kick caught her in the face, sending her sprawling. She tried to rise but her arms slid out from under her. Something was in her eyes and the agony of her nose blinded her with pain. People were screaming now but she could not understand them.

Devon Tremont was laughing and he reached down to grab the back of Penelope's head. He jerked her head up, delighted at the blood on her face. One eye was swelling and her nose looked as though it might be broken. "You'll hang for this bitch!" he yelled at her drawing his fist back to strike her again.

***

I was almost to him when he pulled Penny's head back and the sight of her battered face drove all reason from my mind. I grabbed his fist and jerked him around to face me as I hammered my right hand into his astonished face. The blow sent him reeling, stumbling back, and he fell. I advanced on him, determined to finish what I had started when one of the guards struck me from behind, staggering me.

I turned and saw the man staring stupidly at his broken truncheon. The heavy wooden weapon had snapped when it struck my head. I was glad I had shielded myself when I saw that. "Do that again and you'll regret it," I growled and looked back at Devon.

The young lord was back on his feet now, and my eyes could see he had put a shield around himself as well. He circled me warily, "Someone give me a sword!" he shouted. The guard behind me tossed him his own.

I glared at the guard, "I'm going to remember that." I drew my father's sword as I closed with Devon and we began our deadly dance. I call it a dance, but honestly I am no swordsman, I beat at him like an enraged farmhand with a club. His sword was moving too quickly for me to follow so I ignored it and hammered at him as if he were a side of beef to be cut up for market.

The only thing that saved me was the shield I had cast about myself. I pressed Devon hard, keeping him off-balance with heavy blows, but still his sword kept slipping my guard to strike at me. I would have been bleeding from a dozen places if it could have cut me. Finally we drew back to catch our breath.

I was breathing hard, winded already. My recovery was far from complete and it would not be long before my anger would no longer be enough to keep me fighting. Worse, Devon looked as though he was still fresh. He held his sword in front of him and ran his finger down the blade, *"Thylen"* he said, and I saw a glow appear along the edge.

I hadn't learned that trick yet, and it worried me. From the corner of my eye I could see Rose pulling Penny away. The guards had us encircled now and Sir Kelton was shouting at me to put down my sword. They probably would have rushed me, dragging me down if Dorian hadn't intervened.

"Get back!" His booming voice cut through the din as he broke into the circle. His sword was out and he glared at them from beneath dark brows. "The first man to interfere will find his insides on the floor!" he shouted. Then Devon came at me again.

We traded quick blows but he had me on the defensive now. I was backing as he pressed his advantage and I felt his sword tip catch my cheek, slicing effortlessly through my shield. *Shit!* I was desperate now, he seemed able to cut me at will, and even if I could get past his guard my sword wouldn't pierce his shield.

I had an idea. Stepping back quickly I spoke, *"Shelu Nian Trethis"* and I found myself in utter silence. I had stoppered my ears with a special type of shield, one to prevent sound from entering. My own brilliance amazes me sometimes. I could see Devon's mouth moving but I couldn't hear his words. If I had to hazard a guess I would imagine it was something like, "You stupid fool."

He came at me and I closed my eyes, *"Lyet ni Bierek!"* I said, and I put everything I had into it. The result was astonishing. Light flashed so brightly that everyone watching us was blinded, including I hoped,

Lord Devon. The light was accompanied by a thunderous 'boom' so great that it shook the teeth in my jaw. Everyone within the ballroom drew back reeling, some fell to the floor crying out with shock. I would judge that my 'flashbang' was a success, although I still needed to work out a better name for it.

I opened my eyes and saw Devon sitting on the ground. He was blinking and seemed completely disoriented. His sword lay beside him but his hand couldn't find it. I had created my spell right in front of him, so he should have gotten the worst of it. The flashbang was a creation of pure light and sound, with no force behind it to break or destroy. His shield had not protected him at all, not being designed to do so. In fact his shield still appeared to be around him. *How annoying,* I thought.

I swung at him with my sword, but it failed to do more than knock him sideways. I needed something bigger, heavier. I cast about, looking for a better weapon. My eyes landed on the eastern fireplace. Striding over I looked for the fireplace tools, but someone had taken the iron poker. I started searching the kindling piled next to the hearth instead. The great hall had two fireplaces, and they were so large that the logs were cut almost three feet in length. I selected a sturdy piece fully four inches in diameter. I held it up in a double handed grip, it seemed to have promise.

I headed back towards Devon. He was standing now and still seemed blind, but he didn't need eyes to see me. Using his mage-sight he pointed at me and said something I couldn't hear. White hot flames erupted around me, but my shield kept out the worst. The heat was so great my clothes began to crisp and char about me. I ignored the flames and marched at him, *"Lyet Bierek"* I said again, and a great cracking 'boom' sent him to the floor.

The flash had partly blinded me but I didn't need my eyes any more than he did. The log swung in a great arc as I slammed it into his face. He flew several feet, crashing into a chair near the edge of the room. I hit him again, pleased he was still conscious. I began steadily raining blows on him with my firewood club. He tried to raise his sword but I knocked his arm aside. I thought it might have broken which brought a smile to my face. I smacked him about like one of the dummies the guards practice with, beating him senseless.

Finally he collapsed, unconscious on the floor. As he passed out his shield winked out of existence and

# Chapter 19 – The Ball

I grinned, raising my makeshift club over my head. Someone touched my arm and I almost swung at them before I realized it was Marc. He was shouting something but I couldn't hear him. I removed the sound block from my ears. "...if you kill him they'll have you for murder!" he yelled.

I looked at him stupidly, "Yeah, so what?!"

"You'll be hanged!" he shouted back.

I thought for a second, "If I don't kill him he'll press his case and have Penny hanged!"

Marc looked at me for a moment, "You're right. Kill him." Then Dorian appeared, still blinking his eyes from my earlier spell.

"Let me do it," he said, pointing at Devon with his sword.

We started arguing, trying to decide which of us should finish him off when James Lancaster found us. "Put the firewood down Mordecai. Dorian sheathe your sword!" his tone brooked no delay. I looked down at the piece of wood I held, it was still burning from the fire Devon had used on me, so I walked over to the fireplace and threw it in.

Around the room people were still recovering. Several men were beating out a fire that had started near where Devon tried to roast me. A large tapestry was in flames but it looked like they would be able to keep it from spreading. I walked back to the Duke, his son was arguing with him but he shouted Marc down, "I'm not hanging anyone, not you, not Penelope, not even this piss poor excuse of a lord here! Now shut up and let me think!" I was pretty sure that by 'piss poor excuse of a lord' he meant Devon, but there was a possibility he meant me instead.

I decided to ignore them and started looking for Penny. I found her with Rose, sitting at one of the small tables to the side. They were surrounded by a crowd of people, some of them watched me as I walked over. I showed my teeth and growled at them, "Move!" They cleared out quickly, and a few even ran.

I looked at Penny, she was sitting up but her face looked terrible. One eye was swelling shut and her nose looked like someone had formed it from a badly shaped piece of bread dough. "Oh Mort, your cheek!"

she exclaimed. Her voice had a comical nasal twang, as if she were holding her nose pinched shut.

"Shut up stupid," I said gently. I sat down next to her and touched her face with my mind. Sure enough the bone in her nose had snapped and been driven sideways. My experiments on my own bones had taught me a few things, so I spoke a quiet word first, damping all sensation in her face. Then I moved the bones back into place and reconnected them. My attempt at pain blocking wasn't entirely successful, because she still let out a choked cry as the bones realigned. I couldn't do anything about the swelling but at least she wouldn't look funny when it healed.

I tried to kiss her but that didn't work. Her nose was far too tender, plus she kept going on about my face. Eventually Rose dragged me over to a mirror along one of the walls. I was a horror, my right cheek was drooping, exposing my upper teeth; blood coated that side of my face and ran down my neck. Odd, I hardly felt it at all. I pushed the skin back together and sealed it with my finger and a thought, leaving a red line. I would later regret the rush job, since I still have an ugly scar there to this day.

That was when the screaming and yelling started up again. The doorway to the great hall only had a couple of guards still standing at it. Most of the others were scattered through the crowd trying to calm everyone down. The two by the doors were watching the events inside, so they never saw the men in black leathers who crept up on them from behind. They died quickly, but one of them screamed before his windpipe was cut through. Pandemonium erupted as people scrambled to get back from the doors.

The men spilling into the room were all dressed similarly, in black leather with masks tied over their features, hiding everything but their eyes. They carried sharp knives and long curved swords. I was pretty sure they hadn't come to dance; they had the wrong shoes on. They spread out and began methodically cutting down the guests. People trampled each other in their efforts to get away, making it easier for the men to reach them.

Duke Lancaster was pushing his way through the crowd, he still hadn't seen them yet, "What the bloody hell is going on here!?" He roared as people fought to get around him, then he saw the men. He was nearly cut down then, as he was still unarmed. Two of the men had him caught between them and a fallen table, but Lord Thornbear rushed into them from the side roaring like a bear. He didn't have his sword either, but he held a chair and used it to smash one of the men to the ground. Then he drove the other back like some eastern lion tamer, holding the chair in front of him.

At least thirty of them were already in the room, spreading out, killing anyone they found. I could see many more entering through the main doors. *"Lyet Bierek"* I spoke and the men all around the doorway fell back, shocked and stunned. That bought us some time while Sir Kelton and the guards in the room struggled to form a line between the remaining guests and the men in the room.

The Duke and Thornbear were still cut off from the rest of us, surrounded now by a dozen men. The assassins were still disoriented and Thornbear fought like a maddened bull, swinging his chair back and forth, cracking skulls. Even so they would have been slain had Dorian not come to his father's aid. He charged from the line of men with Sir Kelton and cut his way past those before him to reach his father.

I had never seen Dorian fight like that before, nor do I hope to ever again. He became a demon of slaughter with a sword in each hand. I wondered where he had found the second blade, and it was only later I realized he had taken Devon's sword from the ground. Dorian ran through the men in his way, and as he passed they fell back, dropping weapons and crying out from the wounds he gave them. He went through them like a scythe through ripe grain.

Once he had reached the Duke and his father he paused to toss the sword in his off hand to Lord Thornbear who caught it deftly. The two of them fought on either side of the Duke then, steadily working their way toward Sir Kelton and his men.

During all of this I had taken a position among the guards who were struggling to form a defensive line. Marc was to my right wielding a sword to deadly effect. I tried to do the same but I was far less skilled, if it had not been for my magical shield I would have died several times over. We strove to drive them back but there were too many. Man for man the Duke's guardsmen were better at face to face combat but the assassins outnumbered us several times over. We were driven back, step by step, till they controlled more than half of the great hall, and we were even further from the two Thornbears and the Duke, still fighting for survival.

# Chapter 19 – The Ball

The guards were falling one by one and now we had fewer than thirty men, barely enough to form a line across the room. A few more down and we would be overrun. "Dorian!" I yelled, "Run!" He caught my eye for a second and I hoped he understood. He said something to his father and the Duke and they turned their backs on the men in front of them, charging toward those that remained between them and our line.

*"Lyet Bierek"* I shouted, placing the center of this one behind them. The sound of it would probably deafen them, but at least they were facing away and the men ahead and behind them were blinded. The huge noise even unsettled those before us and we gained a few feet as some of them fell.

Lord Thornbear and his son hacked their way through the stunned men, while the Duke finished those he could with a long dagger he had found. It looked for a moment as though they would reach us unharmed. Five steps, then ten, they were almost to us, when two men managed to time their strikes at Lord Thornbear. He stopped one blade, and almost dodged the other but his age betrayed him and he was too slow. The sword plunged into his chest just below the sternum.

Dorian came of sturdy stock, the elder Thornbear grimaced and grabbed the man who had slain him. Dragging him close he rammed his own sword home before collapsing with his dying foe. I heard a cry come from Dorian's lips, a sound I will never forget as he saw his father fall, but there was no help for it. Lord Thornbear was dead.

Dorian slew the second man and might have charged back into the fray but the Duke stopped him with a hand on his shoulder. Instead they leapt over the last fallen man, reaching our line. I saw my friend's face as he came past, spattered with blood and tears falling from his eyes. I would have spoken to him but I had no words, and the assassins were pressing us harder now.

The Duke armed himself and with Dorian among us our line gained strength, still we were little more than thirty men, and the hall before us held scores, easily a hundred black garbed killers. The conclusion could only be bloody and it would not be in our favor. As we fought I could see some of the women and noble ladies picking up swords from dead men, shoring up the line. Rose and Penny were among them. I even saw Ariadne arming herself, though she did not try to enter the battle.

Genevieve Lancaster stood behind us now, shouting at those unable or unwilling to fight, organizing them to form a barricade of tables and broken furniture, seeing that I had an idea, one that would either save us or kill me in the effort. I have since learned that my ideas are something of a mixed blessing.

# Chapter 20

## Last Stand in the Great Hall

*Traditionally wizards are not known for their ability to heal. The reason for this lies in the complexity of the task. Few mages learn to use their sight inwardly in such a way that they are able to perceive and understand the inner workings of the body; those that do find that attempting to manipulate the processes within results more often in harm than good. Channelers on the other hand do not rely on their own power or intuition, but that of their god. Because of this most acts of magical healing are attributed to saints and holy men. This is not to say that wizards cannot heal, in history a number of accomplished mages have been noted healers, but they are the exception. Most are able to do little more than mend cuts in the skin, some manage to fix broken bones, but few learn the finesse necessary to heal anything beyond that.*

*~Marcus the Heretic,*
*On the Nature of Faith and Magic*

We withdrew behind a makeshift barricade of fallen tables and broken chairs. To call it a barricade was a bit of a stretch, I'll admit, but it gave us a slight advantage. It hampered the men coming at us, making it easier to kill or wound them as they struggled to get over the tumbled furniture. They drew back for a moment to coordinate their final push and the fighting paused.

"Genevieve!" I shouted to the Duchess, "I need your help, I have a plan." She nodded and came quickly to me. She had seen enough to realize that whatever I might do it was better than the alternative.

"What can we do?" she asked me.

"Get the burned logs from the fire. I need a line, as straight as you can make it from one side of the room to the other!" I told her. It took a few more words to explain myself but at last she understood me and soon she had people running to either side of the room, gathering burnt wood to draw the line.

Vestrius' journal had mentioned great wizards of the past using their strength to create huge shields to protect buildings or men during time of war. Often the effort killed them, especially if they did it without proper preparation. My own experiments had already shown me how much more energy was needed to do something without words as opposed to with them. I already knew the words necessary for creating a shield beyond my own body, but there was another method of increasing efficiency, the use of symbols or visibly drawn lines, much like a summoner's circle. I wasn't sure how much help a simple line would be, but it couldn't hurt.

I had impressed upon Genevieve the need for the line to be as straight as possible and one of the men helping her was a carpenter by trade. Soon he was using a board from a broken table to help them rule the line as they drew it across the breadth of the hall. I was glad he had thought of it, the line was much better than what I thought would be possible.

A man spoke out from the men who stood on the other side of our barricade. "If you surrender now I promise we won't kill the women." Devon Tremont was standing behind them, using a chair so he could see us over their heads. "My men could use a reward for their efforts after all."

I looked at Marc, "Next time I kill him first and we can discuss whether it was the proper thing to do later," referring to our earlier argument.

He agreed with me, and then James Lancaster shouted out, "I would sooner die than hand over my people to you!" He was red faced with anger.

"I can arrange that for you my dear Duke," Devon answered him. He closed his eyes and I could see a deep glow forming around him. The power he was radiating now was immense; so far beyond the pale that I could hardly believe he was human. Even the people around me could see it now, and fear ran through the defenders. I began working my way along the line of men and women guarding the barricade, giving quiet instructions. Outwardly I remained calm but the power facing us was so great that I no longer felt the confidence I pretended to. "Mal'goroth, come, use me! Show your wrath to these who would defy you!" Devon shouted.

I looked back at Genevieve, "Is it ready?"

"Almost, we're almost there," she shouted back.

Looking back at Devon my heart quailed. I had learned enough to realize what he was doing. He had broken the most important rule for a mage; he had opened his mind to one of the Dark Gods and given himself over to it. The power of the evil deity was coursing through him now and his body seemed to swell larger with it. I knew that if we did not kill him now he would be the doom of the world. Mal'goroth would use his power to open a bridge, a bridge strong enough for the dark god to enter our world.

Then a voice spoke to me within my own mind. It came from within but I could sense that it originated with the silver star in my pocket, the symbol of Millicenth the Evening Star. *Let me help you. Together we can stop him before it is too late.* In my mind I could see the shining lady speaking to me, and I knew she spoke truly. Without realizing it I drew out the holy symbol, holding it before me in my hand. Almost I accepted her offer, but as I wavered Penny came over and struck the symbol from my hand.

I looked at her, a question in my eyes, "Father Tonnsdale poisoned your family and he tried to poison everyone here!" she shouted at me. I nodded, her words raised many questions but there was no time for them now. I turned back and saw our enemies charging at the barricade.

"For Lancaster!" I screamed at the top of my lungs and every man and woman echoed the cry. Then without warning they turned, ducking down and plugging their ears. *"Lyet Bierek"* I spoke, and then repeated myself, again and again. The sounds were deafening and it felt as if the castle had come under bombardment from cannonade. The enemy attack faltered as men screamed and fell clutching their eyes, some with bleeding ears, and the men and women of Lancaster took several steps back, crossing the line Genevieve and the carpenter had created.

I looked at the doors across the room from us, far behind the men we faced and I spoke the words to create a shield across it, one tight enough to prevent even air from passing. Then I looked down to the line that stood in front of me. Penny watched my face and I wondered if I would die, it seemed such a shame. She started toward me but I held up my hand, I couldn't afford any distractions.

Reaching down into myself I drew out my power and let it fall from my lips and down my arm as I gestured to the line before me. I could feel it flowing outward, filling the line that had been drawn and then I raised my hands upwards. A shimmering screen of light rose from the floor to meet the ceiling, seamless and perfect. Some of the enemy had already charged at us and those who were across the line were cut cleanly in half, limbs and body parts falling to the floor as they died. Those behind slammed into air that had become solid as stone, I could feel the force of them as they struck my shield.

Devon laughed where he stood behind them, purple flames coursing over his body, "Fool! You can't maintain that shield for long! You'll die of the strain and I'll be killing your friends before your body has cooled!"

I glared at him across the screen that separated us, "You don't look so good Devon, did someone rearrange your face for you or were you always that ugly?" Despite the power running through him his face was swollen from the beating I had given him earlier. "Oh that's right I nearly beat you to death with the ugly stick didn't I? Maybe I should finish the job. It could only improve your looks!"

He snarled something at me and I could feel a dark force pressing against my screen, trying to tear it open. That worried me, the strength to maintain a shield is greater than the strength needed to destroy it and he would rapidly burn through my reserves if he kept pushing at it. I looked across the open room and spoke the words I had been saving, words of fire and power.

Nothing happened. I could feel myself weakening and realized I had overextended myself. I didn't have the power left to accomplish my goal. We were going to die. Devon thrust his power against my shield again and I staggered, falling to my knees. Only seconds remained before my strength was gone. I dropped my sword and saw it strike the floor. There at the base of the blade was the maker's mark, the mark of Royce Eldridge. For a moment I remembered his words as he had given it to me. *"I did not make this for your vengeance. I did this to show that even from the ashes of wickedness and tragedy something of beauty can arise. I made this hoping the same for you. Use it for yourself; use it for defending those who cannot protect themselves, as your true father would have. Do not shame either of us."*

I stood up, driven by nothing but my resolve. *"Pyrren nian Aeltos, Pyrren strictos Kaerek!"* I spoke again, this time opening my heart, pouring my life into the spell. Loosely translated the words meant, 'Let the air burn, turning all to ash,' and I meant them. The air beyond my screen bloomed into white hot incandescent flames. I had not directed my spell at the men but the air itself.

## Chapter 20 – Last Stand in the Great Hall

Within seconds the flame was out, and I could feel a tugging at my screen. The air inside had been used up creating a vacuum that pulled against my screen. The enemy were mostly dead, and those still living were suffocating. Devon was still standing, his own shield had protected him, but his eyes were bulging. He gasped as he tried to draw breath, but there was nothing to breathe, nothing but smoke and ash.

He began beating at my shield with his mind, using his power like a battering ram, not even bothering with words. He couldn't speak anyway. The room grew dim as he struggled against me and my vision narrowed, as if I were standing in a tunnel. I held the shield for a long minute before he finally collapsed, and then I held it for minutes more. I had to make sure he was dead.

People were yelling and someone was shaking me, but I ignored them. I would not release my spell till Devon Tremont was dead beyond any doubt. Penny was standing in front of me and I could see her screaming at me, but I couldn't understand her words. Finally she slapped me and the screen collapsed. Smoke and cinders filled the air and people began coughing.

I looked at her, "Why did you do that?" I said.

"Because you were killing yourself idiot!" she answered me, and then the ground rushed up to meet me. She tried to catch me but all she managed was to break my fall. I looked up at her; she had never seemed so lovely.

"Your nose looks like a potato." I said with a laugh and then passed out. Stupid never dies, I thought as I spiralled into darkness.

# Chapter 21

*The biggest factor which makes healing anything beyond simple wounds difficult is a problem of perception. Some wizards manage to heal more complex wounds within their own bodies, but fail when faced with the same problem in other people. Their perception of the inner actions of someone else's body is hampered by the sensations and perceptions of their own body. The few great mage healers found a way around this problem, enabling them to occasionally achieve miracles that some thought possible only for the gods. A great tragedy lies in the loss of the knowledge detailing how they accomplished this.*

*~Marcus the Heretic,*
*On the Nature of Faith and Magic*

I woke in a dark room. I lay still for a long while, trying to figure out how I had gotten there. Gradually I realized that someone lay next to me, and after a moment I identified it as Penny. The snoring is a dead giveaway, and it was worse than ever now, probably because of her nose. I slid my hand over to her and discovered she had a nightgown on. How disappointing. She stirred and the snoring stopped, I could feel her eyes on me in the dark, although I was sure she couldn't see, the room was pitch black.

"Are you awake?" she asked softly.

"I'm not sure, this could be heaven," I replied moving my hand over her shoulder. "I must be awake, because in heaven all the girls are naked."

"Idiot, we thought you were dying," she said, "I thought I would lose you."

"I should have written you a letter first, then you would have felt better." I replied sarcastically. Have I mentioned my unparalleled skills in talking to women?

For a change she didn't react angrily, "I couldn't do it without leaving you something, to explain." I didn't like the sound of her voice, it had a thick sound, as if she were about to cry.

I did my best to divert her, "Exactly why did you try to kill Devon anyway? Are you that interested in getting yourself killed?"

She explained what had happened; her vision, killing Father Tonnsdale, and her resolve to make the most of things by getting rid of Devon Tremont. I listened quietly, amazed at her nerve. This lovely woman had killed the traitor and hidden the fact without me being any the wiser. Then she had planned a murder and kept me completely unaware. I would have been scared to have her in the bed with me if I wasn't absolutely sure we were on the same team.

"At least I had a good reason for everything I did. Unlike you... you tried to kill yourself at the end, even after they were all dead," she finished.

"Not true, I was making sure they were dead," I answered.

"You're an idiot." she shot back.

"You're a double idiot, potato nose!" I replied wittily. Luckily this time she saw the humor in my joke and started giggling, and soon we were both laughing. Fatigue washed over me in waves and I decided I needed more sleep. Before I drifted off I realized I couldn't feel her with my mind. I couldn't feel anything. I was blind, but it wasn't my eyes that weren't working.

I woke early the next morning, amazed at how good I felt. By all rights I should be dead; instead I was hungry and extremely thirsty. Penny was not in the room so I ordered room service, "Hey! Somebody! I know you're out there ya bunch of vultures. I'm not dead! I want food and something to drink!" In point of fact I had no idea if anyone was outside my door, I couldn't sense anything beyond what my eyes could see. But I'm smart you see, I knew that whenever the hero slays a dragon the villagers always wait outside to bring him food and drink. There's usually grateful virgins too, but I didn't think Penny would approve of me asking for those.

Sure enough Benchley poked his head into the room, "You called sir?"

"Yes, thank you Benchley. Do come in," he entered the room with his usual aplomb. I ignored his impeccable manners and started placing my order, "I need you to go kill me a cow. Not a small one mind, a big fat one. Have it cooked and brought up straight away."

He raised an eyebrow, "Certainly sir."

## Chapter 21

"Wait, nix that. Cooking will take too long, just kill it and bring it on up, I'll have it rare."

He nodded and left, cheeky bastard. I had my suspicions that he might not have taken me seriously. Of course I could just as easily have gone down and gotten my own food. My body seemed surprisingly whole, but they didn't have to know that. Not yet anyway.

Since I was alone I took the opportunity to relieve myself. Strictly speaking the chamber pot is for use at night, so you don't have to make the long walk to the privies, but I was feeling contrary. I also examined my face in the mirror.

Ugh! I looked like I had a really bad hangover. Too bad I hadn't actually been drinking. The scar on my cheek was ugly and red and the skin had obviously been put together a bit sloppily. *I can always tell the ladies it's a dueling scar,* I thought. Then I realized it actually was a sword inflicted scar; the events of the previous day seemed almost unreal.

There was a knock at the door so I hopped back in bed. It wouldn't do to give away my healthy condition too soon, "Come in!"

Benchley came in, and as I suspected he had not brought me the cow I had ordered. Instead he had a large tray loaded with roast beef and a variety of fruits and vegetables. "Where's my cow?" I asked reasonably.

"I'm afraid the cow was too fast for me sir. I managed to hack this part off before it got away, I do hope it will be satisfactory," he answered with a deadpan face. *I'll be damned,* I thought, *he has a sense of humor.* I decided to forgive him for cooking it instead of bringing it up raw.

Benchley left and Marc came in soon after. "Still playing sick I see," he remarked.

He always had known me too well. "After yesterday I think I could use a rest," I replied.

"Yesterday? You've been abed for almost two days. The attack was three days ago," he said.

"Oh," I replied intelligently.

Seeing my confusion he began filling me in on the events after my untimely collapse. Once the enemy had been crisped and starved for air they had searched the bodies. Dorian had taken the extraordinary precaution of hacking Lord Devon's head from his shoulders. It seems I wasn't the only paranoid one. They had even burned his corpse, both parts.

The Duke had rallied the outer garrison and they had swept the castle from top to bottom, rooting out the rest of the assassins. They had actually found another forty men scattered throughout the keep and some of the fighting had been long and bloody, but in the end the men of Lancaster had won the day. Dorian had gotten more exercise during that and had made quite a reputation for himself. Some of the men were calling him the 'Demon of Lancaster' now. He had been less than merciful to the enemy. He had also been wounded.

It was just a flesh wound, a dagger through his thigh, but Rose had him in her care now and she was taking no chances. Apparently she was just as protective of him as Penny had been with me. The family physician was probably still off sulking somewhere.

Father Tonnsdale was found dead in his study and it was widely circulated that the assassins had killed him first. Genevieve never mentioned seeing Penny with the iron poker and I'm still not sure if she forgot or if she and Penny had come to an agreement. Women are scary and I'm probably better off not knowing. Timothy's body had not been found, and knowing Penny's story that worried me some, but I didn't have a clue what to do about it.

The teleportation circle that Devon had created was found during the search for assassins. Unfortunately it was destroyed before I had a chance to study it. I would have given a pretty penny to know how it was constructed. I still had hopes that such things might be found further into Vestrius' journal.

All told some thirty seven men and women of the Lancaster household lost their lives, and a considerable number were injured, but it could have been much worse. Close to two hundred assassins had been killed and if Father Tonnsdale's plan had been successful the people of Lancaster would have been unable to defend themselves. It would have been a repeat of the slaughter at Cameron Castle sixteen years before.

Of the noble guests who had come to the Lancaster estate two were dead. Stephen Airedale was killed during the defense of the great hall. The other was Devon Tremont of course, and there was sure to be repercussions for his actions and his death, although it was far from certain what they would be.

Gregory Pern proved that his father's military success was no mere accident, for he acquitted himself admirably during both the defense of the hall and the clean up action after Devon was killed. James Lancaster wrote his Admiral Pern a long letter detailing what had happened and commending him on his son's bravery.

Some of the guests stayed for another week after the disaster, to assist as they could, and to be present at the funerals. Rose Hightower stayed for a month, refusing to leave until Dorian was fully recovered. In fact he could nearly run by the time she left, but we knew there were more reasons for her to stay than just his wound.

The enemy were stacked and burned beyond the castle walls. Only the bodies of Lancaster were buried, and within two days of the battle. The funeral service was almost a week afterwards. It took time to get the castle back in order, and quite a few people had been wounded. It was held on a small grassy knoll near the cemetery, and everyone still able to walk or hobble attended. James Lancaster gave the eulogy, and because so many had died it took nearly two hours to finish. He made a point to speak for several minutes about each person that had died. Frankly I was amazed that he had known them all.

The good Duke was the sort of man who made it a point to know everyone who served him down to the lowest servant, and he had obviously spent long hours working on his speech. Before it was half done most of the crowd were misty eyed, those that weren't already weeping openly. He saved Lord Thornbear for last.

"Gram Thornbear I have saved till now, because I was not sure I would be able to finish if I spoke of him first, for he was my closest friend. In life I knew him from our boyhood days, as a fellow adventurer in childhood pastimes. As a man I respected him as a loyal companion, a loving father, and a wise counselor. In death, I mourn him, for he saved my life and the lives of many standing here now. His action, in the brave defense of the great hall was merely the last act in a long life full of service and integrity. Gram Thornbear's last moments stand out not as an exception, but as an example of how he lived, strong and unbowed by the hardships and trials that cause lesser men to lose their way. He was my first and best friend and I doubt I shall ever know his like again. We will all miss him." James Lancaster's head was bowed as he finished, and I am sure he was crying.

To see him weeping openly affected me deeply, for I had never known him to complain or show sadness. My own face was wet as I held Penny's hand, not daring to look at her, and I vowed to live my life as best I could. To live up to the examples in front of me, Lord Thornbear, James Lancaster, Royce Eldridge, and my own father who I had never known. Only time will show whether I succeed or not.

# Epilogue

It had been over two weeks now since that dark day at Lancaster Castle and life was moving on, as it does. I had used some of my new funds to secretly commission an engagement ring for Penny. She had told me it wasn't important but Rose assured me privately that if I didn't get a ring she would see to it that I suffered painful consequences. I was grateful for the advice, and I'll stick to that story till I reach my grave.

We were gathered now in the chapel. I had some misgivings about that, considering Father Tonnsdale's involvement in the treachery that had nearly killed us all, but the new priest assured everyone that would listen that the man had been acting on his own evil impulses rather than some dark intent given by the Evening Star. I'll keep my own counsel on that, the books I was studying were rather plain spoken with regards to how far the gods could be trusted. In any case the young Father Terragant seemed like an earnest and faithful man.

I stood at the head of the church, directly before the altar. Since this was not a religious ceremony Duke Lancaster stood before me looking down. Following long tradition I knelt before him, holding my hands up before me, palm to palm as if praying. It was the ancient position of homage, given before one's liege-lord. James Lancaster took my hands between his own and I repeated the oath I had been carefully tutored in, "I swear on my honor that I will in the future remain faithful to James, Duke of Lancaster, to never cause him harm. I will observe my duty to him completely against all persons in good faith and without deceit."

James answered me, "It is right that those who offer to us unbroken fidelity should be protected by our aid. And since you, a faithful one of ours, have seen fit to swear trust and fidelity to us in our hand, therefore we decree and command that you shall ever be sheltered by us and given succor in time of need."

The ceremony of commendation was essentially complete at that point, but naturally the occasion demanded some extra pomp and circumstance but I won't bore you with the details. I had spoken with Genevieve before hand and she and James had agreed to let me add something of my own at the end, while everyone was still gathered. When my time had come, I stood and addressed the assembled crowd, "While you are all gathered I have one final and important moment to share with you all."

# Epilogue

Some of the people in the crowd looked at each other questioningly. This hadn't been mentioned previously, but Marc and Dorian nudged each other knowingly. I stepped down from the dais then, and walked to where Penelope sat in the first row. She had been seated there even though she had no standing because the Lancasters already knew of our plans.

She looked a question at me, obviously concerned that I was about to do something foolish in front of the gathering, but I ignored it. Taking her hands I drew her to her feet and then went to one knee, "Penelope Cooper, I have never known a lady so noble, lovely and kind as yourself. Will you marry me?"

She blushed more deeply than I had ever seen her do, "Yes, yes I will marry you Mordecai." The gathered crowd burst into cheering and applause. As the noise rose in volume she whispered to me, "Dummy, you still don't have a ring." But there were tears in her eyes and her smile would have lit the room even had it been the dead of night.

As I looked on her she seemed to glow and it took me a moment to realize my magesight had returned. The subtle radiance around her shimmered with what I can only assume was happiness.

***

A small figure moved through the garden. It had the shape of a small boy, but an observer would note that it moved oddly, some movements too quick, others awkward, as if it were too strong yet unfamiliar with its own body. A full moon lit the landscape as the figure turned, and its face was clearly recognizable. Timothy smiled at the night and walked on, searching for something to satisfy him. He could sense life in the night, the small shapes of animals moving. They weren't much but they would do... for now.

# Coming Soon:

Book 2 of the Mageborn Series

# Mageborn:
# The Line of Illeniel

# About the Author

Michael Manning, a practicing pharmacist, has been a fantasy and science-fiction reader for most of his life. He has dabbled in software design, fantasy art, and is an avid tree climber. He lives in Texas, with his wife, two kids, and a menagerie of fantastic creatures, including a moose-poodle, a vicious yorkie, and a giant prehistoric turtle. This is his first novel.

2582062R00211

Printed in Great Britain
by Amazon.co.uk, Ltd.,
Marston Gate.